FATAL IMPULSE

by

Lori L. Robinett

Printed in the United States of America

First Printing, 2015

ISBN 978-0692401774 (paperback)
ASIN B00UB2U7WS (ebook)

Three Creeks Press
1880 State Road E
Auxvasse, MO 65231

9 8 7 6 5 4 3 2 1

Dedication

This book is dedicated to my friend, Lisa Oliver, and her mother, Cindy March, who helped me plot this story out during our girlfriend getaway in 2014.

Dear Reader,

Thank you so much for taking time out of your busy schedule to read my book.

Do you like giveaways, contests and other free stuff? Do you want to have a chance to read my future work before it gets published, to have some say in what gets published and what doesn't, and to help me choose book covers? Swing on over to www.lorilrobinett.com and sign up for my newsletter. All I ask for is your email address, which I will never sell or give to anyone. In return, you'll get exclusive content and special contests just for special readers!

So . . . pop over to
http://lorilrobinett.com
and sign up now.

Go ahead, I'll wait . . . :)

And you're back? Great! Let's see what's happening in Buccaneer Bay . . .

1

Andi felt her husband's glare from across the room, like a red hot laser boring into her. She nodded and smiled as the gray haired gentleman beside her at the bar talked, but she didn't hear his words.

Instead, she plotted her escape before Chad got any angrier.

She raised two fingers in the air and caught the bartender's attention. "Two red wines, please."

The man continued, his eyes bright with enthusiasm, "There is treasure on this island, just waiting to be discovered. The geology is right for it."

The brunette behind the counter set two glasses on the bar. Andi picked them up by the stems and murmured to the man beside her, "Good luck with finding that tanzanite."

"Tourmaline," he corrected her.

She turned away and froze. Chad stood in front of her, inches away. His steel gray eyes bored into hers, narrowed and suspicious. "Aren't you going to introduce me to your new friend?"

She blinked and turned towards the man. "Chad, this is Mr. Franklin. Mr. Franklin, this is my husband, Chad Adams."

The man stuck his hand out, "Nice to meet you, Chad."

"It's Doctor." Chad grasped the man's hand and pumped it once, "Dr. Adams."

The man hesitated, then said, "Dr. Adams, then. Please, call me Carl."

The chill in Chad's voice matched his eyes. "How do you know my wife?"

Andi handed her husband a glass of wine. "We just met."

"I own a jewelry store in Buccaneer Bay." Carl produced a business card from his breast pocket, "And I'm an amateur rock hounder. Afraid I get so excited about my hobby, I talk about it at every opportunity."

Chad took a sip of his wine, then settled onto her bar stool. "Really, why don't you tell me about it?"

Lightning slashed the sky above them, thunder rolled and the wind swept the rain in sheets across the blackness of the Atlantic that stretched away to the East. Andi hugged herself to calm the shivers. The wipers slapped at the rain while Chad berated her for the way she acted that evening. She stared out into the inky darkness.

He glanced at her. "You act like you don't know what to say or do when we're out in public. You ignored me during dinner, and giggled like a schoolgirl at Carl Franklin at the bar."

He overlooked the fact that *he* monopolized the gentleman's time after dinner, leaving her alone in a sea of strangers. He accused her of flirting with other men on a regular basis, and that night was no different. Hopefully the anger would get out of his system before they got home.

"You make me look bad when you flirt like that," he continued. "It's not like Carl Franklin would ever be in the least bit interested in you, even if you weren't my wife."

It never occurred to him that his wife found the man's hobby of rock hounding to be interesting. His accusations stung, and he didn't always stop with words. The two celebrated their sixth wedding anniversary the previous May, and she was determined to make her marriage work. Her parents raised her to believe marriage is forever, 'til death do you part, so she would not leave him. No matter what.

A sharp bang interrupted his tirade.

The SUV swerved on the wet pavement, throwing her sideways into the door. The seatbelt grabbed and held her in place, and she braced herself against the dash with her hands. Her head jerked from side to side as the vehicle fishtailed back and forth until Chad slowed the Grand Cherokee. He held the steering wheel with an iron grip and guided the vehicle to the side of the road, the blown tire thumping. He set the emergency brake with a sharp yank, then turned to look at her, his dark eyes narrowed. He looked evil in the amber glow of the instrument panel.

The interior light blinked on when he opened his door, bathing the inside of the vehicle with harsh light. He started to get out, then paused, one foot in, one foot out, and turned to stare at her.

"I had control. There is no need to grab the dash like that. As you may recall, this vehicle is equipped with airbags. Had they deployed, your arms would have been broken." That low, smooth voice that had once impressed her now gave her chills. "Snap."

The door slammed shut behind him and darkness washed over her. She bit her lower lip, angry at the tremble she felt at his sharp words. She watched the driver side mirror as he stalked around and opened the back hatch. He shoved his golf clubs to the side and yanked the jack out of the back of the SUV.

She took a deep breath and got out. With winter's last gasp, the rain plastered her thick hair against her head and the clothes against her back. Her thin, sequined jacket did little to protect her from the cold rain that stung like needles where it struck her exposed skin. Her heels sank into the soft shoulder with every step, and the wind pushed her so hard her left leg bumped the steel guardrail. She glanced over the rail. The angry waves crashed into the rocks far below them, but she couldn't see anything but darkness.

He cursed under his breath as she squeezed past him, then said, "Make yourself useful and hold the damned flashlight for me. There's one in the emergency kit."

A dark colored sedan splashed water as it sped by. She reached in the back and fumbled around for the flashlight. Her fingers closed around the black metal barrel of the Maglite. The beam sliced through the night as she took up a position just behind her husband and shone the light wherever he directed. The wind whipped and howled around them. Chills racked her body and her hands shook, which made him madder by the minute.

Finally, he yanked the shredded tire off and lifted the spare on. After a few spins of the tire iron, he let the jack down with a thump and rolled the shredded tire past Andi, then settled the jack and iron back into their places. He stuck out a hand and demanded her jacket.

"What?" She blinked as a raindrop struck her in the eye.

He shook his hand in her face. "Your coat. Give it here. I need something to lay the old tire on so the carpet doesn't get dirty."

She shivered in the rain while he spread her black sequined wrap out and laid the muddy tire on top of it. He slammed the hatch shut, then turned to sneer at her. "It's a wonder I got that thing changed with you shaking that light around all over the place."

She opened her mouth to apologize, but stopped when his eyes narrowed. He grabbed her ponytail and jerked down, forcing her to look up at him."It's a damned good thing you've got me around to take care of you – *you* never could have kept control when that tire blew, and you sure as hell wouldn't have been able to change a tire in good weather, much less in the driving rain like this." He released her ponytail and poked her chest with his index finger, hard. "Stupid bitch."

He laughed that cruel, mocking laugh of his and rocked back on his heels, his head thrown back. Lightning flashed across the sky, and he looked like a madman. His laugh echoed around them, mixed with the roar of the waves, as though the ocean itself was mocking her.

She tightened her grip on the Maglight, and swung it like a baseball bat, just like she'd been taught that summer she played softball as a kid back in Missouri. He blinked and stammered as he stepped backwards. The back of his knee hit the guardrail and he tipped over, his legs flying up in slow motion. He looked at her as he fell, eyes wide with surprise, and then he was gone. His scream echoed against the cliff and then there was silence.

The flashlight felt heavy in her hand.

The emergency flashers continued their steady throb.

Thunder shook the ground beneath her. She stood there, numb, staring down into the darkness.

2

A vehicle approached, slowed and stopped. A power window whirred down. A man shouted, "Need any help?"

Andi stood frozen, raindrops tracing trails down her cheeks, as she faced the guardrail. Unable to move. Unable to talk. The Grand Cherokee's red hazard lights strobed through the darkness.

"Oh, dear!" A woman exclaimed. Shoes slapped against the wet pavement, until she stopped beside Andi. She peered over the guard rail then looked at Andi with wide eyes, "Did someone go over?"

After a moment, the woman put her arm around Andi and gently turned her away from the cliff. No words would come. Andi couldn't stop shivering. The gray haired man pulled a blanket from their trunk and gently wrapped it around her shoulders. The woman held her hand out, palm up, and said, "At least it finally stopped raining."

She patted Andi's arm. The man stood on the other side of the car, talking on his cell phone. He glanced over the top of their white coupe at his wife and the young woman, but turned away when Andi looked up.

He still gripped the phone as he came around the car. He said, "The police are on the way. You're going to be okay."

Andi shook her head. She'd never be okay again. Her legs felt like spaghetti, and the edges of her vision darkened. She felt like she'd been punched in the stomach. She focused all her energy in an effort to keep from passing out. This couldn't be real.

The Maine State Police officers arrived in what seemed like moments, clad in their yellow slickers, quickly joined by a couple of cruisers from the Sheriff's Department. The lights sent beams swirling through the night, the whole scene surreal. They whisked Andi away from the elderly couple and the older officer who appeared to be in charge looked her over. His brown eyes were cold, his tone businesslike.

"I'm Sergeant Watkins with the MSP. Tell me what happened."

Andi sucked in a deep breath, then began, "My-my husband and I were coming back from dinner up at the Clifftop. We had a flat. He changed the tire and then . . . " A chill ran down her body as the memory flashed through her mind.

"And then what?" he prompted, pencil poised over a small spiral notebook.

"He went over the guardrail." Her voice cracked on the last word. She tugged the scratchy wool blanket tighter around her.

He didn't look up from his notepad. Just asked, "How?"

She shook her head and swallowed the lump that threatened to close her throat. "I don't know. I'm not sure what happened. One minute he was standing there and the next he was falling. Screaming. And then there wasn't any sound at all."

His bushy eyebrows pushed together and his eyes bored into hers like lasers. "And where were you when he fell?"

"Right beside him. I held the flashlight for him while he changed the tire." Oh, dear God. Could this be real? She looked down at her mud-splattered high heels and pleaded, "I'm sorry. I don't know what happened."

A younger officer stepped forward and whispered to the Sergeant. The older man's lips pressed into a thin line, then he nodded once and said, "Tell the EMTs they can go, then."

The ambulance had arrived with bright lights flashing, but drove down Highway 3 with only red taillights marking its exit.

That was wrong. Andi could feel it. Panic bubbled up. Eyes wide, she turned towards the Sergeant and grabbed his arm. "Why is the ambulance leaving? Why isn't someone going down to get him?"

"This storm was bad, and the surf's rough. Can't get down from here." He met her gaze, then his tone softened, "I can't risk my men, ma'am. We'll get the Coast Guard to help search in the morning. Buccaneer Bay PD'll coordinate in town. You understand?"

She sucked in a shaky breath, then looked at him, her arched eyebrows asking the question she couldn't bring herself to ask.

He motioned towards the inky darkness to the East, "We may not be able to find him. The currents may pull the body out to sea."

A police detective stepped forward, a thick, sturdy man with a stern face. He swept his hat off, exposing a ring of sparse gray hair fighting to keep baldness at bay, and nodded to her. "Bet the body floats in tomorrow morning. Next day at the latest."

The Sergeant frowned at the older man, "We'll just have to wait and see what tomorrow brings."

The detective harrumphed, then turned to face Andi. "Detective Gerald Johnson with the Buccaneer Bay Police Dept, ma'am."

Andi nodded, but it felt like a dream as she let the younger man lead her to his patrol car. She climbed into the back seat, alone, and watched the full moon peek out from behind the storm clouds as they rolled out across the Atlantic. Numbness began to set in, then there were bits and pieces, sleep and wakefulness, dreams and nightmares, but mostly numbness.

She woke up in their king-sized bed, alone. A half-empty glass of water sat next to an amber bottle of prescription pills on the nightstand. Sunlight filtered in around the edges of the drawn shades. The clock said 10:52. She pushed herself up from the bed, then remembered.

Lightning.

Thunder.

Chad's steel gray eyes, wide with surprise.

Shivering in the rain as she stared down into the darkness.

Her legs turned to rubber and she sat back down with a thump. The edges of the room tilted. She closed her eyes and focused on breathing.

In, out.

In, out.

Blood rushed in her ears. She remembered. Against the blackness of her eyelids, she saw the two of them on the shoulder of that blacktop road, like a movie stuck in an endless loop. He threw his head back, laughing, and she swung. Did he slip on the wet gravel? Did the flashlight hit him? She didn't know. She couldn't remember. Was it murder? Or a horrible accident? Would anyone *believe* it was an accident?

She opened her eyes and pressed her hand to her chest as her heart thudded. It hurt, an actual physical hurt, deep inside. After a few minutes, her heartbeat slowed. Her thick terry cloth robe hugged her as she stumbled across the room. The door swung open with a creak, the doorknob held her weight and blood throbbed in her ears. For a moment, nausea threatened. She hurried into the bathroom and splashed cold water on her face, then waited for the feeling to pass. She ran a brush through her thick, dark hair, then smoothed it back into a loose pony tail. Her movements felt mechanical. Dark circles under her red-rimmed eyes made her look older than her 27 years.

Voices floated up from the kitchen, so she made her way along the hallway and down the stairs. Every step was like slogging through quicksand. The familiar voices beckoned her. Then it occurred to her – how long had it been? Had they drugged her?

Her legs trembled and she sagged against the wall. She wasn't sure she could go on. It took her several minutes to pull herself together before she could face whoever was in the kitchen. She'd had lots of practice putting on a happy face for others over the past few years.

When she appeared in the doorway, conversation stopped for a beat and all eyes turned to her, then a plump, gray haired woman rushed towards her.

"Mama?" Andi cried out and blinked in surprise. The breath rushed out of her lungs, and she reached out for the older woman, fingers clutching at her mother's blouse.

"Oh, baby! You poor thing! I'm so sorry!" The older woman gathered her daughter in ample arms, and rocked her gently. As Andi's sobs dissolved into hiccups, her mother guided her to the table, where she sank onto a wooden chair as everyone bustled around her. The feel of her mother's arm around her shoulders comforted her, and Andi leaned in to her, so glad, so relieved that she was there. Her mother's hand rested on hers, protective.

The whole thing felt like an awful, horrible dream . . . except for the fact that this – this experience brought her mama to her. Live and in person, not a staticky voice on the telephone. She gazed at her mother as if she were a mirage that might evaporate if she looked away. Confusion bubbled to the surface. "But how did you--"

Her mother motioned across the kitchen table. "Your neighbor, Mrs. Harrison, called me as soon as she heard, and I drove to St. Louis and took the first flight they had. I just got here about ten minutes ago."

Gradually, Andi's view of the room expanded.

Mrs. Harrison, the retired librarian from next door sat across the table, perched on the edge of her seat like a bird ready to snatch a crumb. "Luckily, I remembered your mother's name. Didn't take me long to find the right Martha Denton in Missouri." Her small hazel eyes were bright and intense. "I brought a casserole."

Jennie Crawford, Chad's receptionist, looked stricken. A sprig of blonde hair poked out of her usually perfectly coiffed curls. Her naked lips trembled slightly. She half-stood and pushed a plate of goodies towards Andi, "I made some of my wicked good cinnamon rolls."

Andi's mother smiled at the younger woman and said, "They are delicious. I have to get the recipe from you."

"The secret is scalded milk." The blonde's cheeks turned pink as she looked around the table. Her gaze settled on Andi. Her lower lip trembled, then she said, "I can't believe he's gone. I'm so sorry."

"Thank you," Andi whispered. The room swam, and she focused on breathing again, one breath at a time. It was the only thing she was confident she could do at that moment in time. Someone slid a cup of coffee in front of her, and she gripped it with both hands to absorb the warmth.

Carol Graves, one of the local society types who served with Andi on the Friends of the Library Board, cleared her throat and smiled when Andi looked up. Her mouth opened, but then closed without a word when Mrs. Harrison began talking about storm damage from the night before. No one mentioned Chad. What could they say? Martha sat next to Andi and clutched her arm with both hands as if she were an apparition that might disappear into thin air.

God, it felt good to be held. Andi missed her mother even more than she'd realized. Gray streaked the older woman's hair, more than last Christmas. No, Christmas before last. With a start, she realized she hadn't been home in over a year. Why had she let Chad keep her from going?

An assortment of pies and casseroles and plates of cookies covered every available flat surface. The aroma of homemade chicken noodle soup mingled with the sweet cinnamon smell of apple dumplings. Comfort food. Her hand dropped to her hip, where all the calories would land.

She jumped when her cell phone chirped. Everyone's heads swiveled from her to the phone on the counter and back again. No one ever called her, besides Chad. Her mother started to stand, but Andi put her hand out as she pushed away from the table. "I've got it." Her voice sounded small in the big kitchen.

She glanced at the screen. Anonymous. She hesitated, but swiped the screen.

The gruff voice on the other end of the line got straight to the point. "Detective Gerald Johnson with the Buccaneer Bay Police Department. Coast Guard is out already. No sign of remains yet."

She sucked in air and held it for a beat, then shivered as a chill ran down her spine. "You'll let me know?" Until that moment, she hadn't considered that the fall might not have killed him. But the cliff . . . the rocks. Even if he survived the fall, the icy Atlantic would've claimed him quickly. "And what if they don't find him?"

He took a drink of something, swallowed loudly, then answered, "We'll find him, all right. Don't you worry about that."

Silence echoed in her ear. Unease curled up in the pit of her stomach as she stared at the screen. Finally, she sat the phone on the counter. She took a deep breath, then turned back to her guests. Everyone stared at her expectantly.

She struggled for words, then finally murmured, "Thank you all for coming. It means a lot to me." She couldn't do this anymore. Her vision narrowed. Darkness closed in on her, and she fought to maintain focus. No one met her eyes.

The linen tablecloth needed to be ironed.

Sunlight reflected in a chip in the red glass vase centered on the table.

A deli tray sat on the breakfast bar, the plastic wrap pulled back.

The sun shone brightly through the vertical blinds on the sliding glass door, but wet spots still glistened on the deck.

A dog barked in the distance.

And the tunnel began to close.

Her mother grasped her arms and guided her onto a chair, then herded everyone else out of the room. "Thank you all for coming. We do appreciate it so much, but my daughter needs her rest now." The hushed tones of conversation drifted out with the small group like a cloud, and finally the two women were alone.

"I take it that was the police?" The older woman stepped close and rested her hands on her daughter's shoulders, then massaged them gently. "Honey, I don't know how much you remember . . ."

Her voice trailed off and she waited. Andi blinked, not sure how much was real and what was the product of her overactive imagination. A chill ran up her spine at the hazy memory of the accident.

A little voice whispered, *it wasn't an accident.*

But that wasn't true. It *was* an accident! Her heart threatened to burst. Guilt ate at her gut. For so long, she hid the signs of abuse, ashamed of her weakness, afraid to leave, afraid to be alone. Yet she *had* been alone, isolated from her friends and family.

And now she was truly alone.

Tears filled her eyes and she felt as if she'd been sucker punched. She swiveled to face her mother. "Oh, God, Mama, he's dead, isn't he?"

Martha nodded and Andi leaned back into her plumpness, letting her mother envelop her in a hug. Her mother whispered, "What did the officer say?"

"He said they're looking for the body." Andi melted into her mother, warm and soft and safe. Real tears began to flow and deep, racking sobs shook her body. She squeezed her eyes shut and willed herself to stop. Feeling sorry for herself would do no good. Chad had been her husband, her life, but he had also been cruel.

Andi pushed herself to her feet and turned toward her mother. Martha held her daughter and rocked back and forth. "It's going to be okay."

Andi sucked in a deep breath. "I--I don't know what happened--"

Her mother gently pressed a finger to her daughter's lips, "Shush, baby. What's done is done."

Andi snapped her head up to look into her mother's eyes. Did she know? Did she suspect there was more to it than a simple accident? No judgment lived in those big brown eyes, just love. Her mother held her hand sandwiched between hers, and memories of Andi's childhood tripped over themselves in a rush to the surface. Making peanut butter cookies. Mama's hands balling the dough, criss-crossing the tops with a fork. The quilt they pieced when she was in high school, made from her favorite childhood clothes.

That was so long ago. She sniffled. "What am I going to do now? What happens next?"

"You can always move back home." Martha gently squeezed her daughter's arm and said, "But first things first. We've got to get the arrangements made and then we'll get through the funeral together."

"But there's no body yet." Andi turned away and lifted the coffee cup to her lips, savoring the warmth and bitterness. The liquid burned all the way to her stomach.

Somehow, she would get through this. She had to. The thought of being alone overwhelmed her. But for right now, all she had to do was hold it together until they found his body, and then get through the funeral.

She turned, looked over the lip of her cup at her mother and asked, "Does his mother know?"

"The police notified her. She called here while you were asleep and I talked to her. Told her we'd call her when the arrangements were made."

Andi's eyebrows arched, "And she was okay with that?"

Martha harrumphed and stood up, then tugged her simple blue dress down to straighten the wrinkles and said, "Guess she had to be."

The corners of Andi's mouth twitched up as her mother turned away. Mama never had liked the overbearing and snooty Cora Adams.

She'd been so focused on her own situation, she hadn't even thought to ask about her sister. She asked, "How's Mandy?"

"She's fine. Busy as ever. Little Jakey is running a fever, so she had to stay home and take care of him."

Martha busied herself at the counter, wiping crumbs away with a quick hand, then turned to face her daughter, "But she wants you to know she's thinking about you and she'd been here if she could've. She sends her prayers."

"Her family comes first," Andi regretted not being closer to her family. Moving away when she got married had been difficult. She and Chad had such a whirlwind romance, that summer after her junior year in college. She'd shocked everyone when she didn't return to college that fall and got married instead. Chad asked her to marry him and move to Maine, and she'd been over the moon.

Martha frowned and sighed, "Don't be petty, hon."

"I'm not. Really, I understand." Andi got up and refilled both coffee cups, then added creamer and sugar to them and stirred.

Martha put her hand on her daughter's and shook her head. "Honey, you don't have to do everything for me. I'm not Chad."

Andi froze. With the mere mention of his name, grief washed over her like a wave. Her husband was gone. She nodded and walked out of the room, stood in the living room for a moment, then lowered herself into a chair. What would life be like after Chad? She'd never been alone.

Her mother followed her and sat on the couch. The two women sipped their coffee in silence. Andi gazed out the window and wondered how she ended up here. She'd been so happy when she'd married Chad, so eager to please him. But as he grew more demanding, she struggled to keep up appearances. She'd been careful not to let anyone know how difficult her life had become. She couldn't let her mother know the marriage had been a mistake, no more than she could let the women from the

Library Board know that her handsome husband was a petty bully behind closed doors. Even with him gone, she didn't want anyone to pity her.

After the coffee was gone, Andi stood and took Mama's cup, then walked towards the kitchen. On the way, she caught her reflection in the hall mirror. Her dark ponytail fell to the center of her back, because Chad liked long hair and didn't want it cut. Long bangs hid her blue eyes, and her round face made her look plumper than she was. Chad called her Chipmunk Cheeks. Claimed it was a pet name, but it hurt and he knew it.

"Need any help, honey?" Martha called from the living room.

"No," Andi answered, as she turned away from her reflection and walked into the kitchen, "Just filling the dishwasher."

Her cell phone chirped again. She wiped her hands on a dishtowel and glanced at the caller ID. Anonymous. She answered.

"Mrs. Adams?" The voice on the other end was gruff.

Her stomach fluttered with unease. "Yes."

"Detective Johnson. You comin' down or not?"

She straightened and the muscles in her back tensed. "Did you find him?"

"Not yet. Told you the Coast Guard has already got cutters out searching. Half o' Buccaneer Bay is out on the water helping search."

She opened and closed her mouth like a fish out of water. "Um, sure. Of course. I'll be there as soon as I can."

Martha held out her hand and motioned for the phone. Andi blinked, then turned it over.

The scowl on Martha's face matched her voice when she spoke. "Who is this?" Her eyes narrowed as she listened. "You may be the law, but I'm her mother. The poor child had the shock of her life last night and the doctor had to give her pills to help her sleep."

Martha pressed her lips into a thin line as she listened, then she broke in. "I'll bring her down in a bit, if she's up to it."

Andi's eyes widened at her mother's insolence. Her mother pulled the phone from her ear and looked at it, then handed it to Andi and shrugged. "I don't know how to turn the gol-danged thing off."

Andi took the phone and pressed the red button, then looked at her mother with wide eyes. "I can't believe you spoke to him like that."

Martha's heavy eyebrows scrunched together. "And I can't believe he never did nothing about your good-for-nothing husband."

Andi's eyes widened in surprise. She opened her mouth to speak, but her mother held up her hand, palm out. "Don't want to hear anymore about it, but maybe we should go down to the harbor and see if they can find the SOB's body."

3

Though her mother insisted on driving, Andi convinced her that she could get them to the harbor quicker and would know where to park. They drove down Main Street, rounded a curve and the harbor appeared before them. Tall masts sprung up from the boats like a forest of toothpicks, and white sails billowed in the salty breeze. As they turned into the parking lot, Andi was blown away by the number of cars already there. Parking would be at a premium after the tourists arrived after Memorial Day, but early May was still quiet. She drove down three aisles before she found a parking space.

They got out of the car and walked towards a clump of people gathered on the pier. An unmarked police car slanted across the two end spaces.

As they walked, the crowd parted for them. Several folks murmured their apologies and sympathies, but some simply stared and others whispered behind their hands.

Andi pointed to a long white boat with a red stripe along its side. "There. That's a Coast Guard boat."

The two women walked out to the end of the pier, towards the boat. With every step, Andi's dread grew. As they reached the end, a thick-set older man stared at them. He stood facing them with his feet planted far apart and his arms crossed over his chest.

He pointed at the sun hanging low over the little village of Buccaneer Bay. "Wondered if you were ever going to get here."

Martha opened her mouth to speak, but Andi placed a hand on her forearm and murmured, "I'm sorry. It's been a rough day."

He narrowed his eyes and looked her up and down. "You remember anything new about last night?"

She shook her head. "Have you had any luck today?"

He swept his hand to indicate the harbor. "Coast Guard is running a grid. Been having trouble all day 'cause so many folks is out there trying to help and doing nothing but gettin' in the way."

Her mom stepped forward. "We don't want to be in the way. Is there someplace we can wait?"

He snorted. "Right here."

Andi gazed out into the harbor. He was right. A constant parade of boats flowed out of the harbor, and nearly all of them turned north. She lost sight of them as they rounded the bend, but she knew they would cruise along the craggy cliffs that rose up out of the sea to the north of Buccaneer Bay. That might be a good thing, because the cutters were big and couldn't get in as close as some of the smaller vessels, but she hoped they were careful. Rocks jutted up out of the ocean at odd angles, and some lurked just below the surface, waiting to tear a hole in an unsuspecting boat.

One of the waitresses from the Black Sails Diner brought Andi a cup of black coffee, which she gladly accepted. She wrapped her fingers around the warmth and sipped occasionally, glad for the bitterness. It fit her mood. Seagulls swooped around her, snatching crumbs dropped by those who hung around, hoping to catch some news. The people were as bad as the seagulls, she thought. Looking for crumbs.

After some time, she became aware of Martha's heavy sighs. Andi glanced at her mother and noticed her shifting her weight from foot to foot. "I'm sorry, Mama. You need to go sit down. Do you want to take the car home?"

Her mother shook her head. "Of course not. I'll stay here with you."

A young female officer with a long blonde ponytail stepped forward. "Ma'am, if you'd like to wait up at the Coast Guard Station, there are some benches up there."

Her mother glanced back towards the white building with sun-bleached red shingles near the base of the pier, then looked at Andi. "Want to go wait there?"

Andi shook her head. She looked from her mother to the blue water, then back again. "I'd rather wait here, but you go on ahead."

The young officer said, "I'll walk with you."

Her mom's eyebrows rose and Andi nodded, then turned to gaze out at the sea again. Her eyes swept the harbor, looking for any sign that anyone might have found anything. She watched boats come in and boats go out. Felt the warmth being chased away by the lengthening shadows, and shivered. A part of her still expected to wake up and find this was all a bad dream. She paced the wooden deck. Why hadn't they found his body yet?

The detective passed her several times, but never spoke. He talked into his radio constantly. Andi could make out words here and there, but nothing of consequence.

The young female officer approached her when the sun had nearly set behind Cadillac Mountain. "I'm going to get sandwiches from the Black Sails. Thought I'd get your mother something. Want me to pick anything up for you?"

Andi shook her head. The way her stomach fluttered, the thought of food was not appealing. As the blonde turned away, Andi called out, "Wait! Can you see if someone can give my mother a ride home? There's no reason for her to stay here."

"Why? You think we're not going to find anything?" The detective's gruff voice startled her.

She turned to find him standing less than a foot behind her. She stepped back. "They haven't found anything yet."

"So why are you sticking around? Think they won't find anything?"

"No!" She stuttered and blinked, rapid fire. "Well, because they may find something."

He pursed his lips and studied her. "We'll keep looking. And if there's anything out there, the Coast Guard'll find it, if the crabs and sharks don't find it first."

Her hackles raised at his callousness. She narrowed her eyes. "It? That is my husband you're talking about, not chum."

One corner of his mouth twitched up, then he turned on his heel and marched back to the end of the pier where the Coast Guard officials were gathered. She fought to control her temper, but the blood pounded in her ears. That man infuriated her. He seemed to enjoy getting a rise out of her. Pushed her buttons just to see her react.

She clasped her hands behind her back and braced her feet wide, then stared out at the darkening sea. That man would not get to her. Instead, she turned her thoughts to her husband. What if the sharks had gotten to him? She hoped he died quickly. No one deserved a slow, painful death. Not even Chad. What if they couldn't find him? What if there was no body?

The reality of the situation began to sink in. The antagonism of the detective worried her. Did he think she'd killed her husband? Could he charge her, even with no evidence?

After a while, her legs began to ache. She sat down on the pier and dangled her legs over the side. She gripped the rough wooden edge, almost glad for the uncomfortable sensation. It gave her something to think about besides Chad.

She watched as her shadow reached out and stretched over the blue-green water. A stream of boats returned from their search. As the sun sank behind her, the Coast Guard cutter appeared around the bend and chugged to the pier, where it slid into its slip. The crew disembarked and filed past her. The captain, a middle-aged man with a deep tan, approached the detective and the two of them huddled together. The older man turned and looked at her over his shoulder, then shook the younger man's hand. The captain walked along the pier and touched the brim of his hat with his fingertips when he reached her. Neither of them spoke to her.

Andi watched the sea until the sun had set behind her and she was alone on the pier. She wasn't sure what she was waiting for. Going home to an empty house? At least her mother was there. But what would she do when Martha went back home to Missouri?

4

The funeral director, a slight man with wire rimmed glasses perched on a hook nose, pulled a large map from behind his desk and spread it out between them. He spoke with a voice, cultivated to sooth those in mourning. "Most of our clients choose to be buried in Bayview Cemetery. Your mother told me over the phone that she did not believe you and Dr. Adams had yet purchased plots?"

Names filled the creased map, so neat and orderly. Andi opened her mouth, struggled for words, aware of his eyes upon her, then shook her head.

"Let's choose a place you can visit whenever you want, a place to go to remember your husband."

Andi looked down at her hands clasped in her lap. The cluster of diamonds on her left finger reflected the light. Remembering her husband wouldn't be a problem. Forgetting all he'd done to her might be. She took a deep breath and glanced at the map spread out between them, "How much for a plot?"

"A double plot would be-"

She cleared her throat and asked, "How much for a single?" She'd never worried about money during her marriage, but it had been on her mind since the accident.

Mr. Bolan blinked rapidly behind his round glasses. The clock on the wall ticked away the seconds. "It is traditional for a married couple to have a double plot."

The thought of a headstone with her name and year of birth on it made her queasy. Martha grasped Andi's hand and squeezed, then tapped one finger on the map. "He's right, honey. Double plots are traditional."

Thoughts tumbled through Andi's mind. What if she remarried? What if she moved back home to Missouri? The silence of the room closed in around her, the only sound was the squeak of leather as her mother fidgeted in her chair. Finally, she nodded.

Martha sighed and Mr. Bolan pressed his thin lips together as he wrote up the contract for the double plot. Andi signed the contract and asked, "What next?"

He centered a printed form on his desk and poised his pen, "We pride ourselves on providing a remembrance service that honors the memory of your loved one. A funeral is, after all, for the living."

So many of Andi's memories were locked away in a dark corner of her mind. She and Chad had kept their private lives private. Keeping it private would be her way of honoring his memory. Besides, she couldn't bear for people to know the truth. People would think she was weak, or deserved it.

He asked about surviving family members and where they lived, then asked, "Were there any civic organizations Dr. Adams was involved in?"

"He was a member of a fraternity in college, but I don't recall the name." The more questions he asked, the more she realized she didn't know her husband. She could feel the wiry man's eyes boring into her. "I'm sorry, I'm drawing a blank."

He tapped his pen on the desk, then said, "Well, we'll come back to that. Why don't you consult with family or friends and then get back to me?"

The whole thing felt surreal. Andi couldn't believe she was making funeral arrangements for her husband. What would she do? How would she make ends meet? Then it hit her like a ton of bricks. Her eyes widened and she spun to face her mother. "His office. His patients. We need to go by the office."

Martha nodded as she plucked a tissue from the box on the desk and tucked it into her daughter's hand. She said, "We can run by there before we go home."

Mr. Bolan paused for a moment, a small smile hovering, but not quite lighting, on his lips. After a beat, he asked, "Now, about memorials. Many times our clients request that a donation be made to a local charity. Is there a charity you would like to list, perhaps one that Dr. Adams felt strongly about?"

He felt strongly about a lot of things, but the only charity that came to mind was the local animal shelter. Someone abandoned a cat in the neighborhood the previous summer. The lanky orange tabby cat looked like an awkward teenager. Andi fed him, afraid he'd never make it through the harsh Maine winter. Chad hated the cat, which he referred to as "it." The kitty disappeared just as he'd started to fatten up. Although Chad never admitted to it, she suspected he'd gotten rid of the poor thing.

She took a deep breath, sat up straight in the chair and said, "Yes, as a matter of fact, I think donations to the Buccaneer Bay Animal Shelter instead of flowers would be nice."

Martha stifled a cough and looked at Andi, eyebrows arched, but didn't say anything. Mr. Bolan jotted the final notes in his book, then slapped it closed and pushed his chair back. "Might I suggest that you stop at the masonry shop to pick out a stone? We have some brochures with a variety of options available--"

The rest of the morning passed in a fog. Being a widow hadn't even begun to sink in. Andi floated along on auto-pilot. After they finished with the funeral home and the mason's, they drove to the south edge of town. They pulled into a small concrete parking lot and Andi stared at the squat red brick building with white columns and black shutters. Chad's receptionist's yellow Subaru sat alone in the lot.

Martha stepped out of the car. "Did you bring your key?"

Andi shook her head. "I don't have a key." She examined a sheet of copy paper taped to the front door, then read it out loud. "Office closed until further notice due to an emergency."

"Then whose car is that?" Martha slammed the car door harder than necessary.

Andi tugged on the front door and it swung open. "Jennie's. Remember? You met her at the house yesterday."

"So he trusted her and not you?" Martha rolled her eyes. "I always thought he spent too much time at work."

Andi glanced at her mother, but didn't comment.

Martha followed her daughter into the building. The waiting room, decorated in soothing shades of blue, had an air of relaxed sophistication. Dark blue fabric covered chairs lined the walls. White sponged clouds formed a border along the top of the walls, and a rainbow mural decorated the area blocked off for children. Though Andi had suggested a children's area, he dismissed it as ridiculous, yet when his receptionist offered to paint the waiting area and surprised him with the clouds and rainbow, he praised it as a brilliant move.

That hadn't surprised her in the least.

The two women followed the sound of Jennie's voice, and found her sitting in Chad's brown leather chair in his office, on the telephone with a patient. Her long blonde hair cascaded past her shoulders in loose curls, and her slightly smudged mascara was the only visible imperfection in her cosmetic armor.

Chad's dental certificate from the University of Missouri-Kansas City hung on the wall directly behind his desk, along with his undergraduate degree from the University of Colorado. A large color photo of him and his fraternity brothers on a ski trip hung on the wall to the right. Several of them had autographed it, and the words "Winter Break 1998" were written in large slanted script in black magic marker at an angle at the top right of the photo. He still talked fondly of his frat brothers, and kept in touch with several of them. They got together for ski trips, and the occasional golf trip. Someone should contact them, but she didn't even know their names. He referred to them simply as his "brothers."

His big oak desk looked as if he'd just left it, with the black flat-screen monitor on one side and papers stacked neatly in the chrome in-tray and out-tray. His small, precise doodles in the margin framed his neat handwriting on the blotter. The only personal item on his desk was the chrome business card holder Andi gave him for a birthday gift a few years ago. The room looked as if he might come walking in the door at any moment, ready to handle his patients.

Andi and her mother stood in the doorway until Jennie glanced up with red, puffy eyes. She smiled sadly and nodded a greeting, then murmured, "I'm so sorry."

Andi nodded again. Her eyes should be puffy like that. But her eyes were dry, so dry they burned. She gestured towards the telephone and said, "Thank you for doing this. I really appreciate it."

Jennie flipped the notebook closed, then kept her hand on top of it, fingers splayed. "It's the least I can do. I hope you don't mind. When I left your house yesterday, I thought about all that you have on your mind, and you don't need to worry about this stuff." She swiveled in the chair, then pushed to her feet with an exhausted sigh.

"You're right. I haven't had time . . ." As Andi's voice trailed off, Martha cleared her throat. The three women stood there, the silence buzzing around them.

Andi motioned to the ski trip picture, "Do you know how to get in touch with Chad's friends from college?"

Jennie nodded and said, "Doctor kept his contacts in his agenda. I'd be glad to send them a letter if you'd like."

Andi nodded and looked around the office. Thoughts tumbled in her brain, disconnected. Chad handled everything himself. He'd kept all aspects of the business close to the vest. But now, he was gone. And she would have to pick up the pieces.

"Jennie, I know this puts you in a tough position, but can you help wrap things up with the practice? And, of course, I'll do anything I can to help you get another job."

"I know. And I appreciate that. I don't know what I'm going to do." The last word rose into a whine. She sucked in a shaky breath and closed her eyes for a beat, then produced two business cards. "I went ahead and called our accountant and corporate lawyer. I'm sure they'll be in touch."

Andi nodded and rubbed her thumb across the embossed cards. The familiarity in Jennie's voice rubbed her the wrong way, and from the look on her mother's face, it irritated her, too.

She touched her mother's arm. "Come on, Mama. We've got a lot to do."

Martha lowered her chin and stared at the busty blonde for a beat, then turned and marched out of the room with Andi in tow.

As they drove north towards home, Andi considered telling her mother that she suspected Chad of having a fling with his receptionist. She couldn't even elevate it to an affair in her mind. Chad laughed and denied it when she asked him about it, but the thought nagged at her. Still, she didn't want to say it out loud. Saying the words made it seem real, tangible. Besides, her mother hadn't liked Chad and would never let her hear the end of it.

At least the girl would take care of things at the office, which Andi couldn't handle on her own. The practice needed to be closed and the business wrapped up. Maybe there'd be a little money in it.

Money.

Her blood ran cold. She hadn't worked since she waitressed at Pizza Hut back in Missouri. No work experience. No degree. Who would hire her? How would she survive? She swallowed hard. Perhaps it would be possible to sell the business, maybe to a new dentist moving in. Dana would know about that. Andi missed her best friend. She couldn't wait to talk to her.

Just as it had throughout the day, fear niggled at Andi, taunting her. For the hundredth time, she closed her eyes and watched her husband topple into the ocean. Surely it had been an accident. She wanted to believe that, but felt guilty that she'd wished him gone many times.

Martha's voice roused her from her reverie. As they turned into the subdivision, Martha said, "She seems like a nice girl."

Andi nodded. "She is." She stepped on the brakes and signaled as they neared the white, two-story house.

Her mother sighed heavily. "She seems very close to Chad."

"She is," Andi repeated.

"Do you think he was ever unfaithful to you?" Mama glanced at her, then added, "It just seems that he spent a lot of late nights at the office, and she's a pretty girl."

"She is." Andi turned into the concrete driveway and stopped in front of the double garage, "And I would be lying if I said I never suspected anything. But it doesn't matter anymore."

"Do you trust her to help you close the business?"

Andi put the gearshift in park and turned the engine off. She sat for a moment and took a deep breath, then got out before answering. "The practice needs to be closed. She knows more about it than I do, and I think she'll do the right thing. So, yes, I trust her."

Martha swung out of the car. "With the business."

"Yes," Andi said, "With the business."

"You ought to talk to Dana about the business stuff. She's works for a lawyer, right?" The older woman rounded the front of the sedan, then ambled up the sidewalk, grunting with each step.

"Yes, she does." Andi trusted her best friend more than anyone. "She's on vacation right now. I didn't want to bug her, but I sent her a text that I need to talk to her when she gets back. I'll ask her before I let Jennie do anything."

Andi inserted her key in the lock and pushed opened the heavy dark green door. Mama followed her daughter in and said, "I'm glad. Trust Dana. She'll steer you right."

Martha followed Andi through the tiled foyer and into the living room. "Have you thought about what you want him to be buried in?"

"They haven't even found him yet." Andi dropped onto the sleek gray couch. "I wonder if I should be out there. I should be, shouldn't I?"

Martha shrugged, "They'll call when they find the body."

"If they find the body."

Martha shook her head. "Think positive, sweetheart."

Andi let her head fall back and closed her eyes. Chad would want to look his best. His appearance and what others thought mattered to him. It seemed like such an odd thing, though, to worry about what a dead person would be wearing for eternity. How long would the clothes last? Would they rot, like his body would? Or did embalming keep the body from rotting? What would he look like if the insurance company questioned whether or not it was an accident and insisted that he be – what was the word they used? Disinterred? – in six months so an autopsy could be performed?

Andi took a deep breath and let it out in a huff. “I guess one of his suits. He has a charcoal gray suit that looks nice. Guess I’ll go get it together so it'll be ready when they find him.”

As if on cue, her cell chirped. She took a deep breath and answered.

The detective's gruff voice greeted her. "Body washed up. Old couple walking the coastline up near Black Bear Cove found it."

Andi's fingers turned white as she gripped the phone. She met her mother's concerned eyes and nodded.

"You there?"

She nodded, then said, "Yes. Yes, I'm here."

"Medical examiner's takin' the body. After he's done, he'll send it over to the funeral home. Be a day or so."

A chunk of ice settled in her gut and the cold spread throughout her body. A lump formed in her throat and she swallowed hard. "Do I need to identify the body?"

He snorted, "No need. We got dental records waitin' at the morgue."

The phone went dead. She lowered her hand and stared at the phone. No pleasantries whatsoever with that man.

So, they found him.

Her husband was dead.

She shivered, then squeezed her eyes shut, but no tears fell. Maybe that would happen at the funeral.

Martha cleared her throat and said, "Well, then. I guess we need to make sure those clothes are at the funeral home." She scooted forward on the sofa as Andi pushed herself to her feet. The two walked upstairs. Martha kept one hand under Andi's elbow as if she were the elderly person that might fall at any moment and break a hip.

When they reached the master bedroom, Andi turned to her mother and said, “I need to do this myself. Alone. Okay?”

Martha gave a quick nod and said, “I’m tired. I think I’ll go take a nap. Call me if you need anything.”

What Andi really needed was to talk to Dana. She’d call when she got back. Andi didn't want to bother her or worry her. Hopefully she’d get back in time for the funeral. It wasn’t like Dana could do anything, it'd just be nice to talk to her.

In the meantime, there were things that needed to be tended to, though, so Andi took a deep breath and turned her attention to picking out something for her husband to be buried in.

Neutral shades gave the bedroom a modern, but elegant look. The room was longer than it was wide, with a sitting area in front of the deep bay window. It would have been the perfect place for a reading nook, with a comfortable chair and a side table just large enough for a book and a cup of tea. Instead, Chad set up his treadmill there. Andi walked to his closet, the larger of the two closets in the room, and tugged the double doors open. She selected a dark gray suit and the ivory button down shirt that hung with it. She stood for a moment fingering the smooth silkiness of the suit, remembering the day he bought it.

He spent more on that one suit than she spent on clothes in a year, but when she mentioned that she’d like to get a new shirt, too, he pointed out that he made the money, and her contribution was zero, so he would spend his money any way he saw fit. She reminded him that he would not let her get a job.

She touched her jaw with the tips of her fingers, remembering how it had popped painfully when he responded with a closed fist.

She sighed, grateful he would not be able to hurt her again.

The telephone on the nightstand jangled and demanded her attention.

"Hello?"

"I know what you did."

"Who is this?" Her nerves tingled. "What do you want?"

"I want those documents." He breathed heavily into the phone. "You thought they were worth killing for and I have no problem doing whatever I have to do to get you out of the way. I'll be in touch."

The phone went dead and she dropped onto the bed, her mouth hanging open. What the heck? That made no sense at all.

Martha hollered from across the hall, "Who was that?"

Andi blinked and stared at the phone. "I don't know."

"Do you need help picking out something?"

"No. No, I'm fine. I'll do it." Someone's idea of a bad joke?

She shook her head and turned to the dresser to open his valet box. He would want to be buried with his diamond cufflinks, even though no one would see them. Two rough pink and green rocks sat next to his cufflinks in a little velvet lined compartment. She frowned. Seemed like an odd thing for him to keep there. She scooped up the diamonds and clipped them to his dress shirt. She opened his top dresser drawer to get a monogrammed handkerchief for the suit pocket, then slammed the drawer shut, a bit harder than she intended. Something rattled. She frowned, opened the drawer again and rummaged through the contents. In the back of the drawer, tucked under the lining, she found a small brown envelope. She squeezed it open and a key on a beaded chain dropped into her palm.

What could it possibly open?

5

The metal felt cool in her palm. She flipped the small, gold-colored key over, but there was no writing on either side of the round head. It didn't look familiar.

The doorbell chimed and Mama hollered that she would get it. Andi stuck the key in her jeans' pocket, then grabbed the suit and shirt and went downstairs.

Mrs. Harrison stepped inside and held out a basket of muffins. "I thought you might like some of my wicked good chocolate chip muffins."

Andi's mother accepted the basket.

"Again, Andi, I'm so sorry for your loss. You know, I lost Mr. Harrison several years ago, so if you ever need to talk or want someone to go to dinner with, you just let me know." Mrs. Harrison's hand fluttered at her chest. "Poor dear had a stroke and hung on for nearly a year. Awful way to go, that."

Andi wasn't sure how to respond.

Mrs. Harrison's thinly drawn eyebrows inched up her forehead. "Thought I'd stop in and offer to take the clothes up to the funeral home for you."

Andi blinked, "I'm sorry?"

The woman smiled, exposing a smudge of red lipstick on her front tooth. "I heard they found the body. I'm sure that was a mess, after being in the water, what with all the crabs and sharks and lobsters nibbling away."

Anger flared, but Andi took a deep breath and kept her voice steady, just as she learned to do with Chad. "I'm not really sure. The police notified me that the body had been recovered and would be delivered to the funeral home." She bowed her head slightly and let her dark hair fall forward to hide her face.

The wiry woman plucked the clothes out of Andi's hands and draped them over her arm. "Closed casket, I assume?"

Andi stepped forward and started to close the door. "Yes. Thanks again."

Mrs. Harrison craned her neck forward, but Andi closed the door before the woman could ask anything else. A shiver ran up Andi's spine. She leaned back against the door for a moment, then followed Martha into the kitchen.

"I'll add Mrs. Harrison's muffins to her list. She's already brought over a casserole and a fresh loaf of bread." Martha scribbled the addition to her detailed list of those who had stopped by to offer their condolences in the form of a casserole or pan of lasagna.

"Thanks, Mama. I'll get thank you notes out after the funeral." It was one of the niceties of small town living that Andi treasured. It was nice to not have to think about what to make for dinner for a change. She glanced at the menu displayed on the refrigerator, started to walk away, then stopped. She pivoted on one foot, then tore the paper off and wadded it up.

Her meals would never be dictated by a menu on the refrigerator again now that Chad was gone.

Friends and neighbors dropped by throughout the day, most bearing food, and all curious. Playing the part of the grieving widow sapped her energy. Life had been turned upside down, and Andi found it difficult to keep from withdrawing into herself. She wanted to escape to her room with a good book. Instead, she made her way around the room with a tray of little individual quiches. Virginia Fable, the nosy neighbor at the end of the block, stopped Andi. Virginia arrived earlier in the afternoon with her infamous ziti casserole, which she took to every church dinner and potluck in town. And which she packed home nearly full every time because she never actually cooked the ziti.

She waggled a crooked finger under Andi's nose and chided, "It is not appropriate for you to play host when you've just lost your husband. You should be sitting there crying."

Stunned, Andi dropped her chin and hid behind her dark hair as it fell forward. The heat in her cheeks frustrated her. Head still down, she glanced around and made eye contact with her mother. Martha met her eyes and nodded towards a chair. Andi sighed, then sat down and played the part that was expected. Except for the crying. The tears still wouldn't come.

Two days later, Martha drove her daughter to the funeral home for the visitation. Mr. Bolan greeted the two women at the entry and led them down a plush hallway to a hushed room. The casket sat at the front of the room, the polished steel gleaming. Martha had suggested the funeral director close the casket before they arrived, and Andi was glad for that.

She hadn't seen her husband since he disappeared over the cliff. Had no desire to see him again, either. In a way, she'd already grieved the loss of her husband. That process started less than six months into the marriage, when the fairytale evaporated into thin air as the real Chad revealed himself. The tears weren't there to fall anymore.

A red sash that said simply "husband" wove through the large floral arrangement draped over the top of the casket. Another funeral spray, slightly smaller, sat next to the arrangement Andi had picked out. No card, no banner. Odd. Andi made a mental note to ask the funeral director about it, or perhaps the florist, in case the card had been dropped. She wanted to make sure everyone who sent flowers was properly thanked.

One of Chad's professional photos, the same as on his business card, sat on an easel propped up next to the casket. His smile, his best feature, was at least partially responsible for his success as a dentist. Martha held Andi's elbow as they walked to the front of the room, then stood in front of the casket. Andi reached out and caressed the cold metal with her fingertips, wondering what he looked like inside the darkness, then she turned away.

Mr. Bolan led them to the front row. The two women sat quietly. Andi's gaze lit on the casket, but her thoughts were elsewhere. Numbness spread throughout her body, and she wondered when she would begin feeling again.

A strangled sob broke the silence.

She turned to see a tall, thin blonde staggering up the aisle, a thick man with a dark tan at her side, gripping her elbow. Seeing her mother-in-law always made her feel inadequate. Cora was everything Andi wasn't - elegant, cultured and gorgeous. Andi smoothed her thick dark hair self-consciously, then tugged at her black dress. It clung to her generous curves and reminded Andi of Chad's description of her. Round. She sighed and faced forward, anxious to avert her eyes from her perfect mother-in-law.

Martha had called Chad's mother to pass along the details of the arrangements, but the last message from Cora indicated they were flying into Portland and renting a car so no one would have to pick them up. They lived in California, never visited Maine – Chad always flew out to see them -- and rarely called. When Cora did call, she didn't talk to Andi. Being an only child, Chad was the center of her life. And he outlasted three husbands.

"Oh, my baby! My baby!" Cora fell forward, pressing her rouged cheek to the casket.

When she finally stood, she kept a protective hand on the smooth metal, as though it connected her to her son. She squared her shoulders, then turned and pinned Andi with cold, gray eyes. Andi felt as if she were looking into Chad's eyes again.

Grant released Cora, and turned away from the casket. He smiled sadly as he stepped forward, then leaned down to give Andi an awkward hug.

"I'm so sorry. So sorry," he whispered against her hair.

She squeezed back, thankful that he wasn't searching for just the right thing to say. That seemed to just make things worse. Several people had lamented her husband's untimely death. What was that supposed to mean anyway? It's not like you jot it down in your DayPlanner. Andi was sick of hearing what a wonderful man her husband had been from people who knew nothing of the man she shared her home and bed with.

"I know. It's awful," she whispered back. For the first time, she felt tears threaten, but none spilled over. She sniffled and looked up as Grant straightened. Cora moved to stand beside him and wrapped her bony hands around his arm, then stared at Andi.

Martha motioned to the cushioned pew. "Please, have a seat."

Grant sat next to Andi, with Cora beside him. An occasional sniffle broke the silence. The doors opened and people started filing in, some Andi knew and some she didn't, but all insisted on telling her what a shame it was to lose such a wonderful man before his time. She nodded, accepted hugs and let Martha handle the questions.

Cora nattered on about her "baby," and occasionally broke out in a high-pitched wail that hurt the ears.

At last, Andi spotted a friendly face, and waited anxiously for her best friend to pay her respects. Dana looked completely put together as always, in a black suit with a beige blouse and a simple strand of pearls at her neck. Freckles sprinkled across her nose and cheeks gave her a youthful appearance. Her red hair was shoulder length, straight, shiny and healthy.

Dana leaned in and gave Andi a real hug, a tight, caring embrace. Dana whispered, "I'm sorry – I know you've got so much to think about right now. I'll call and we'll get together tomorrow."

Andi introduced her best friend to Martha, then explained, "Dana works for Edward Jordan's firm here in Buccaneer Bay. She's his paralegal."

"So nice to meet you. Andi has told me so much about you. I'm going to have to get back to Missouri soon, so I'm depending on you to help my little girl through this." Martha put her arm around her daughter's shoulders, "Unless I can talk her into moving home."

Dana patted Andi on the arm and said, "That's what friends are for. And probate and estates are what I do for a living, so I'm glad to help."

Just then, Cora let out another gasping, theatrical sob. Dana looked at Andi and winked, then moved on to give her condolences to the grieving mother. Andi sent up a prayer of thanks for such a good friend, and turned to the next person in line, a sad smile tugging at the corners of her mouth. It felt as though her face might break under the strain.

Jennie gave her an awkward hug, then pulled her companion forward. She said, "You remember my husband, Jeff?"

"Yes, of course. Good to see you again, Jeff." Andi accepted yet another awkward hug and felt the man's ribs through his cotton dress shirt. No matter how many times she had met them, Jennie insisted on introducing him as her husband. Andi continued, "I don't think I've seen you since you were at our house for dinner just before Christmas."

He nodded and his eyes darted over the faces that surrounded them. His eyes brightened and he waved at a familiar face, then quickly excused himself. Jennie glanced over her shoulder at the casket and her brown eyes welled with glistening tears. She pulled a tissue from her purse and disappeared into the crowd.

When Andi and her mother finally got home, they were greeted by peace and calm. Andi escaped to her bedroom to change out of the black dress that made her feel like the Michelin man, and slipped on her favorite flannel pajamas. Martha followed suit.

Andi went downstairs and looked in the refrigerator, filled to overflowing with dishes and plates and pans of every shape and size. All that food. All those calories. She sighed and closed the door. When Martha came downstairs, she shooed her daughter out of the kitchen, so Andi settled into her favorite chair in the living room and looked out the front window.

She fell in love with this house because of that big picture window, and had been so excited when Chad finally agreed to buy it. From her first visit to Maine, she had been drawn to the depths of the Atlantic. The deep blue-green water called to her. She loved the view from their house, perched on top of a hill. She pulled the fleece throw closer around her and watched the beam from the lighthouse sweep across the darkness.

Martha carried in a tray of goodies and flipped the light switch. She set the tray down on the coffee table and dropped onto the sleek gray sofa with a grunt. Andi leaned forward to get a mug of cocoa. Mini-marshmallows bobbed merrily in the foam, and she smiled. She hadn't had marshmallows in her hot cocoa in years.

Martha blew on her steaming beverage, then said, "That was quite the experience. Looks like you and Chad have a lot of friends here in Buccaneer Bay."

Andi nodded and sipped her cocoa.

"Things are going to be tough for you now."

Andi nodded again, her thoughts turning to the last funeral she'd attended…her father's.

"I went through hell when your daddy died, mostly 'cause I didn't want to accept help from anyone." Martha stared out the window, focused on a spot far in the distance.

"I'm sorry. I should've been there for you," Andi whispered. Losing her daddy during her freshman year of college had been hard, but she hadn't given much thought to how it affected her mother.

Mama shook her head, "I wouldn't have let you anyway. Thought I had to be tough. But you don't have to do it alone."

"I know."

"Why don't you move back home?"

"I need to stay here," Andi glanced at her mother, "For now, anyway. I need to wrap things up. The dental practice and all. How long do you think you'll be able to stay?"

Her mother shrugged. "I'll head back after the funeral."

The thought of her mother leaving, of being left alone, disturbed Andi more than she wanted to admit. She thought about all the things that would come in the days to follow, the adjustment to being a widow and she ventured, "Do you think you could stay another week? We haven't seen each other in ages and it would be nice to have the company."

"No, your sister has already had a time trying to cobble together daycare." Mama leaned forward and sat her mug on the coffee table. "She can't afford to miss work and can't afford to pay a baby sitter."

Andi grabbed a cork coaster from the end table and slipped it under her mother's mug. "Don't you think Mandy could find somebody for just a few more days?"

Mama laughed, "No, she depends on me to be there when Jakey and Romy get off the school bus."

Andi frowned. "She takes advantage of you."

Her mother shook her head, "No – I'm glad to do it. Being a grandma is a blessing!"

Andi merely grunted in response, not sure what words could express what she felt. Even though she understood in her head, it still hurt in her heart. She was the oldest, the responsible one, and Mandy was the baby of the family that needed looking after. But she had her husband and her two kids. Andi had no one.

"What'd you say?"

Andi's voice trembled when she replied, "It's just that Mandy has you all the time, and I need you now. It's my turn."

"Now, Andrea, that's no way to talk. You know I dropped everything to be here, and I will stay until the funeral's over. But then I've got to get home. I have responsibilities there," Martha said, kindly but firmly. She waited until Andi met her stern gaze, "I'll buy you a plane ticket. Come home with me."

Andi sighed and shook her head, then flipped the television on. The two sipped their cocoa as they watched the news and gossiped about folks back home. They talked until the wee hours of the morning, something they hadn't done once since Andi'd gotten married after her junior year at college and moved out to Maine with Chad.

The next day Andi buried her husband, which was much harder than she'd anticipated.

6

The funeral service was brief, and tasteful, even though Cora's outbursts and theatrical sobs interrupted the eulogy a couple of times. Andi sat on the front row, tissues clutched tightly in both hands. More were tucked into her purse in case she needed them. Martha sat to her left, and Dana to her right.

Andi glanced around at the mourners, wondering how they knew her husband, how well they knew him. Watching them made her feel isolated. They were her husband's friends, not hers.

Her mind wandered, thinking about their courtship and the marriage, and wondering how it had all turned so sour. She didn't know. The framed portrait on the easel next to the casket showed a tanned, healthy man with a beautiful smile, but that smile never touched his cold, gray eyes.

Finally, they climbed into the black limo and left the historic old Yager-Wilson Funeral Home, up Second Street past the fire station. Half a dozen firefighters stood at attention as the procession passed. The hearse turned right on Maple, then a quick left onto First Street. Police cars with flashing lights blocked the intersections. Children played in the playground at the school, oblivious to the mourners passing them.

The procession continued north until it reached the arched iron gate. The limousine turned right and the cemetery sprawled before them, neat rows of gravestones marking the final resting places of the dead. Ahead and to the left, Andi noted the white tent that had been set up to cover Chad's grave. The black Towne Car glided to a stop.

Martha gave Andi's hand a squeeze. "You're almost through it, honey. Let's go get this over with."

Andi nodded and got out of the car. The long black hearse squatted directly in front of them, the back open. The pallbearers carried the casket to the gleaming gurney waiting under the shade of the tent. She turned away, directing her gaze at the long row of cars winding through the cemetery behind them. Dana's tan Impala was five cars back, and Andi was relieved Edward gave her friend time off work to attend the funeral.

The funeral director led Andi and her mother to the white folding chairs facing the yawning black hole. Everyone gathered around, their whispers lost in the cool spring breeze. The minister said a few words and led them in prayer, then approached Andi and whispered words meant to console.

She tried to focus on the words, but simply couldn't. Instead, her thoughts turned to the insurance policy Chad had insisted they buy. Everywhere she looked, she saw bills. The gleaming casket. The concrete vault in the ground. The tent flapping overhead. The gravediggers waiting discreetly behind a stand of oak trees. Worry niggled at her. How would she survive without Chad? People milled around, then the crowd drifted away from the tent in small groups. Andi wanted to leave, but was anchored in place by mourners paying their respects.

Off to the side, Detective Johnson stood by himself, his feet planted shoulder width apart and his thick hands clasped in front of him. His gray suit looked as if it had been purchased off the rack at Sears, and the front of his jacket didn't meet. His eyes were hidden behind dark glasses, but Andi could feel him staring at her.

The Towne Car waited, and Andi escaped to it as quickly as possible, winding her way through mourners who watched her with sad eyes. The cop stepped into her path. Before he could utter a word, the limo driver slipped between them and took Andi's elbow. She got into the car, and her mother followed.

Martha yanked the door shut and frowned, "That was rude. Why would he do such a thing?"

Andi shrugged. She stared out the tinted window and watched the detective walk away, his gait stiff. Dana walked past and Andi waved, but her best friend continued on, talking with a short, curvy woman with strawberry blonde hair who worked at the library. She had never felt so alone.

As they drove off, and Martha talked about how nice everyone was, Andi glanced back and watched as they lowered the polished casket into the ground.

7

Andi poked her head into the guest bedroom. "Want me to carry your bag?"

Mama stood next to the bed, beaming. She held out a white envelope. "Surprise!"

The return address was the Buccaneer Bay Travel Agency. Andi turned the envelope over. Her name was written on the outside. "What is this?"

Her mother clapped her hands together, as excited as a child on Christmas morning, "Go ahead - open it!"

Andi slipped her thumb under the flap and popped it open. She pulled out a boarding pass, then asked again, sounding out each syllable, "What is this?"

"Come home with me." Martha spread her arms wide. "We'll get someone to help box up the stuff you want to keep and we'll have it shipped. The rest of the stuff can be auctioned off."

Andi shook her head and stepped back, blinking rapidly. "Mama, I can't go back. This is my home."

Martha snorted. "Don't be ridiculous. Missouri is home." She stepped around Andi and walked across the hall to the master bedroom.

Andi hurried after her, anxiety building in her chest. Panic began to set in. "Mama, listen to me. I'm staying here."

Martha opened the closet and leaned forward to peer in. "We'll just pack a few things now. Everything you need is back home. You can have the basement if you don't want to stay in your old room."

Andi's breath came quickly. The last thing she wanted was to go back to the way things were. It would be like she'd never left. She'd worked hard to build a life for herself here. Served on the Board for the Friends of the Library. Took pride in her flower garden. She grabbed her mother's arm and tugged until her mother turned to face her. "Mama, I said I am staying here."

Martha's gray eyebrows pushed together and she wilted. Her shoulders slumped and her jaw dropped. Her voice was little more than a whisper. "But . . . But I already bought you a ticket."

Andi almost gave in, then swallowed the lump in her throat. Her mother couldn't afford this grand gesture. Though her mother would be hurt, Andi had lived for everyone else too long. "You'll just have to come out for another visit. I'm sure we can get the airline to issue a credit."

Her mother sighed and seemed to shrink two inches. She stared at Andi for a beat, then pushed past her and hurried across the hall. Andi followed, feeling like a heel for dashing her mother's hopes. Martha snagged her blue bag and dragged it off the bed, so it hit the floor with a thump. Andi reached for the carry-on, but her mother yanked it away then stomped down the stairs.

After they got into the Toyota, Martha fastened her seatbelt and asked, "My flight isn't until 4. Could we go up Highway 3?"

Andi nodded and smiled. "That's about the only way to get there. We're on an island, remember?"

Her mother dug in her purse. "Do you want some gum?"

Andi shook her head. She refrained from warning her mother about the dangers of the sugary treat.

"You sure?" Martha held out the package. "You used to love gum. Were always digging through my purse for a stick of gum."

"I'm not a kid anymore."

Martha tucked the gum back in her purse and stared out the window at the expanse of sea off to their right that appeared and disappeared through the trees. The ocean drew Andi toward it like a magnet. There was something majestic and awesome about the way it stretched to the horizon.

“You are so lucky,” Martha breathed.

Andi had to agree with her. Even though the locals still considered her an outsider, she felt like a Mainer. “Why don’t you come back out next month?”

Martha smiled, then patted Andi on the forearm. “I'd love to, but it's so hard for me to get away.”

Andi knew the answer before she'd asked. Maybe that's why she asked. She got points for asking, without dealing with the guilt trip. Suddenly, the evergreens gave way to water as they crossed over to Thompson Island. That little stretch of road had surprised her when she first moved to Mount Desert Island. On the map, it looked like there was a bridge. In reality, the highway straddled a muddy bit of land between the two islands. Crossing Thompson Island took only minutes, and then they were again surrounded by water as they crossed over to the mainland. In a few weeks, the tourists would start pouring in and Highway 3 would be slow-going.

At the Hancock County-Bar Harbor Airport, the two said their goodbyes and hugged several times before Martha disappeared through the security checkpoint. After she passed through the metal detector, she turned to wave one last time, and Andi blew her mother a kiss. Her mother would be in Boston and then on to Kansas City soon, and Andi would be left all alone in Buccaneer Bay.

But she still had Dana, she reminded herself. Thank God for Dana.

Shortly past the bridge at Hancock, a little red coupe zipped around her. The speedometer indicated she was driving nearly ten miles an hour under the speed limit, which was the exact opposite of how she usually drove. Andi sighed and shook her head to clear it, then glanced in the rearview mirror.

A light gray sedan followed a car's length back. The driver wore dark sunglasses, but Andi thought she recognized Detective Johnson. Why does one always feel nervous when followed by an officer of the law, even when doing nothing wrong? She pressed down on the gas until she was up to the speed limit, and he matched her speed. Sweat trickled down the back of Andi's neck, and she swallowed hard. She set the cruise just under 55, hoping he would pass, but even at that reduced speed, he kept following her. A chill ran down her spine, and she tried again to swallow the lump that had formed in her throat. She wished he would just pull her over.

He followed her all the way to her house, turn by turn, but continued on when she pulled into the driveway. As she forced herself to walk casually up the brick walk, the sedan's engine rumbled behind her. She glanced over her shoulder as she inserted the key in the front door, just as he turned right at the end of the block and disappeared from sight.

Once inside, she collapsed against the door and waited for her heartbeat to return to normal. Her head tipped back against the door and she stared at the ceiling. Her imagination ran wild, imagining what the police were after, that she was going to be arrested, that her freedom was short lived.

She'd done nothing wrong. Why was she freaking out? Her legs shook, but she pushed away from the door and peeked out the sidelight. No sign of the police. She shook her head and frowned. He was trying to shake her up, that was all. She had nothing to hide.

At least, she didn't think she did.

She knuckled away the tears that threatened to spill over. Chad was gone. She was a widow, and she had to find a way to continue without him.

She dragged herself up the stairs one step at a time. Her legs felt heavy as lead. She gripped the handrail tightly and pulled herself along. The emptiness in the house surrounded her like a living, breathing thing. It still didn't feel real, being a widow. She'd never lived alone, and she dreaded it. How would she survive? What would she do?

Upstairs in the bedroom, the red message light blinked on the answering machine. As expected, there were several messages, including one from Mrs. Harrison who had received some of Andi's mail, and one from Detective Johnson, who said he had some routine questions. The first message was pleasant in its pure normalcy (Mrs. Harrison collected their mail "accidently" on a regular basis), but the second was cold as black metal.

Andi called Mrs. Harrison and told her she'd be over later, but decided to put the other call off until she could talk to Dana.

But before Andi talked to Dana, she wanted to look through Chad's den. He kept that door closed and locked. He hadn't even allowed her in the room to clean.

To her surprise, the handle turned easily and the door swung open to reveal his den – his retreat, he called it. The smell of fine quality cigars lingered in the heavy tapestry drapes. The humidor she'd given him for Christmas a couple of years ago sat on his desk, along with a crystal ashtray and a black coffee cup rimmed with gold. The large mahogany desk dominated the room, with a burgundy leather executive-style chair behind it. It was turned slightly to the side, as if Chad had just stood up and left a few moments before. The room was too dark for her taste, all mahogany and deep reds and greens. She tugged the drapes open and sunlight streamed in.

A picture of Chad and Andi on their wedding day, in an ornate silver frame, and a small paperweight from the Trump Tower in Atlantic City huddled together on the desktop. An oversized book on Maine gems sat atop the credenza. She flipped through the slick pages idly, admiring the photography. A post it note poked out, marking a page with the word "pegmatite" jotted on the yellow tag. The word was vaguely familiar, probably from the gentleman at the dinner party who talked about some of his legendary finds in the surrounding mountains. She pulled the tag off and crumpled it up, then took the book out to the living room to display it on the coffee table.

By the time she finished going through Chad's desk, the shafts of sunlight on the worn Oriental rug reached the opposite wall. Neat, tidy piles gave her some sense of what needed to be dealt with. Mostly bills. The credit card bills were the most worrisome, so she flipped through them page by page. She reached the American Express bill, and stopped cold.

A charge to the Sapphire Star in Atlantic City for the first weekend in April caught her attention. The weekend of her birthday. The weekend she spent alone because Chad had a dental conference in Boston that he just couldn't miss. There were also a couple of restaurant charges in Atlantic City.

Tears welled in her eyes. She'd suspected he cheated on her but she'd never had proof. This hurt like a knife through her heart. Her shoulders drooped under the weight of this new knowledge. She sucked in a deep breath, then blew it out in a huff. This wasn't fair. She couldn't even confront him.

She shook her head, dropped the file folder on the floor and tugged open the wooden file cabinet beside the desk and flipped through the hanging folders. Her eyes drifted to the Insurance folder, but she forced herself to be methodical. The thin Auto folder contained paperwork on the Grand Cherokee, saying he refinanced it in March. That was odd. It would have been paid off in August. She examined the signature on the promissory note. Her signature on the loan papers looked suspiciously like Chad's receptionist's writing, round and almost juvenile.

She flipped ahead to the Insurance folder.

Both policies were in the file folder. She pulled his out and skimmed it. When finished, she leaned back against the wall and stretched her protesting legs in front of her. It appeared to be a $250,000 life insurance policy with a clause that said if he died in an accident, the policy paid double. Relief washed over her like a wave. She'd have enough to pay the bills! She'd be able to keep the house!

If the insurance company paid.

The phone jangled and she pushed herself to her feet to answer it, stretching and massaging her tingling legs to restore the blood flow.

She was pleasantly surprised to hear Dana's voice. "Hey, things are quiet here at the office and Edward said I can take the day off. I'm about ready to wrap things up at work and head for home – mind if I stop by?"

Andi rolled her shoulders and smiled, "Not at all! I've got a couple things I want to talk to you about anyway."

8

She set the insurance policy on top of the desk and returned to the hanging files in the file cabinet again. The file marked "Legal" contained photocopies of their Wills. Chad's small, neat print on the bottom of each indicated that the original was in the safe deposit box at Harbor Regional Bank. She pulled his copy out and laid it on top of the insurance policy, and continued through the files. Just as she was about to close the drawer, a plain manila file folder stuck in the very back of the cabinet caught her eye. The hand-written label simply said, "Will." She frowned and leaned in to get a closer look. The blue manuscript jacket indicated that it had been drawn up by an attorney in Bangor by the name of Benson Harrington III.

She scanned the document, shocked to discover he specifically excluded her from his estate. Explicitly. He left everything to his trust, and named the attorney as Trustee.

She flipped to the last page. The signature was dated only three weeks before.

Why would he do that to her? Had he hated her that much? He was such a perfectionist, so concerned about image. He had told her on more than one occasion that he would never, ever, get a divorce because he did not fail. What changed his mind?

Then a horrible thought entered her mind.

What if divorce wasn't his plan?

Her heart thudded in her chest, and the blood rushed in her ears. She stared at his stylized signature, thoughts swirling in her head. Regardless of his plans, she had to deal with reality. How could she survive with nothing? Chad had never let her work. She had no savings, no money of her own. After all she'd been through, he left her high and dry.

The musical chime of the doorbell broke Andi's reverie. She leaned back in the chair and peered out the bay window. Dana's Impala sat in the driveway. Andi bit her lip, folded the new Will up and stuck it in the back of the right hand drawer, tucked beneath Chad's dental stationery.

She hurried to the front door and let Dana in, who immediately enveloped Andi in a hug. "How are you? Really?"

Andi's words froze in her throat. Years of saying what others expected to hear kicked in, and she said, "I'm fine. Or, I will be."

Doing what's expected is a tough habit to break.

The other woman tilted her head a bit and nodded. The concern in her emerald green eyes was genuine. "I can only imagine how difficult this is for you."

Andi didn't want to be pitied, and she didn't feel like small talk and gossip. “I’ve been going through Chad’s office. Would you have time to give me some guidance, maybe point me in the right direction?”

“Of course!” Dana's features relaxed as she dropped her Tory Burch purse on the hall table and followed Andi to the kitchen. Andi made Earl Grey tea and sweetened hers with honey while Dana dunked an English Teatime bag into her cup, then helped herself to a lemon wedge from the plastic container in the refrigerator door.

Dana squeezed the lemon then dropped it into her tea and took a sip. "You're still slicing lemons for Chad?"

Andi stopped cold. She laughed, a short, harsh sound. "Guess I don't need to do that anymore."

She led her friend to the den and gestured towards the leather armchair. Dana took her seat and Andi dropped into Chad's chair behind the desk. She explained briefly what the stacks contained, but stopped short of telling her friend about the new Will. She wasn’t sure she should tell anyone about that.

Maybe it’d be better to just shred it and pretend it never existed. Could she do that?

Dana sat her cup down on the corner of the desk, and scanned the insurance policy. A couple of times, her eyebrows arched and she made a little sound of surprise or understanding. Andi sipped her tea, watching her friend's facial expressions. Dana put the thick sheaf of papers down, then picked up the copy of the Will, perusing it in the same way. Finally, she laid the document on the desk and picked up her tea, still sitting on the edge of her seat. Andi chewed on lower lip and waited for her friend to break the silence first.

"You understand, I'm not an attorney, so I can't give you legal advice."

"I know, but I thought maybe you could tell me what I should do next, maybe tell me whether or not I need a lawyer." Andi's forehead furrowed.

"OK," Dana leaned back in the chair, the leather creaking slightly with her movement. "You need to file the Will with the court. My firm can do that for you. We'll open an estate and help you through the process."

"Probate, right?" Andi pursed her lips, worried at the thought of the courts being involved. How much trouble would she be in if she hid the new Will?

"Yes, but there probably won't be much to it. I assume you owned everything jointly?"

Andi thought of the more recent Will and the refinancing of the Grand Cherokee and wondered if that was indeed the case, but nodded.

"That's the next thing you need to do – put together a list of your assets and how they're titled." Dana motioned towards the file cabinet and the stacks of papers beside it, "Looks like you've already started to go through the paperwork. Look for deeds, titles, that sort of thing."

"I have copies of the titles to the cars." Andi pulled them out of the shorter stack on the edge of the desk and slid them across the desk. Both copies had a notation on the bottom that the originals were in the safe deposit box. But did the refi affect that?

Dana glanced at them, then set them aside. "Good. They're titled in both names, and/or, so they're both yours immediately."

The two discussed assets for a couple more minutes. Andi wanted to know about the insurance policy, but was afraid to ask. Dana suggested she go to the Recorder of

Deeds office to get a copy of the house deed, since it hadn't been in the file cabinet. Andi's stomach churned at that thought. Had he done anything about the house? When Dana nodded towards the insurance policy, Andi's fingertips whitened as she gripped her teacup tighter.

"The funeral home will get death certificates for you. You'll probably get them in the mail in a few days."

Andi nodded, "The guy at the funeral home said he ordered ten."

"That'll be plenty. Call the insurance company and find out what forms they need you to fill out in order to collect. Let me know if you need help filling it out." She pointed to the policy, "Have you read the policy?"

Andi shrugged. "Skimmed it, but don't really know what I'm looking at."

Dana scanned the policy and smiled, "It's a double indemnity."

"Which means?"

"It means that because Chad died in an accident, you'll be able to collect double."

Andi nodded, and bit her lip. Inside, she was cheering. Half a million dollars was like winning the lottery. But it also sounded like motive.

At least, it would to Detective Johnson.

"That means you will probably need to get a copy of the accident report. I know it happened out by the Clifftop. I assume the Highway Patrol was on the scene, so you'll want to contact them and get a copy."

The idea of asking about an accident report made Andi's stomach turn. Every time she closed her eyes, she saw her husband topple over that guardrail.

She imagined his body crashing into the rocks below.

No one deserved to die like that.

"I'm sorry." Dana leaned forward and touched Andi's arm. "We don't have to do all this now. Why don't I call the insurance company and the highway patrol for you?"

Andi sucked in a deep breath and words tumbled out, "A police detective is asking questions. He was at the funeral. He followed me when I took Mama to the airport."

Dana's green eyes widened. "Is he harassing you?"

"No, not exactly," Andi tipped her head forward and hid behind her long dark hair. "But he left a message on my answering machine earlier today, something about having questions for me."

A frown furrowed her friend's brow as she straightened the papers in front of her. She hesitated, then said, without looking up, "Did he say what kind of questions?"

Andi looked up through the fringe of hair and watched her friend closely, then shook her head. She tucked her hair behind her ears and sucked in a deep breath.

Dana looked up, then her chin dipped once, "The police probably just want to make sure they've got the accident report filled out completely. Everything is going to be fine. You know I'll help with anything you need, but we've talked about this enough for now." Dana avoided Andi's gaze, as she stood and glanced at her watch, "I've got about half an hour before I need to go meet Derek for dinner."

Andi stood and stretched. Dana grasped her arm and steered her out the door, then whispered conspiratorially, "Let's go sit in the living room for a bit and catch up on gossip. Have you talked to Jennie lately, besides dental office stuff? I heard that the pro wrestler she used to be married to is in town and Jeff has moved out . . . "

9

After a sleepless night, Andi pulled Detective Johnson's card from her purse and called him. He said he was close and would stop by shortly, so she walked next door to Mrs. Harrison's house to pick up her mail. The old woman was the type of neighbor you always waved to, and occasionally talked to when you both happened to be doing yard work, but you always remembered that you had something in the oven you needed to check when she offered to show you her bunions.

The old woman shook her head and clucked her tongue. "Did you hear about Tobias Peabody?"

Andi shook her head.

"He slipped in his bathtub and snapped his neck." She snapped her fingers. "Lucky bastard."

She stopped cold when an unmarked police car swung into Andi's driveway. “Oh, my! Is something else wrong, dear?” Her bony hand fluttered at her chest like a bird.

“Just routine police business,” Andi assured her, and cut across the yards to meet the cop in the driveway. He stood at the front of his car, hands at his side, chin up. His weathered skin hinted at years of being exposed to the harsh Maine weather.

“That was quick,” She said, brushing past him on her way to the door.

He grunted. “I was in the neighborhood.”

He paused to wipe his shoes on the doormat, then followed her into the house. She suggested they go to the kitchen, then started a pot of coffee while he settled in at the table. He produced a small spiral notebook and a cheap Bic pen from his pocket, and jotted a few notes before he spoke. She pulled out the chair across from him and sat, folded her hands in front of her, and waited.

He cleared his throat and began, “Appreciate you taking the time to talk with me.”

Her heart thudded in her chest. “Of course.” She fought the urge to hang her head and hide behind her hair, and instead looked him in the eye.

His voice was like gravel. “Take me through the events of the night of May 15.”

She cocked her head and narrowed her eyes. "Again?"

He grinned. There was a gap between his two front teeth, yellowed with nicotine. "Humor an old Mainer."

She took a deep breath and explained that they'd been to a dinner party with some of Chad’s business acquaintances up at the Clifftop. She closed her eyes as she related the events of the evening. As she described the flat tire, it was almost as though she were there again. She saw the jagged lightning bolts, heard the booming of the thunder, and felt the goose bumps pimpling her skin as she remembered the cold rain, the blowing wind. She saw Chad throw his head back, heard the mocking cruelty of his laugh.

A chill ran up her spine and she huffed out a breath. She opened her eyes and the officer stared at her, pen poised above the paper. He made a rolling motion with his hand.

“He was laughing.” She squeezed her hands together to keep them from shaking. “And he was off-balance, I guess. He bumped against the guardrail and tipped over. It all happened so quickly.”

"Wait." He held up his hand, palm out. “He was laughing?”

She nodded.

His bushy eyebrows pushed together. “During a thunderstorm. On a cliff with a storm raging. Changing a flat tire in the dark. And he was laughing?”

“Yes, sir.” She chewed on her lower lip. She honestly couldn't remember what Chad had said. Something mean, she was certain, that he thought was funny.

He settled back in his chair. “Why?”

She opened her mouth, closed it, then shrugged. “I-I don’t remember.”

He leaned forward and wrote on his pad. “Who changed the tire?”

“He did.” She leaned forward, mirroring his actions.

He put his arm around the spiral notebook, like a kid in grade school keeping others from copying. “Where were you while he was changing it?”

“Standing beside him, holding the flashlight.” Her knuckles had been white. She remembered that clearly.

His cheap pen scratched across the paper. “Anyone see you that night?”

She thought for a moment, then straightened, “Yes! A car passed by. I remember because it splashed water on us.”

He scribbled, “Make? Model? Color?”

“It was dark. Four door, maybe.”

He ran a hand over his nearly-bald pate. “License number?”

"No." She shook her head, then raised her index finger, “Wait! There was a dent in the door. Passenger side.”

He asked a few more questions, where the vehicle was, which direction it was going, what she was wearing that night, had they been drinking.

The chair squeaked as he pushed away from the table. "Need to see the vehicle, ma’am.”

She led him outside. "Someone drove it home for me that night. They parked it beside the garage."

She watched while he examined the SUV from bumper to bumper, inside and out. The blown tire still laid in the back, on her sequined jacket.

The detective fingered the wrap. "This yours?"

She nodded. He looked at her with narrowed eyes, but didn't comment. After about ten minutes of watching his methodical search, she left him to it and returned to the house.

When he finished, he walked into the kitchen and watched as she sliced cookie dough from a refrigerated log. She placed each one on the cookie sheet exactly 1 ½” apart, precisely 1 ½” from the edge of the pan. Convincing Chad that cookies cut from a log were acceptable had been quite the accomplishment on her part, and she suspected the consistent appearance of the cookies had been the thing that tipped the scales in her favor.

"Neat," the detective said.

She paused with a cookie hovering over the pan, and looked at him with wide eyes. "I'm sorry?"

He nodded towards the round bits of dough. "Precise."

She shrugged. "Habit, I guess."

"May have more questions for you later." He hooked his thumbs in his waistband and tugged his dark blue pants up.

"You know where to find me."

He held up a small brown paper bag. "Took samples out of the car for analysis. That okay with you?"

She nodded and slid the cookie sheet into the oven, wondering what the samples were of. "Is this routine?"

"Yep. Anytime there's a suspicious death."

She let the oven door slam shut and turned to face the gruff cop. "Suspicious?"

"Yes, ma'am." He spoke slowly and watched her face as he said, "Dr. Adams had a gambling problem. Did that affect your marriage?"

He was baiting her, and she felt herself tense. "Gambling problem? What are you talking about?"

"Had a bad run of luck in A.C. Turned it around though." He pulled the little notebook from his pocket and flipped the cover back. "'Bout the time he started seeing his mistress. Out of his league, if you ask me. Probably helped him out of that jam. Or would have, after she got her inheritance."

10

Andi stammered and stuttered, unable to form an intelligible word.

The detective continued to press, "How did your husband meet Ms. Woodson?"

She shrugged and blinked as she tried to wrap her mind around his words. "Who?" Her world began to crumble. The trip to Atlantic City. The credit card receipts.

He ignored her question and hammered away with his own. "Did he have life insurance?"

"We both had life insurance. That's not a crime." Her cheeks burned, and she fought to keep her voice calm. Panic rose like bubbles in her chest.

"No, ma'am, it's not. Does tend to make folks suspicious, though. Did you know about your husband's affair?"

She glared at him. "No." Which was true. She hadn't known for sure until that very moment.

"That's all for now. I'll see myself out." He turned to look at her and held her gaze. "The insurance people will start an investigation of their own before they pay out."

Her nostrils flared and she clenched her fists at her side. "They're welcome to do that. I have nothing to hide."

"Don't leave town without checking with me first."

His footsteps echoed in the hallway, then the front door opened and closed. It wasn't until his car rumbled to life and gravel crunched as he backed out of the driveway that Andi realized she had been holding her breath. Her palms ached where her fingernails dug in, forming crescent moon indentions.

It took her a few minutes to regain her composure. The clock on the wall showed noon, straight up. Dana would be at lunch. Andi flexed her hands, then picked up the phone and dialed her friend.

Dana was supportive, but cautious. "It was a tragic accident, but I know the hell you lived through with him. If that comes out, people may wonder." The line hummed as she paused, then, "Did you know he was having an affair?"

Tears threatened at the reminder and Andi sniffled. "No." It came out as a strangled whine.

Silence stretched over the line for several heartbeats. "I'm coming over as soon as I can get away."

Andi busied herself with straightening the house while waiting for her friend to arrive, and went over every word that had been said, over and over, in her mind. She wasn't stupid. Chad screwed around on her, but she assumed it was his receptionist. The detective mentioned someone young about to inherit a lot of money. What name had he said?

That would be just like Chad, to leave her for a rich, young trophy wife. He had been the user, the abuser, but the police were questioning her. Suspicious death, that's what the detective called it.

Suddenly, a loud screech sounded. She pressed her hands to her ears and looked around. Smoke alarm. Cookies. Damn! She forgot to set the timer! She raced into the kitchen, grabbed a potholder and jerked the oven door open. Black smoke rolled out and she coughed as she snagged the cookie sheet and dropped it into the sink. She tugged the kitchen window open and waved a towel at the blaring smoke detector.

By the time Dana's tires crunched in the driveway, Andi had thrown the cookies away and the cookie sheet soaked in suds in the sink. The smell of burnt cookies lingered in the air as the two women sat at the kitchen table and sipped coffee.

"I know it isn't funny," One corner of Dana's mouth tugged up in a grin. "But I can't help it. I burn stuff all the time. Nice to see that you, Ms. Perfect Cook, do too!"

Andi shook her head and rolled her eyes, "I haven't done that in years."

"Don't worry. The smell goes away pretty quick." Dana's tone turned serious. "Now, tell me what happened with the cop."

Andi related the conversation with Detective Johnson to her friend. Occasionally, Dana interrupted to ask a question.

Once Andi finished, Dana folded her hands in front of her and leaned forward. "Now tell me about the night it happened. Every single detail you can remember."

Andi took a deep breath and told her everything. Bits and pieces were unclear. The memories was cloudy, foggy.

The incriminating holes in her story made her look bad, she knew, but the memories simply weren't there. When she finished, Dana took a deep breath and puffed her cheeks out.

"Wow," she said, "I don't know what to say."

Andi swallowed hard and hugged herself. "It was just a horrible accident, right? I'm not a murderer, am I?"

Dana caught Andi's gaze. "You are not a murderer. Don't even think that way."

Andi swallowed and hoped her friend was right. Memories of her imperfect marriage flitted through her mind. Her husband demanded she wipe out the sink every time she ran water, so there wouldn't be water spots. She had to remake the bed if the hospital corners weren't crisp enough. Did anyone else wash their sheets every day – and iron them? His insistence that she iron his underwear – that one always did astound her. His voice as he chastised her for not holding the flashlight still in spite of the driving rain. Her favorite jacket covered with mud so the carpet in his precious Grand Cherokee wouldn't get dirty.

The pain in her chest was real.

Tears spilled over and ran down her cheeks.

"It was an accident, Andi. Let yourself off the hook. And think how much time you'll have to spare now that you're not catering to his every whim." Dana reached across the table and grasped Andi's hand. "Did you suspect he was having an affair?"

Andi sucked in a deep, quivery breath and nodded, "But I don't know who. For sure, anyway. I thought him and Jennie, maybe."

"And what was the name the cop asked you about?"

"Woodward? Wood-something-"

"Woodson?"

That clicked, and Andi said, “Yes, but how did you know?”

“Woodson. Think about it. One of the most powerful names in New England. They own most of the state. Well, from here down to Kennebunkport, at least.”

Of course. Those Woodsons. Images of mansions and fancy dresses and hobnobbing with celebrities filled her mind. Andi got up and refilled their mugs, then dropped into her chair. Surely Chad couldn't have been involved with folks like that.

Dana said, "Let's talk legal stuff. Do you know how probate works?"

The two sipped while they talked about what had been, and what was yet to come. Dana's legal knowledge made Andi feel much more comfortable about all the things that she'd have to deal with over the next few months. Her friend promised to help her through it all, and Andi knew she would.

Dana glanced at her watch, then pushed her chair back. “Now, the insurance company may have a few questions for you. Just remember that you did not do anything wrong, but I’d leave out the part about swinging the flashlight.”

Dana winked at Andi and they hugged. Before Dana left, Andi gave her the life insurance policy and a business card for the funeral home so she could file the necessary paperwork. Dana offered to sit in with Andi if the insurance company insisted on an interview. Andi's heart was much lighter when she waved goodbye to her friend from the front doorway.

Her stomach growled, reminding her that she hadn’t eaten anything substantial all day long. She headed for the kitchen to make herself a sandwich.

After she finished her sandwich, she rinsed the plate and put it in the dishwasher. She glanced at the clock, then picked up the phone and called her mother. It was almost bedtime back home, so she thought it might be a good time to talk.

She was wrong.

Martha answered with a curt, "Hello?"

Andi's spirits rose just hearing her mother's voice, "Hi, it's me!"

"Oh, hi, honey." Something crashed in the background and Martha sighed heavily. "What are you doing?"

Andi plucked a clean dishcloth from the drawer, ran it under hot water, and said, "Nothing. Dana came by earlier for coffee and helped me go through some paperwork."

"That's nice of her," Martha grunted as if she'd lifted something.

"Yes, it was." Andi scrubbed the countertop, moving canisters out of the way as she cleaned left to right, back to front. "And then a police officer came by."

"That's nice. Oh, I got some pictures developed the other day. Got some good ones of little miss Romy." There was another crash in the background. "Jakey! Put that down right now and get back in bed!"

Andi's jaw dropped. She stopped scrubbing and said, "Did you hear what I just said? I said a *policeman* came by!"

"I'm sorry, honey. Guess I was distracted. Jakey has the flu and has been puking all day and I just can't get him to sit still long enough for his tummy to settle down. Jakey! I said NOW!" Martha sighed again. "Now what were you saying?"

Andi massaged her temple in a vain attempt to relieve the pressure starting to build. "Nothing important, Mama. Sounds like you've got your hands full."

Martha laughed, then there was a moan in the background. "Oh, no! Jakey, aim for the bucket! Sorry, honey, I've got to go."

Andi stood there for a moment listening to the dial tone, then pushed the end button and sat the phone in its dock. The clock on the wall said 8:32 p.m. Mama said she had sent some pictures of Romy, and Andi was anxious to see them. She hadn't gotten the mail yet, so she hurried out to check the box. As she walked back to the house, she tipped the envelopes towards the porch light. One envelope caught her eye. It was from a law firm in Bangor.

The firm that prepared the new Will in Chad's desk.

11

No pictures from home, and nothing else but bills and junk mail – and the mysterious legal mail. She sighed and took the mail in, dropping most of it on the breakfast counter. She slit the linen envelope open and pulled the letter out. A self-addressed, stamped envelope fell onto the granite. She read the letter, then perched on a bar stool to read it again.

The attorney had been notified of Chad's death, and his client had told him he would keep the Will at home, so the attorney wanted Andi to deliver the original to him so he could file it with the Probate Court. He added that the Will nullified all previous Wills and that it would override any other Wills that might be filed with the Probate court.

Andi didn't want to get in trouble for not filing it, but also hesitated to mail it back to some attorney she didn't know. Of course, it was too late to call the office. Why had she waited so long to check the mail? She meant to get it when she ran next door to get the mail that had been delivered to Mrs. Harrison, but the cop distracted her.

She shut off the lights and went upstairs. It was going to be a long night, and the words in that letter scrolled through her mind over and over.

At exactly 8 the next morning, she picked up the phone and punched in the number printed on the letterhead. She asked the receptionist for an appointment with Benson Harrington. She was transferred to his secretary, who offered an appointment at 1:30 that afternoon.

Andi gave her name and the woman asked her to repeat it, then placed the call on hold. She wondered if she should've called Dana first. The instrumental version of Singing in the Rain entertained Andi until the woman came back on the line. "May I ask the purpose of the visit?"

"I have a Will that Mr. Harrington wishes to file with Probate."

"Sounds good. We'll see you at 1:30. Do you need directions?"

After Andi placed the phone in its cradle, she stared at it, hoping she was doing the right thing.

That afternoon, she found herself sitting in the elegant reception area of Harrington, Jefferson and Biggs, P.C. The only other time she'd been in an attorney's office was when Chad took her to sign their own wills and powers of attorney. This office was much nicer, tastefully decorated in muted tones, understated and expensive. The chairs looked plush, but were hard as a rock.

She gripped her purse tightly, as if the Will would escape at any moment or someone would snatch it away from her.

A tall, athletic-looking woman with cascading brunette curls, perhaps a couple of years older than Andi, appeared in the hallway and asked Andi to follow her. She led Andi into the conference room and offered coffee or a cold beverage, diet or otherwise. Andi declined. The woman left and returned a moment later with a portly older gentleman with cold, dark eyes, a deeply lined forehead and a bulbous nose lined with broken capillaries. The two sat down across from Andi, the polished expanse of the table stretching between them.

The attorney spoke first, his voice deep and cultured. "Thank you for coming in today, Ms. Adams. I understand that you have a Will for me?"

"It's Missus Adams." She smiled, her handbag clutched in her lap. It took a couple of false starts, but finally she spit out the words, "I have a few questions first."

His frown lines deepened and his assistant glanced at him, then down at her legal pad. His voice was low, but powerful. "You are welcome to ask, but attorney-client privilege extends beyond death, so I don't know if I will be able to answer your questions or not."

"You represented my husband?" She folded her hands and rested them in her lap to keep them from shaking.

He nodded, "I can confirm he was a client."

Of course he was a client. Why else would he have sent that letter? "For how long?"

He shrugged, "A while."

She chewed her lip and asked, "And you prepared this Will at his request?"

"Yes," he said, then raised his eyebrows and stared at her. Was that a challenge?

Andi's brain wasn't working like she wanted it to. There was so much she didn't know, she didn't even know the right questions to ask. “Did you prepare any other documents for him?”

He nodded once and pursed his lips.

“What other documents?” She glanced at the big brown file pocket sitting directly in front of him.

He bit off his words as he said, “I’m not at liberty to discuss that with you.”

She took a deep breath and plunged ahead. “I assume you prepared a trust, because it is referenced in the Will as being dated on the same day as the Will.”

He hesitated a beat, then nodded.

Her tongue stuck to the roof of her dry mouth. She asked the question she'd been afraid to articulate even to herself. “Did you prepare divorce papers for my husband?”

His assistant’s eyes opened wide and the attorney blinked. Bingo. Andi could feel confidence welling inside her. She tucked her hair behind her ears and raised her chin.

The furrows in his forehead deepened again. “I’m not at liberty to say.”

There had to be a way to find out more. She kept at it. “So you do divorces in addition to estate planning?”

“For certain clients, yes.”

She took a shot in the dark and asked, “Clients such as the Woodsons?”

A muscle in his cheek twitched. “My clientele is none of your business, Ms. Adams. Now, do you have the Will?”

She wondered if she had any options, and wished that she'd confided in Dana and asked her advice before she made this trip. She looked from the attorney to his assistant. His eyes were cold, but hers were warm. Her forehead was pinched. Andi sensed an ally, and focused on the assistant. "If I read the Will correctly, everything my husband owned goes into his trust. I have a sneaking suspicion that I am not the beneficiary of the trust. So, can you explain to me why I should provide the Will to you for filing?"

The assistant's eyes flicked to the attorney, and he nodded. The woman produced a plain white envelope from underneath the legal pad in front of her. Andi's name was typed neatly on the front of it. The brunette handed it to him, and he slid it across the polished table. Andi accepted it, opened it and her jaw dropped.

The check, drawn on the law firm's trust account for $10,000, shook between her fingers.

It was made out to Andrea Adams. No notation in the memo line. "What's this?"

"My client instructed me to provide you with that check to reimburse you for any expenses that you may incur in relation to the Probate process."

Andi narrowed her eyes. She fingered the check for a moment, then folded it in half and tucked it into the inner zippered compartment of her handbag.

This felt surreal. She should be home mourning her husband, not sitting in his attorney's office. She noticed the coffee carafe sitting on the console against the opposite wall and slid her chair back. "If you don't mind, I think I will have some coffee after all."

The woman started to stand, but Andi held out her hand. "Not a problem, I'll get it myself."

She bent down and pulled the blue-jacketed Will out of her purse, then walked around the table. She dropped the document onto the table between the attorney and his assistant. Mr. Harrington immediately opened it to inspect it. Andi busied herself with the coffee, adding cream and sugar, while she peered over his shoulder at the file jacket. Three folders peeked out, one labeled, "Estate planning," another "Dissolution," and the final one, "Corporate / Flatlander Holdings, L.L.C."

Andi stirred her coffee and walked back around to her seat, as she repeated the words on the labels to herself over and over to memorize them. So, that was it. Chad planned to divorce her, and set up this new Will so that everything would be all tied up in a nice neat little package. But she'd never heard of anything called Flatlander Holdings. How could he betray her like that?

She sat down and took a sip of sweetened coffee. Mr. Harrington handed the Will to his assistant. "We'll get this filed right away."

The tall brunette picked up the file and walked out of the door without raising her gaze. Andi asked the attorney, "Do I owe you anything for the filing fee?"

He leaned back in his chair and crossed his arms. "It's been taken care of."

Her brow bunched in a frown. "By whom?"

His lips curled up. "I'm not at liberty to discuss that." He pushed away from the table and stood, indicating that the meeting was over.

Andi stood, also. He thanked her for her time and exited the room. His assistant appeared as if on cue. She swept her arm towards the door and said, "This way, please."

When the two women reached the reception area, Andi stuck her hand out. "Thank you. I'm sorry, I didn't catch your name?"

The assistant's grip was firm. "Amanda. Amanda Dobbins."

"Well, thank you, Ms. Dobbins. I appreciate your making this as easy as possible. Do you have a card?"

Andi fingered the crisp business card in her pocket as she walked to the parking lot. She felt as if she were floating through unknown seas, a boat with no anchor. Flatlander Holdings. Why hadn't she known anything about any of this? Not only was her husband cheating, he planned to divorce her and hid money in a holding company – at least that's all she'd ever heard about holding companies. It seemed like that old movie with Tom Cruise as a young lawyer had something to do with holding companies.

The visit left her with more questions than answers.

When she passed through Ellsworth and the road opened up in front of her, she called Dana at work and left a message on her voicemail. The drive south on Highway 1 was boring, but after 1 broke off to the east and she continued south on Highway 3, the tree-lined blacktop with power lines running alongside reminded her of growing up in Missouri. The road was relatively empty this time of day, save a dark sedan a little ways behind her.

Suddenly she remembered that odd phone call right after Chad died. She glanced in the rearview mirror again and couldn't squelch the unease settled in her gut.

As she passed the Hancock airport, her thoughts turned to her mother and home. It would be so easy to go home and leave all the drama behind, but that would mean giving up her newfound independence. Chad would've been shocked that she'd gone to see that attorney on her own. She slowed and looked out into the bay when she reached the bridge to Thompson Island and immediately felt the pull of the ocean. Maine was home. She couldn't go back to Missouri.

She blinked when she reached Mount Desert Island. She had been driving on auto pilot. She glanced in the rearview mirror and saw the same dark sedan still behind her, but not close enough for her to make out the driver. She eased her foot off the pedal and the car slowed.

Her phone chirped and she swiped the screen when Dana's name flashed on the screen. How secure was a cell phone? The whole situation made her nervous, and she didn't want to risk having anyone else hear about what had transpired with the attorney.

Dana asked Andi to dinner, and they arranged to meet at the law office when Dana got off work. Andi glanced at the clock on the dash. She should get there about 5:15. Hopefully Dana would have the office to herself.

She turned south on Pine Street and pulled into the law firm's parking lot just as Dana's boss walked out the door. As Andi got out of her car, she looked back. The dark sedan slowed and she caught a glimpse of a man wearing sunglasses before he sped up and continued south.

Edward opened the door to his red BMW as he waved and said, "Dana's waiting for you, just go on in. She's got some paperwork for you for the estate."

She thanked him and went inside. Dana tapped away on her computer, surrounded by stacks of work. She smiled and held up a finger without looking up. Andi sat down in the extra chair to wait for her friend to finish her train of thought.

When Dana finished, she reached to turn her computer off.

Andi scooted forward. "Just a sec, don't shut it off yet. Can you help me track something down?" She didn't want to tell her friend that her internet had been shut off. That was one expense she'd cut immediately.

Dana straightened in her chair and opened her browser. "Whatcha looking for?"

"First, what do the initials 'L.L.C.' stand for?"

"Limited liability company. A pretty common form of company nowadays. People used to form corporations, but now we usually recommend limited liability companies instead. It's easy for an individual or a partnership, good way to protect assets."

Andi clutched her purse in her lap and asked, "Can you find anything about a limited liability company by the name of Flatlander Holdings?"

Dana tucked her red hair behind her ears then started typing. She clicked and typed, then sat back and grunted.

Andi frowned and scooted forward. "What?"

"It says here that Flatlander Holdings was organized by Benson Harrington III. The LLC form lists an address right here in Buccaneer Bay." She pointed to the screen, then she turned to Andi and said, "Isn't that Chad's dental office?"

Andi stood up and moved around the desk to look over her friend's shoulder. She was right. It was his work address. That made sense. Of course he would've had everything sent to his office to keep it from her.

Dana navigated a few more screens, and printed her findings. Flatlander Holdings owned half a dozen lots at Big Bear Cove, the new development just north of town. She stood up and grabbed Andi's arm. "Come into the library. I think we've got a plat map in here."

Andi followed her friend into the bookshelf lined room, where Dana pulled a stack of large, spiral bound books from a shelf. She spread them out on the conference room table, shuffled through them and said, "Here. This one."

Dana opened the book, flipped pages back and forth and finally pointed to a map. "Right here. These are the lots he bought."

Andi squinted at the small, slanted script, trying to make sense of the lines. She followed the coast line with her finger. "This is the harbor?"

Dana nodded. "And these lots he bought are on Big Bear Cove, just outside the city limits."

"Close to where they found his body." Andi's chest rose and fell with a heavy sigh. "The new condos where that little fishing village used to be."

Dana tapped the deed she'd printed. "And this says the mineral rights were included in the deal. That's tough to get landowners to sell, with the number of semiprecious stones found up there."

Andi raised her eyebrows and wondered if the rocks in her husband's valet were valuable. The dots were starting to connect.

Dana glanced over her shoulder and asked, "So you didn't know anything about this company?"

Andi chewed her lip. There wasn't even anything she could think of in hindsight that would've pointed to anything he'd been up to. "Not a thing."

Dana dropped into a chair and asked, "Mind if I ask how your finances were before his death?"

"He handled everything. I thought we were doing fine." Andi pulled out a chair diagonally from her friend. Something nagged at her, but she couldn't quite grasp it.

Dana twisted a strand of red hair around her index finger and frowned. "But where could he have gotten enough money to purchase something this big?"

"There's no way he would've had that much money." Then it clicked. The paperwork where he had refinanced the Jeep Grand Cherokee. But no, that wouldn't be enough. Unless he'd mortgaged their home, too. "But, I found out after he died that he borrowed money without telling me. Refinanced our Jeep. He even forged my signature to do it, so he wouldn't have to tell me."

Dana looked at Andi and frowned. "He was trying to come up with cash for an investment opportunity. And you think maybe the Woodson girl loaned him money, or cosigned for him, or something? What else did you find out at this attorney's office today?"

Andi gave her friend the condensed version, and told her Chad had gone to the attorney for at least three different matters – the divorce, the Will and Trust, and this company. Then she unzipped the inside pocket in her purse and held up the check. "And they gave me this for 'my troubles'."

Dana gasped and her chin dropped. "And you took it?"

Andi shrugged and smoothed the check on the table. "Why not?" Given the state of her bank account, how could she not take it?

Dana opened her mouth, then pressed her lips together. Doubt clouded her expression. Finally, she said, "Why, indeed."

The two sat there looking at each other. A light bulb in the ceiling buzzed loudly. Andi folded the check and slipped it back into the zippered pocket of her purse. She stood up and slung her handbag over her shoulder. "I won't use it unless I absolutely have to."

Dana pushed to her feet, too, and led the way back to her little office. As they walked, Andi asked, "Is there a way to challenge the Will?"

Dana leaned over to retrieve her purse from under her desk. "Most wills have a no contest clause. Benson Harrington would've done that, too."

Andi followed Dana out the back door. "So if I contest it?"

"You automatically lose any inheritance that you might have been entitled to."

Andi's shoulders drooped. "At least there's the life insurance."

"About that." Dana's eyebrows pushed together. "I called the insurance company and they want to see the police report and newspaper clippings."

"Newspaper clippings? Why?" Andi felt as if every nerve were on fire.

"Standard procedure when there's a suspicious death." Dana paused. "Have you seen the Morning Sentinel today?"

Andi let out a breath and deflated. "No. Don't know if I want to."

Dana patted Andi's arm and said, "It's going to be okay."

Tears welled in Andi's eyes as she stared at the ugly gray carpet. She'd been so busy, she hadn't allowed herself to think about what okay might mean to her. "People keep telling me that, but it's really hard to believe. Do you have a copy of the paper?"

Dana nodded. "In the reception area out front."

Andi pushed to her feet and walked down the hallway. It felt as though she were outside her body, watching herself go through the motions. The headline screamed at her as soon as she rounded the corner.

"Pillar of the Community Dead After Suspicious Fall"

How could anyone write something like that? She glanced at the byline, but didn't recognize the name. This wasn't good. Everyone would think she murdered her husband. She turned to Dana. "This is awful. I didn't do it!"

Dana covered the distance between them in two quick strides and wrapped Andi in a hug. "Oh, sweetie, I know you didn't."

Tears coursed down Andi's cheeks as she melted into her best friend's embrace. After a minute or so, she pulled back and sucked in a shaky breath. She blinked the tears away and angrily swiped at her eyes. She murmured a thank you, then turned away and snatched a handful of tissues from the box on the side table.

Tears. Finally.

Dana stood quietly as she rubbed Andi's back. After Andi's sobs turned to sniffles, Dana whispered, "I'm so sorry you're going through this."

Andi swallowed the lump in her throat and nodded. "Thanks. I appreciate your support."

One corner of Dana's mouth tugged up in a half smile. "You've definitely got my support. Now, what do you say we forget about this for a bit and get something to eat?"

Andi nodded. "I am a little hungry."

"Good. You can leave your car here and ride with me."

Dana hurried through the office turning off lights, then locked the door behind them. Andi hopped in with Dana and they headed down towards the Harbor. Dana took a left at Main Street. "How does Jolly Jack's sound?"

"Great. It's a beautiful afternoon -- maybe Faith can get us a table on the deck."

Dana pulled into the parking lot and they walked past the old wooden lobster traps and nets towards the green canopy emblazoned with a skull and crossbones. A few tourists sat around, but it was still a little early for them. They stepped into the cool interior and were met by Faith Sullivan, the owners' daughter.

"Hi, ladies. Two?"

Andi said, "Any chance we can get a table on the deck?"

Faith glanced at her chart, then over her shoulder. "Give me a minute to clean off a table for you."

Dana grinned. "No problem."

Faith hesitated, then inclined her head towards Andi. "So sorry for your loss, ma'am."

The young woman led them through the dining room and out to the back deck. Though the sun hadn't set yet, the lights strung around the perimeter were already twinkling. While waiting for the table to be cleared, the two friends leaned against the railing and looked out at the harbor, enjoying the salt air. Though Andi had lived in Maine for years, she was still amazed at the instant relaxation she felt at the water's edge.

Once they sat, Andi glanced around. The woman at the table next to them quickly looked down. A couple across the deck leaned together and whispered, then both looked over at Andi and Dana. After that, Andi kept her head down, all too aware of the whispers that swirled around her, taunting her. Maybe it was too soon to be out in public. To Andi's surprise, her friend chatted as if this were any other girls' night out. She even suggested that it was time to consider getting on with life.

As Dana swirled a shrimp in cocktail sauce, she said, "You weren't happy with Chad, so it's not like you have to serve required mourning. You want to figure out what he was doing – and I get that – but you need to put it behind you."

"I'll try," Andi promised, but didn't know how she could. She needed closure. She'd just lost her husband, but she had so many questions.

"I bet the insurance money comes in soon." Dana gave Andi a pointed look, "Use that money for you. Your new life. Put Chad behind you."

That evening Andi went to the living room, sat in her favorite chair, and pulled the ivory chenille throw around her. She snuggled into its softness and rocked herself. The darkness crept in and surrounded her, and she welcomed it.

She slept in the chair that night, unwilling to sleep in the bed she had shared with Chad. Finding out about her husband's indiscretions and secrets after his death left her feeling cheated. There was no argument, no confrontation. It ate at her, but there was nothing that could be done about it.

No one understood.

How could they?

Gradually, it became easier to move through the house without thinking of him with every step. By the end of the first week, she slept in the middle of their king-sized bed, which she still made carefully each morning. The crisp corners and plumped pillows were just as they'd been when he was alive.

At the end of the second week, she caught herself redoing a corner three times to make it perfect. She stood back and looked at the bed, beautiful and elegant and precise. She yanked the comforter askew, mussed the sheets, then grabbed the pillows and threw them on the floor. As she walked out of the room, she smiled – really smiled – for the first time in weeks.

12

It had been nearly three weeks since the accident, and she was learning to adjust to living alone. She had just put a load of towels into the washing machine when the doorbell rang. She answered it, and a young couple stood there smiling. Both were dressed casually, in jeans and t-shirts. The sandy haired man hooked one hand over the woman's shoulder in a possessive gesture.

She didn't recognize them. "Can I help you?"

The man said, "I realize we should have called first, but we wondered if now would be a good time to look at the house?"

She blinked, "I'm sorry?"

The blonde at his side craned her head, attempting to look inside. "If now isn't a good time, we can come back."

Andi shook her head and blinked rapidly. The man pointed to the yard. "Should we call the agent to make an appointment?"

Andi stepped forward and looked in the direction he pointed.

At a For Sale sign posted in the front yard.

She laughed and shook her head. "I'm sorry, there must be a mistake. This house isn't for sale. The agent must've put it in the wrong yard."

As the couple backed their tan Honda out of the driveway, Andi walked through the dewy grass and tugged the sign out of the ground. She leaned the sign against the side of the house, went inside and moments later she was talking to the agent whose name was prominently displayed on the sign.

"I'm calling to let you know there's been a mistake. My house isn't for sale, but a sign with your name on it has been put in the yard by accident."

Gabby Martin said, "That's odd. I place all of my signs myself. Can't imagine how I would've put a sign in the wrong yard. What's your address?"

After Andi gave her address, Gabby sounded as confused as Andi felt. "I'm sorry – that house *is* listed with me. And who are you again?"

A feeling of dread began to build in Andi's gut. "Andi--Andrea--Adams. I own this house."

"I'm sorry, Ms. Adams. Let me pull the listing here." Papers rustled in the background, "Here we go. The listing contract was signed by Benson Harrington, Trustee of the Chadwick Adams Trust. I ran my usual check, and he is the title owner of the property."

Andi mumbled something and disconnected, then frantically pawed through the pile of mail on her breakfast bar. Moments later she was holding for Benson Harrington.

As soon as he got on the line, she cut him off. "Why is my house for sale?"

He responded with a slow, deliberate cadence. "I'm sorry, I don't know what you're talking about. Who is this?"

"This is Andi Adams and there is a for sale sign in my yard. Would you like to explain that to me?" Panic caused her voice to rise and she fought to keep it even.

"I'm not at liberty-"

"Not at liberty?" Her heart raced and she felt lightheaded. "This is my house. My husband and I bought this house together six years ago."

"And as the Trustee, I'm happy to offer you the opportunity to continue living there until the house is sold, as long as you pay your rent on time-"

"Rent?!" She couldn't believe her ears. She trembled with anger.

"Yes, my client set his trust up so that you could continue to live in the home as long as you paid rent in the form of mortgage payments to the bank, but he also specified that the home be sold after his death. The home has been listed as he directed."

She slammed the phone down and paced the hallway, scared and frustrated. Chad had covered every base. How could she have lived with him and not known what he was planning? How could he have been so duplicitous?

She snatched up the phone and called Dana on her cell. Dana answered on the third ring. Quickly, Andi relayed what happened. Dana gasped and Andi could hear Derek asking who it was. Dana whispered Andi's name, then told her the bad news. "He very well could be right. We haven't seen a copy of the trust. It's not normal, but it's also not completely unheard of."

Andi's breath expelled in a rush. Blood pounded in her ears and stars floated in front of her eyes. “So I have to get out.”

“Unfortunately, probably yes. Let me call my boss and then I’ll call you back. Don’t move.”

Andi literally didn’t move. Didn’t even put the phone down. When Dana called back, Andi answered on the first ring. Dana's boss agreed to call the attorney in Bangor. They were acquaintances, but Edward hadn’t sounded optimistic. Andi hung up and walked around the house, taking a mental inventory of everything and wondering what was hers and what wasn’t.

And she wondered where she would go.

Alone.

Unemployed.

Homeless.

Later that day she received a polite but brief and to the point letter from Mr. Harrington stating that the home would be sold, and all the furnishings would be sold at public auction, upon the sale of the home, pursuant to the terms of Chad’s Trust. The polite tone of the letter didn't make up for the fact that he listed the home without informing her first.

Just as she tossed the letter in the trash, the telephone rang. She snatched it up when she saw Dana's name on the caller ID.

Her friend wasted no time. "I hate to saddle you with more bad news, but I called the insurance company to make sure they got everything they needed. Turns out, the adjustor is holding the check until the investigation is complete."

Andi dropped into a kitchen chair and sagged against the table. "Investigation? What investigation?"

"The adjustor contacted the Buccaneer Bay Police Department for more information and the detective apparently told them he hasn't cleared you yet. The adjustor can't pay out on the policy until the police complete their investigation."

"How long will that take?" Andi massaged her temple with her fingers.

"Hard to say. I asked her worst case scenario. She said it sometimes takes a couple of years."

Andi sat up and stared at the basket of bills on the kitchen counter. More came in the mail every day. How could she possibly keep up?

Dana said, "I'm sorry. I've asked her to do everything she can to expedite the claim."

"I know. I appreciate it. I really do." Her heartbeat pounded in her ears. Her blood pressure was probably through the roof. "I've got something on the stove. Got to run."

She gripped the receiver in white knuckled hands. Though she'd told herself not to count on that money, she had been. Every scenario she imagined included using that money to pay off her debts. What would she do now? What could she do?

She shook her head. No sense wallowing in self pity. She grabbed the Morning Sentinel and went to the den to peruse the classified ads and apply for jobs. Most jobs that offered benefits and decent pay required a degree and, even more often, experience, which Andi sorely lacked. One job promised "interesting work with new challenges every day for the person with good interpersonal communication and research skills, possibility of working out of home." It sounded great, but was for a private investigator by the name of Jimmy Webster out of Bangor.

It sounded good, but she didn't think she could work for a grown man who still went by the name Jimmy. He was either awfully young or a mobster.

She kept reading, and another ad caught her attention. The local tourism office needed someone to hand out brochures and direct people who needed assistance. The pay wasn't great, but they weren't picky about qualifications, either. It would mean an income, though piddly, but more importantly, experience.

Andi sat down at the computer and created a resume. It needed massaging, since she didn't have any work experience. At least she could include things like serving on the Friends of the Library Board, and other charitable functions she'd helped with since she'd been in Buccaneer Bay. The printer beeped to alert her to add paper, so Andi opened the top drawer of Chad's desk to retrieve his linen stationery. When she pulled out a few sheets, a sheaf of papers of a different color caught her eye. She pulled them out of the drawer.

They were photocopies, and poor ones at that. Whoever copied them had done a sloppy job, resulting in crooked pages. The top of the first page was cut off, but the words "Woodson Enterprises, Inc." were printed right below whatever was missing. It looked like some sort of accounting document, with columns and numbers – lots of very big numbers. She flipped to the back page and saw that it had indeed come from a CPA's office, and had been copied to Benson Harrington III - the same attorney who prepared Chad's new will.

She scanned the document again, but paid more attention to the last paragraph, which was entitled "Summary of Valuation." It said there were 50,000 authorized shares of common capital stock in Woodson

Enterprises, Inc., with each share valued at $10,000. She raised her eyebrows and whistled. No small potatoes. A table with names in the first column – August Woodson, Caren Woodson, Portia Woodson, and other names were too blurry to read - included a list of certificate numbers in the second column, and a final column that said 'total number of shares'. A thick, bold circle highlighted the words Initial Public Offering at the bottom of the page. It was all Greek to her, but she'd seen enough movies and read enough books to recognize that whoever owned those certificates owned the company – and the company was worth a hell of a lot of money.

Like most people down east, she'd heard of Woodson Enterprises. Who in this part of Maine hadn't? But she couldn't for the life of her figure out what Chad would be doing with something like that, even if by some strange quirk of fate he actually had been having an affair with a Woodson. The quick photocopy job made Andi wonder if he was *supposed* to have it. Right behind the valuation packet was a legal pad with notes written in Chad's small, neat print. There was a notation about current value of tourmaline, something about a geological survey and mineral rights, and then a bunch of numbers - 44°25'34.2"N 68°14'47.9"W - next to the words "pegmatite dike."

None of it made sense, but the stuff about the pegmatite dike reminded Andi of the sticky note she'd found that marked a page in the Maine gem book. She hurried out to the living room and opened the book. It fell open to a picture of a large crystal that looked similar to the rocks in the valet with Chad's diamond cufflinks. According to the author, pegmatite dikes were elongated veins of gems that could be anywhere from half a foot to several feet thick, and the veins could run for hundreds of feet.

If Chad found what she thought he had, it could be worth more money than she could imagine. But what did that have to do with Woodson Enterprises?

The telephone rang and she picked up the receiver from the end table. The recorded voice, a woman, likely chosen for her kind but firm demeanor, calmly told her that her phone service would be disconnected in five days unless payment in full was received.

She sighed, then squared her shoulders and returned to the den, where she tucked it all back in the drawer and made a mental note to check it out thoroughly after she dealt with the more immediate issue – the necessary business of finding a job. She filled the printer, printed her resume, and headed for the Chamber of Commerce.

The woman at the Chamber was very nice, and seemed sympathetic to Andi's situation. Mildred Stevens was closer to 60 than 50, with close-cropped silver hair. "I'm afraid we don't have much in the budget for salaries."

Anything was better than nothing. "I understand."

"I'm afraid there aren't many benefits, either. We do offer six days off a year, for whatever reason you need, sick or personal or vacation." She peered at Andi over her reading glasses. "But we don't get holidays off."

Andi'd already gotten a call about the phone. The internet and cable had been disconnected. How long would it be before the electric was shut off? "I understand."

The older woman smiled apologetically and tilted her head, "And the hours aren't regular. Are you sure you are interested?"

"Absolutely," Andi bobbed her head, then stopped, not wanting to appear too needy. "When do you expect to interview for the position?"

The woman reminded Andi of the local librarian who taught her a love of books when she was a child. She glanced around the cramped office overflowing with files and loose papers, all in neatly organized stacks. The older woman motioned for Andi to sit in a straight-backed wooden chair, while she took a seat behind the desk.

"I'm Mildred Stevens, the office manager." She peered over her glasses just as the librarian had when Andi was twelve and had asked her where to find the book about the dog by Stephen King. She pulled the glasses off and let them dangle on a beaded strand. "What do you know about local tourism?"

"I moved here with my husband six years ago, and have had a wonderful time exploring the area. This island has so much to offer. As an outsider, I know what appeals to the tourists, and what questions they don't know enough to ask."

The woman narrowed her eyes and chewed on the tip of the earpiece of her glasses. "That's an interesting take."

"I'm eager to work, and willing to do whatever needs to be done." Andi pressed her lips together. She didn't want to seem too eager.

The woman crossed her legs and knocked over a stack of books. The toppled stack reached nearly to the edge of her desk. Andi immediately slid from the chair and began to restack the paperbacks. She held up one of the novels. "Lea Waite - I love her Antique Print series."

Ms. Stevens nodded her approval. "I'm a fan, also." She bent to help restack the books.

Andi said, "You know, there are a lot of writers from Maine. Have you ever thought about having writers come to the Harbor Fest?"

"Of course. You know, Bangor attracts a lot of readers as tourists, but that has slowed down a bit since Stephen King moved to Florida."

"Well, there's Lea. Paul Doiron. I bet they'd help us get in touch with other Maine writers."

"Interesting idea." The woman straightened in her chair, then picked up an elegant burgundy fountain pen and began to tap it on her desk. "Perhaps Portia Woodson would be willing to help. She's become a bit of a patron of the arts."

"Is she part of the famous Woodson family? From up by Bangor, right?"

"Yes, she's August Woodson's granddaughter. So sad. Her parents were killed in a horrible automobile accident a few years ago, and her father was the only son of August Woodson. That girl and her sister will inherit a fortune when he passes away."

"That's so sad," Andi murmured. Chad would have been set for life if he had survived. Once he divorced her, of course.

"Yes, it is. And it sounds like Auggie Woodson isn't doing well. The poor girl and her sister will have a lot on their shoulders when the old man passes away."

She shook her head slowly, then slipped her glasses back on and studied the application centered on the desk in front of her. After a moment, she peered at Andi over the rims and said, "Aren't you the woman whose husband just died?"

"That's right." Andi squared the stack of books and slipped back into her seat.

The woman pursed her red lips. "You sure you're ready to start a new job?"

Andi nodded.

Mildred raised her thin eyebrows and lowered her chin even more, "It's been quite a while since you've held down a job, Mrs. Adams."

"Yes, ma'am. I assure you, I'm motivated. I need a job. Frankly, I need the money."

The older woman snorted and frowned, "Well, this isn't a charity. And this isn't a counseling service for new widows. You work for me, you work. Understand?"

Andi suppressed a smile and nodded. "If you take a chance with me, you won't regret it. I'm a hard worker."

"You'll have to be. Tourist season is upon us." Ms. Stevens pulled a paper from one of the folders on her desk and slid it across to Andi, "Fill this out, then I'll give you a set of keys. Report to work Saturday morning at 9 o'clock sharp. Any questions?"

Andi neatly filled out the W-9, then handed it to Ms. Stevens, who gave her a quick rundown of what to wear and what exactly the job would entail. The urge to sing the Mary Tyler Moore theme was overwhelming as she left the building, and headed home, proud of herself for getting a job. The very first job she applied for. It took her the rest of the week to decide what to wear on her first day of work.

The job itself wasn't much of a challenge, but it gave her a regular schedule. She had a purpose, someplace to go, a reason to get dressed in the morning. Her new "office" had a storefront that looked like a little white cottage. Various potted plants and two Adirondack chairs filled the front porch. Inside, there was a display counter showing artifacts that had been found in the area, a few examples of rough gemstones for the rockhounders, and a display on lobstering. Pictures of happy people fishing, sailing and otherwise enjoying the water hung around the perimeter of the room. The tourists who came in were nice for the most part, though sometimes tired and cranky.

In her free time, Andi read the brochures and discovered that there were a lot of attractions in the state that she didn't know about. Her mother always said that about Missouri, too – lots of great things to do and see within driving distance, but everyone thinks they've got to leave the state when they go on vacation.

Andi collected brochures and studied the maps, making plans to explore the area on her days off. One of the proudest days of her life was the following Friday, when she arrived at the little office and discovered an envelope in the drawer with her name on it. She slipped her thumb under the flap and tore it open to find her very first paycheck. Sure, she'd had part-time jobs when she was in high school and college, and worked as a waitress during college. But she'd never had a real job before, nothing full time. Once Chad entered her life, there was never another thought of a career.

It had been a whirlwind romance, and he was offered a thriving dental practice in Buccaneer Bay before he even graduated, thanks to his family's connections. Her mother had been heartbroken when Andi dropped out of college to get married. He insisted that there was no need for her to finish school, since her job would be to take care of him. At first, she'd been happy to go along with him.

But now she *was* making it on her own, delighted to discover it was a good feeling. She photocopied the check before depositing it, framed the copy and hung it in the den.

Shortly after she got the job, she was running errands in town when she spotted the colorful window display at Bunch o' Blooms. Instantly, she remembered the second, smaller funeral spray. The older woman behind the counter had slightly gnarled fingers and sharp blue eyes.

Andi explained, "My husband, Chad Adams, died in May, and you prepared the floral arrangements for his funeral."

"Ayuh." The woman stared at Andi through narrowed eyes.

"There was a smaller arrangement that was so thoughtful. I'm working on thank yous, and want to make sure I send a note to the person who sent it, but the card got separated from the arrangement." Andi stopped when she realized the words were tumbling out too quickly.

"You're not from 'round these parts." It was a statement, not a question.

Andi shook her head. It wasn't the first time she felt like an outsider. Locals tended to think you were a stranger if you weren't a third generation Mainer. Andi's shoulders dropped and she turned to leave.

"Most young folks don't get the importance of hand writing thank you notes anymore." The woman looked skeptical, but pulled a stack of order slips from beneath the counter and flipped through them.

Andi froze.

Finally, the woman said, “Ah, here it is. Ordered by someone at Woodson Enterprises. Home office in Bangor is the billing address. No name.”

Andi nodded, thanked her for her time, and wondered how her husband had ever gotten involved with an heiress. Detective Johnson seemed to know more about

Chad than Andi did, but it wasn't as though she could ask him about it over coffee.

As each day passed, she began to worry less about her dead husband, and began to think that she might truly survive by herself. The burden of being a widow, of being alone in the world became a little easier to bear as time went by, even on a shoestring budget. At least her water and electric hadn't been shut off. Detective Johnson hadn't made an encore appearance, the sun shone brightly, and bright dandelions dotted the yard. Andi's tennis shoes crunched in the gravel as she walked down the curved driveway to the mailbox. The mailman returned her wave as he continued along his route.

She pulled the various envelopes and catalogs out of the box and flipped through them as she walked back towards the house. Her feet stopped moving of their own accord when she saw a plain brown envelope. She swallowed past the lump in her throat and her stomach did a little back flip. She slipped her thumb in and tore the envelope open, then pulled a single sheet of paper out.

"I know what you did, and you have something I want. I will be in touch."

Ever since she'd woken up in bed after the accident, there had been the nagging fear that the police would come and take her away to live out her days in a small concrete cell, and now this. The weight of the world crushed her like a bug.

Now it wasn't just the police she had to worry about. She looked up and down the quiet residential street. Someone was out there, watching her.

Was that person following her?

She jogged up the driveway, heart and mind racing.

13

Twenty minutes later, she stood in line at Harbor Regional Bank, the check from the attorney and a completed deposit slip gripped in her hand, the paper crinkled and moist from her sweat. When her turn came, she slid the crumpled check and deposit slip across to the teller, a well-endowed young woman who looked like she was trying too hard to be attractive. The blonde peered at Andi, then at the deposit slip, then examined the check carefully. When she looked down, her fake eyelashes lit on her cheeks like butterflies.

The lashes fluttered up and she pursed her lips. "It'll be just a moment, Mrs. Adams."

She stepped around the counter, hurried across the lobby and whispered to a man in a glass-enclosed office. The two peered out at Andi, then bent close and whispered some more. The woman pointed at the check, then hooked her thumb towards the lobby. Panic began to build. Andi glanced at the door, and debated for a moment on running. Her eyes slid back to the suited man. He nodded, then he and the teller came out and approached Andi. She swallowed hard, hoping that the others in line couldn't hear her heart thudding in her chest.

"Mrs. Adams, could I see you a moment?" The man said as he motioned for her to follow him to his office.

As she strode across the lobby, she felt the eyes of everyone in the bank on her back. She held her head high and walked with all the confidence she could muster. He sat behind his desk and she took a seat in a poorly cushioned blue chair that was surely uncomfortable on purpose.

Her voice cracked when she asked, "Is there a problem?"

"Oh, heavens, no! I simply wanted to suggest some options for you." He pulled some brightly colored brochures from a stand on his desk and spread them out like a deck of cards.

It took every ounce of self-control to keep from letting her breath out in a whoosh. He started by saying that he didn't intend to pry, and then did just that because he assumed the check drawn on the attorney's trust account was an inheritance. After a brief explanation on Andi's part, he proceeded to tell her about the various investments available, and explained that an interest bearing account would be to her benefit. He jotted a few figures down for her, and it dawned on her that she knew nothing about money, how to invest it or spend it wisely. Her head swam with figures and decisions.

Chad had taken care of the finances. He gave her an allowance, enough for groceries and household supplies.

She'd muddled through things since the accident and succeeded in keeping a roof over her head and the electricity turned on, but that was the extent of her knowledge. She worried that she shouldn't be doing this, but she needed money in the bank. It was time to look out for herself.

After asking a few questions, she followed the banker's advice, filled out the appropriate paperwork, and left the bank with a new checkbook and a slick folder full of information to look over. After she left the building, the blonde teller pushed out the door and ran after her.

The girl grabbed her arm. "Mrs. Adams?"

Andi stopped and turned. "Yes?"

The blonde's buttons pulled on the front of her shirt, showing a peek of white lace underneath. "I just wanted to say how sorry I am. For your loss, I mean."

"Thank you."

She looked down at her pink pumps. "Chad was a wonderful man. I understand he died quickly?"

Andi stood, finger poised over the unlock button on the key fob, and looked closer at the young woman. A dark streak down her part marred her blonde hair, and her brown eyes were sunken and hollow.

Something clicked in Andi's brain and she narrowed her eyes as she examined the blonde. "I'm sorry – do I know you?"

"No. Not really. I just knew your husband from when he came into the bank." She shrugged and smiled tightly, "He was always very nice. I'm sorry. I shouldn't have bothered you."

She spun around, took two quick steps to the entrance of the bank and yanked the door open. As Andi watched her hurry away, she wondered if that girl was the type to go away to Atlantic City for a weekend, then stepped into the Grand Cherokee and pulled out of the lot. Without consciously deciding where to go, she headed out of Buccaneer Bay and found herself at Harbor Chrysler. Right there in front was a beautiful Sahara package Jeep Wrangler, dark green with a tan soft top, just begging to be driven along the shore. Andi wheeled into the lot and sat looking at it, as her thoughts turned to Chad.

It had been a Saturday. He planned all week for them to get a new car, and spent hours researching the specs on various vehicles. She'd wanted a Jeep for years, so she'd lobbied the entire week to go look at them. She found a red one with a black soft top that was perfect for them, since they didn't have kids yet, and didn't plan to start a family for a couple of years.

When the salesman approached, she asked about the red Jeep. Chad smiled as if to apologize, then told the salesman they were interested in a Grand Cherokee Limited.

"But, honey, could we test drive both of them?" she'd asked.

He smiled again, lips stretched tight over perfect teeth, then apologized to the salesman for the interruption. When the salesman pulled a Grand Cherokee Limited around for a test drive, Chad opened the back door and motioned for her to get in. She did. He and the salesman chatted in the front seats, and the young man glanced uncomfortably at her more than once.

That afternoon, after the paperwork was complete, they walked onto the lot to drive the new Grand Cherokee home. He led her around to the passenger side. For a moment, she thought he was being chivalrous, but should've known better. They were alone. The only time he opened doors for her was when he was performing for someone.

He stared at her with cold, gray eyes, then opened the back door. It was his way of putting her in her place.

She shook her head to clear the memory. He couldn't treat her like that ever again. If anyone had known how he really treated her, they probably *would* think she'd knocked him over that guardrail on purpose.

Maybe she had, without even realizing it.

She sat in that very same Grand Cherokee, looked at the Wrangler and thought about Atlantic City, blondes and back seats, until a young man in khakis and a blue dress shirt strode across the lot. She parked and got out, waving at him. He waved back and headed her direction.

He ran through his sales pitch, but all she could think about was the freedom that Wrangler represented. She'd done everything Chad wanted for so long, and now that he was gone, she felt an uncontrollable need to do something for herself. She was ready to declare her independence. The salesman offered her his card, and asked, "Will your husband be coming by for a test drive?"

"No." *I'm a widow*, she thought, as she pointed to her vehicle, "I'm thinking about trading the Grand Cherokee in."

It felt good to take control, but she was terrified. Buying a vehicle was a big step. Chad always handled things like this. A short time later, she clutched her purse in her lap while she talked to the salesman and the sales manager. If they recognized her name when she filled out the paperwork, they gave no indication.

She wrote the check for the Wrangler that afternoon, and waited nervously as the finance manager called the bank to confirm that the funds were there. Of course, they were, and she was treated like a queen. Though it scared her to spend that much money, the doubts dissipated as she spent the remainder of the afternoon driving aimlessly, and ended up pulling off the side of the road and watched the sun paint the sky pink, red and orange over Eagle Lake.

14

Dana pushed through the doors of the Black Sails Diner and Andi waved at her. As Dana slid into the red vinyl bench seat, she set a wrapped package on the table. Andi looked at her and cocked her head, but Maggie showed up to take their orders before she could question her friend.

As the older woman walked away, Dana urged, "Go ahead, open it!"

Andi leaned back in her seat. "What's this for?"

Dana shrugged her shoulders. "Consider it a 'welcome to your new life' gift."

The paper tore easily, revealing a first edition of *The Maine Woods.* It showed Andi just how well her friend knew her. Simply holding the book in her hands made her feel independent. Chad hadn't encouraged her love of exploring, but she felt as if she were beginning to spread her wings. She nodded her thanks, not trusting her voice.

Right on cue, Maggie appeared with their order. Andi had just taken a big bite of her burger when her cell phone rang. She pulled it from her purse and glanced at the number while she chewed. She swallowed, then swiped her finger across the screen.

"Ms. Adams, it's Jake, from the dealership?"

She looked across the table at Dana and shrugged, "Hi, Jake, what can I do for you?"

"Just wanted to remind you that I still need the original title to the Grand Cherokee you traded in?"

She frowned as her stomach did a back flip. "I'm sorry. Got so excited about my new Wrangler, I forgot about that. I'll go get it out of the safe deposit box this afternoon and bring it up to you."

After she hung up, she relayed the story to her friend.

Dana wiped a bit of ketchup from the corner of her mouth. "Do you know where the key is to the safe deposit box?"

Andi blinked. "I didn't even think about needing a key. Chad always did the banking. I just assumed they opened it up for you and let you in."

Dana laughed. "You have a key and the bank has a key, and it takes both to get into a safe deposit box. Do you know if your name is on the signature card for the box?"

A chill ran through Andi. "I don't know."

They paused while Maggie refilled their drinks. After she walked away, Andi sat up straight. "Wait! I found a small key in his dresser drawer right after . . ." A chill ran up her spine at the reminder of Chad's death.

Dana reached across the table to pat Andi's hand. "I bet that's the key to the safe deposit box. Do you want me to go to the bank with you?"

Andi felt silly, but she didn't want to go alone. "Do you mind?"

Dana grinned. "Not at all. You going to let me drive that Jeep?"

Andi grinned back. "Maybe one of these days. But I'm not ready to give up the keys just yet."

As soon as they paid for lunch, Dana followed Andi to her house. Andi left her friend in the living room while she ran down to the basement to look for the key. She'd stuck it in her jeans' pocket the day she found it. Her mom did laundry while she was visiting, so hopefully she pulled the key out before washing clothes.

Andi shuffled through the clothes stacked on top of the washer and dryer. Chad's clothes were stacked there, waiting for her to bag them up for donation. At the bottom of the stack she found a broken dish filled with loose change, a couple of safety pins and a button that had fallen off in the dryer, and, at the very bottom, the key. She tossed it in the air and caught it with a flourish and a grin.

As they walked into Harbor Regional Bank, she was glad Dana had come along, because the entire affair intimidated her. The bank officer led them to the vault, then swept his hand for them to go first. "Please accept my condolences for the loss of your husband."

Andi nodded her thanks.

He continued, "Chad had such a fine sense of humor."

Dana shot Andi a look and cocked an eyebrow, but didn't say anything. The suited man handed Andi a clipboard and pointed to a red x. "Sign here."

Chad's signature appeared many times on the sign in sheet. She scanned the list quickly. He visited the bank box nearly once a week during his last few months of life.

Finally, the man stepped halfway down the bank of drawers and inserted his key into a lock box. Andi looked at Dana, who nodded. Andi took the key from her pocket and stuck it in the other lock. It turned easily in the mechanism. The man tugged the box out of its cubby and took it to a small cubicle where he sat it down with a loud clank.

"Please push the button when you're finished." He swept a red velvet curtain closed behind him, leaving the two women alone.

The bright fluorescent bulbs above them gave off a garish light. The lid opened with a creak. Inside stacks of bills had been rubber banded into neat bundles. Andi picked one up and flipped through it. All hundreds. Her eyes widened and she glanced up as Dana let out a low whistle. Dana looked up at her, eyes wide. "Where did all that money come from?"

Andi glanced nervously as the flimsy curtain behind them. "I have no idea." Seemed like every time she turned around, she learned something new about Chad. She'd been married to a stranger.

The money distracted her so much, she almost missed the small cloth pouch with a drawstring top tucked into one corner of the metal box. She loosened the drawstring and poured the contents into her cupped palm. Several rocks tumbled out, long crystals of green and pink. She wasn't exactly sure what they were, but knew they must be valuable if they were hidden in a safe deposit box.

"What are they?" Dana plucked one green nugget up and squinted at it.

Andi shrugged. She wasn't sure herself, but suspected they were tourmalines. Once they were polished and cut, they'd be worth a lot of money. She dropped them back in the pouch and tucked the bundle into her purse, with the intention of looking up that man she spoke to at the Clifftop about them. He could probably tell her what they were, if she could remember where he said he worked.

Dana said, "I don't see any vehicle titles here."

Andi shook her head, thinking about the refinancing paperwork in Chad's file cabinet. She stacked the bills back in the narrow metal box. Without knowing where the money came from, she didn't want anything to do with it.

Dana said, "If you're finished, I'll buzz the guy."

Andi nodded. A shiver ran down her spine. The situation still seemed surreal. As an afterthought, she flipped the case open and grabbed a bundle of cash, then stuffed it in her purse next to the crystals.

Once the safety deposit box was put away and they were escorted out of the vault, Andi put her hand on her friend's arm. "Can you come with me while I talk to someone about a loan?"

Andi turned to the gentleman who'd been helping them. "I need to talk to a loan officer. Is there anyone available?"

He directed them to a glass enclosed office, where an older man with gray hair and a double chin sat. He half-stood when they entered his office.

She dove right in. "I traded my Grand Cherokee in on a Wrangler. The young man at the dealership told me that he needs the title. As you may know, my husband just died. I thought the title would be in our safe deposit box, but it wasn't."

As she spoke, she watched his countenance carefully. Recognition dawned on his face, and she knew her suspicions were correct. He nodded slowly, and typed as she spoke. When she finished, she clasped her hands in her lap and waited.

He leaned forward and peered at the screen, then clicked his mouse. “I’m sorry, Ms. Adams. Your husband refinanced that vehicle at the end of last year, so we have the title in our files here at the bank. You owe approximately $20,000 on it. He was only making interest payments. We will need that amount in full before we can release the title.”

Her shoulders sagged, and she thought about the bills sitting in the safe deposit box. Without knowing their origin, they could be dangerous to use, especially at a bank. She closed her eyes and focused on breathing. After what she'd spent on the Jeep, she had very little left from the check the attorney in Bangor had given her. When she opened her eyes, the older man stared at her.

She took a deep breath and plunged ahead, "I don't have enough money to pay it off. I thought it was paid for and I traded it today for a Jeep -- it's used, it's not brand new -- but I spent nearly everything I had to buy the new Jeep--" She purchased that vehicle on a whim, a burst of independence . . . and now it felt like a lead weight around her neck.

He held up one hand, palm out. "Mrs. Adams, I think I can help. You can fill out a loan application for the difference you owe, accounting for the loan on the Grand Cherokee."

His words swirled through her head like smoke. She couldn't quite grasp the meaning. She deflated. "That'll be an awfully large loan."

Dana leaned close and whispered, "But not really so bad. What you already paid is the down payment."

Andi chewed her lower lip. "How does this work? Then you'll use my new Jeep as collateral?" Chad always handled the money, but the more she learned, the more she wished she'd been more involved. Not that it would've done any good. The more she learned, the more lies were discovered.

The banker nodded. She swallowed the lump in her throat. Should she take a chance and use the cash? She glanced at Dana with raised eyebrows and pointed to her purse. Dana's eyes narrowed and she shook her head no.

Nearly an hour later, she tucked the title to the Grand Cherokee safely in her handbag and her bank account was anemic.

Dana waited until they got outside, then grabbed Andi's arm and leaned close. She whispered, "Don't even think about using that money. You don't know where it came from or what it's tied to, but you know it's nothing good."

Andi jerked her arm away, immediately defensive. "But what am I supposed to do for money? I've got bills to pay and Chad left me with--"

"I know. It sucks. But you're going to have to buck up and get on with life. Chad is gone." Dana marched towards her car. "You're going to get burned if you're not careful."

Andi frowned as she trailed Dana down the sidewalk. She'd expected Dana to support her no matter what. "But why shouldn't I use some of that money? What could it hurt?" The whine in her voice made her angry. She clamped her mouth shut.

Dana didn't say another word until she dropped Andi off at her car. Dana rolled down her car window. Her flashing emerald eyes matched the intensity of her flaming red hair. "You know that much cash couldn't have come from anything good."

Andi looked around at the picturesque town, the quaint shops, the gaggles of tourists meandering down the sidewalks. She felt as if she were living in a dream, or had stepped into an alternate reality. "I don't know where that money came from."

"Exactly my point." Dana's red curls swung as she shook her head. "Doesn't matter if you know the source or not. You need to tell somebody about that money."

Heat crept up Andi's cheeks. "Who do I tell? Everyone in this town already looks at me with suspicion in their eyes. They think I'm an outsider, and they don't know what he was like."

"Just be careful. You're playing with fire." Dana's window zipped up and she drove away as Andi got into her car. She sat for a moment, heart pounding, before she backed out of the drive. She swung by the dealership to deliver the title to Jake. As she drove, she took deep breaths to clear her head. Dana didn't understand. How could she? Dana had friends and family who loved her, and they'd be there for her no matter what. Andi didn't have anyone. She was alone and on her own, with no one to depend on but herself.

15

Andi stepped out of the shower and dried herself, then leaned over and wrapped her long tresses in the towel. As she stood up and flipped her head back, she thought about her day. Work would be busy, but hopefully she'd get off early enough to swing by the grocery store. Spots on the bathroom mirror drew her eye, and she opened the cabinet door to get the cleaning spray. Her finger froze just as she began to squeeze the trigger.

She didn't have to do that. Not anymore.

As she blow dried her hair, she could almost feel Chad grabbing it in his fist and yanking. He liked that, controlling her. Hurting her. After she'd finished her hair and makeup, she left home without even stopping for a cup of coffee or bowl of cereal.

Someone pulled out of a parking space just as she turned onto Oak Street. That was lucky, particularly during tourist season. She wheeled the Jeep into an empty space in front of the Morning Sentinel and walked through the throngs of people meandering along the sidewalk until she reached Gloria's Locks.

Without allowing herself to over think it, she pushed the glass door open and approached the reception desk. "I'd like a cut and style, please."

The young girl perched at the counter twirled her blonde hair around her index finger. Her perfectly arched eyebrows rose as she glanced down at the calendar spread out in front of her. "Do you have an appointment?"

Andi shook her head.

The girl ran her finger down the list of names and phone numbers scrawled across the appointment book. "I can get you in a week from tomorrow with Marilyn."

"My next appointment cancelled, if you want me to fit you in."

Andi looked up at the woman who spoke. When she saw the purple streaked hair, she started to shake her head no, but stopped. This might be just the person to help her. This bold woman might be able to work miracles.

She looked at the girl who shrugged and went back to twirling her hair.

The stylist stepped forward and extended her right hand. "I'm Jackie. Come on back."

Andi sat in the chair and clutched her purse in her lap. Jackie ran her fingers through Andi's long, thick hair and said, "Mmmm. Whatdaya have in mind? Just a trim?"

"No. I want something completely different."

Jackie grinned as she wrapped her fingers around a ponytail of hair and pulled it back from Andi's face. "You know, we could take off a few inches, or we could go with a pixie cut. With your round face, you'd be cute as all get out. You'd look like that actress in Once Upon a Time."

Andi's brown eyes widened in the mirror, and she shocked herself when she nodded. "Let's go for it."

"You're sure?" Jackie cocked her head and raised her eyebrows. "No going back."

"No going back," Andi repeated. *In more ways than one.*

As Jackie moved around her, snipping with her silver scissors, Andi felt lighter with every lock of hair that fell to the floor. For so long, she'd done everything Chad wanted, from keeping his house perfect to looking the way he insisted she look. He was gone now, and she could live the life she wanted. Her spine straightened and she lifted her chin. She would be okay.

After Jackie finished blow drying Andi's hair with a round brush, she handed Andi a mirror and spun her in the chair so she could admire her new look. A grin spread across Andi's face as she turned her head this way and that. Joy overwhelmed her. She handed the mirror back to Jackie and wiped away a tear. "Thank you. I can't even begin to tell you what this means to me."

"Some folks say your hairdresser is like your therapist." The stylist swept the cape off with a flourish. "In some ways that's true, and it's pretty clear to me that you needed a fresh start. I'm glad I could help you do that."

The two women walked to the front of the salon and Andi gave her new stylist a generous tip, then made an appointment for a trim in five weeks. She pushed through the door and stood on the sidewalk, giving her eyes time to adjust to the bright sunlight. Her smile was so wide, her cheeks hurt. She turned and walked towards her Jeep, excusing herself as she dodged tourists. Just as she opened the door, someone shouted, "Hey! Get away from that

Jeep!" The door froze in mid-swing as she paused and looked around.

Dana jogged across the street, then pulled up abruptly. "Andi?"

"Hey! What are you up to?"

"I didn't recognize you!" Breathing with the exertion, Dana shook her head. "I thought somebody was trying to steal your new ride."

Laughter bubbled up. "What do you think?" She flipped her head left, then right.

"It looks amazing. You look just like Snow--"

"White!" Andi tossed her head and said, "I know, right?!"

"It's really something." A sigh escaped Dana's lips and she shook her head slowly. "You look like a totally new person."

"I feel like a totally new person. I feel lighter, happier, better than I have in ages."

"I've got to get back to work." Dana threw her arms around Andi in a bear hug. "You deserve this, you know."

"Thanks," Andi waved as her friend crossed the street. It was true. She did feel like a new person. Getting a new haircut was symbolic. She'd shed the last remnants of Chad's control with those long tresses Jackie swept up and threw away.

16

Preparations for the Harbor Fest kept Andi busy that next week. Mildred told Andi how excited everyone was about the expansion of the event to include fine art and, at Andi's suggestion, local writers.

The Chamber rented big tents for the artists to display their wares in the park, and Andi spent all day Friday making sure everything was ready for the vendors to set up. She focused the majority of her time on the main tent with rollup sides, and strung white twinkle lights all around it. Mildred arranged for It's Thyme to cater the event. By the time the shadows lengthened across the park, guests filled the magical setting. Artists and townspeople chatted as they nibbled on lobster rolls and sipped champagne from flutes.

Mildred approached Andi and said, "You've done a fantastic job with this. Why don't you take a break and get a bite to eat before the lobster rolls are all gone?"

Right on cue, Andi's stomach growled. "Thanks, I think I will."

She looked around and spotted Dana sitting at a round table at the back of the tent. She wove through the crowd, greeting those artists that she recognized. She pulled out a chair at Dana's table. "Looks like it's going to be a success."

Dana nodded and waved towards the crowd. "You've done a great job with this."

"Thanks." A grin spread across Andi's face. "It was a lot of work, and I really only did a little bit of it, but I think it'll be worth it. We have over 75 artists entered."

Dana raised her champagne flute. "To a successful Fest."

"Cheers." Andi raised her own glass and took a sip, then, "You need to find Kate Murphy's booth tomorrow. Her husband, Pete, is a glassblower, and she makes these amazing glass beads over an open flame."

"Sounds neat. I love that kind of stuff." Dana looked over Andi's shoulder and waved. "There's Edward. I'm going to go say hello - be right back."

Andi glanced over her shoulder as Dana greeted her boss. She took a moment to simply revel in the party atmosphere that she'd helped to create. Being part of something bigger than herself always appealed to her. That's why she enjoyed serving on the Library Board so much. Maybe she'd get involved again, now that her life was returning to normal. Then again, none of those women reached out to her after Chad's death. They avoided her like the plague.

She shook it off, closed her eyes and took a deep breath. The air was crisp and clean, fragrant with lobster and salt. Andi leaned back, letting her cares and worry float away. She felt lighter than she had in ages.

A shadow fell over her. She opened her eyes to find a dark haired man with piercing blue eyes standing over her. "Are you one of the artists?" His Wranglers were crisp, and his denim shirtsleeves were rolled up, exposing muscled forearms.

"No, I work for the Chamber." Her eyes wandered to the tanned triangle of skin revealed at his neck by a couple of buttons left undone. She looked down, but this time she didn't have enough hair to hide behind. She took a deep breath, lifted her chin and met his gaze.

He pulled out a chair and sat. "I don't remember seeing you at other Chamber events." His ice blue eyes crinkled when he smiled, exposing nearly perfect teeth. He was what most would call ruggedly handsome, probably in his mid to late thirties. Forties tops.

Her heart thumped in her chest. "I just started recently."

He motioned to the artfully stacked lobster cages that she'd strung with red and white lights. "You've really captured the feel of Buccaneer Bay. That'll make a good impression on all the artists."

She felt her cheeks heat under his praise, and looked down. "Thanks." Her stomach did a little flip. It was too soon to be attracted to a man, but she couldn't deny the tingle she felt in his presence. Besides, she felt as if she had wasted years of her life with Chad.

After they chatted a few more minutes, he leaned forward. "I realize this is a bit forward of me, but could I give you a call sometime?"

She hesitated, then gave him her phone number and he entered it in his phone. He slipped the phone back into its holster just as Dana returned to the table. She nodded at him once, then glanced at Andi with one eyebrow arched. "Am I interrupting anything?"

"Nope." He grinned and pushed to his feet. He glanced at Dana. "Good to see you again."

Dana narrowed her eyes and tilted her head. "And you."

"Such a beautiful night for a party." His manner was easy and relaxed. He hooked Andi's hand with his and brought it to his lips. "You are to be commended on a job well done. Hope the rest of the event is as successful as tonight."

He excused himself. Andi watched him walk away, thinking about Wrangler butts for the first time in years.

17

As soon as he disappeared into the crowd, Dana interrogated Andi about her new friend. "How do you know him? Are you going to see him again?" She sounded like a mother, a mother with a teenage daughter.

"Oh, Dana! I don't even know his name, much less anything else about him! But he's got a cute butt, doesn't he?" Laughter erupted like the bubbles in the champagne bottle in the ice bucket and she clamped a hand over her mouth. She felt new, alive. Like a new person.

Dana narrowed her eyes and focused on Andi. "I'm surprised you didn't recognize him. I figured you knew him. He's one of the execs with the Chamber. Supposedly he's a big time public relations guy from Boston originally. Moved here because of his wife."

Andi shrugged. “I don’t have much to do with the Chamber itself. They just send me my paychecks.”

A frown still creased Dana's forehead and her jaw clenched and unclenched.

“Dana?” One of the great things about Dana was that she was always honest, sometimes brutally so. Whenever a straight answer was required, Andi went to Dana. But this time it looked like she was holding her tongue for some reason. Andi pressed, “What is it?”

She shook her head and glanced around at the crowd. "I really shouldn’t say anything, because I don’t know for sure.”

“Shouldn’t say what?”

Finally, she spit words laced with venom. “Didn't you hear me a minute ago? He’s married.”

It was like getting a bucket of cold water dumped over her head. Andi frowned, determined not to let it get her down, and turned her attention to the artists drifting in and out of the round tables. "It's not a big deal. He was just chatting." Why did this bother her? Chad only been in the ground a month and it was too soon to be looking at men like that anyway. But the possibility of someone exciting and new was, well, exciting. A handsome man approached her and spoke to her like an equal, without a trace of the condescension in his voice.

The good-looking guy didn’t cross her mind again until the following Wednesday. She was cleaning the downstairs bathroom when the phone rang. She ran and picked up on the fourth ring.

She huffed out a breath, then said, “Hello?”

“Hi,” The voice was deep and a little rough, as if he had just woken up. “You probably don’t remember me, but we met at the Harbor Fest.”

Her skin tingled at the memory, “Right, but I don’t think we ever exchanged names.”

“I thought about that after I walked off." He laughed. "Anyway, my name is Paul - Paul Thompson. And you are?”

“Andrea Adams. But my friends call me Andi.” She caught her reflection in the dresser mirror. A flush of heat colored her cheek like apples. With her new haircut, she looked like an entirely different person. And felt it.

“Does that mean I get to call you Andi?” That gravelly voice gave her chills.

A butterfly did a back flip in her stomach as she walked back into the bathroom. “Sure.” She slid down to the floor and leaned against the cool tile of the tub.

“Good."

Silence hummed between them. Her tongue flicked out to moisten her full lips. "I think we kind of work together."

"Do tell."

"I work at the tourism center, at the Chamber of Commerce." Her job, so low on the totem pole, embarrassed her a bit, but he didn’t react.

"We probably have walked right past each other, then. I do some PR work for the Chamber."

After a few minutes of small talk, he took a deep breath, then plunged into the meat of the call. “I’m thinking about taking a trip up to Witch Hole Lake this weekend to take some pictures for a brochure. Would you like to come along?”

“Who all is going?” The butterfly did a double back flip.

“Just me. And you, if you want to go.”

She closed her eyes and pictured the two of them, alone in the wilds of Maine, on a deserted lakefront. Just the sound of his voice gave her thrills. What would she do in an enclosed space with him?

"Still there?" His voice, barely more than a whisper, gave her chills.

"Yes." Two sides of her tussled about his offer, until she decided it was best to confront things head on. Her voice came out more abrupt than she intended. "Are you married?"

The phone line hummed quietly as her heart thumped in her chest one, two, three, four times.

Finally, he spoke. "Yes. Yes, I am. But we are separating."

"Oh." Oh, God, did that mean he was available? He said separating, present tense - not separated, past tense. She'd have to ask Dana for a judgment call on this one.

He plunged ahead. "I mean, I don't want you to think this is a date or anything. I just thought it would be fun for you to go along. And it would actually be helpful to have your perspective."

Of course! It was business, not a date. She squeezed her eyes shut, thankful they weren't face to face. "Oh," she said again, then cursed herself. He worked with words, and all she could come up with was 'oh.' The internal debate continued, while they talked about photos that would appeal to tourists.

They reached an awkward silence, and he said, "I should let you get back to your day."

The lonely voice in her head won the battle. She swallowed hard and took a tentative step forward. "You know, I've been reading about that lake, but I've never been there."

His voice brightened immediately. "Oh, it's great. There's a little picnic area and a small beach, all surrounded by woods, with amazing carriage trails. It's an easy hike. We might even get lucky and spot a moose or a bear!"

She laughed at his excitement. "Okay."

"Okay, as in, okay, you'll go?" His voice was hopeful.

She nodded, then realized he couldn't see her. "Yes."

They made arrangements to meet at Caddy's Quick Shop the following morning. Guilt tugged at her, but she squelched it. After they hung up, she sat on the cool tile floor, hugging herself and grinning at her brazenness. Was going with him the right thing to do? Would she be able to do the right thing and keep this at a friendship level?

How horrible would it be if she didn't?

18

Andi called Dana and told her about the call. Her friend's demeanor was a bit cool, but to her credit, she wasn't judgmental.

"I know how difficult it is for you to be alone." Dana kept her tone even. "But, it's only been a month since Chad died."

"I know." Andi winced at the whiny tone in her voice. "And that's why I'm feeling guilty. But I want to put that chapter of my life behind me -- and it's not like this is a date. It's for work."

"Just be careful. Don't jump in to something too fast."

"I won't," Andi assured her. She appreciated her friend's concern. "But I feel like I wasted so much time with Chad. Our marriage ended a long time ago."

"I get it. Really, I do." Dana's sigh reached through the phone. "But what's the deal with his marriage? Did you ask him?"

The corners of Andi's mouth curled up. "Yes, he's separated." *Separating*, a little voice in her head insisted.

The next Saturday morning, she pulled into a parking spot at Caddy's Quick Shop. She ran inside to get a soda. Marilou Young perched on her stool behind the cash register, tapping a stubby yellow pencil on the counter. In all the years Andi'd lived there, she'd never seen Marilou leave her roost. She was old and cranky, and knew every one of her customers by name.

Wally Morton leaned across the counter, his voice sharp. "You tell Burt to make sure he uses new antifreeze when he flushes my radiator this time."

Marilou swiped Wally's keys off the counter. "Will do."

"I'm not kidding around. If I find out he used that old stuff again, I'm going to tell everyone in town. I know that shed in back is full of ancient antifreeze and he's trying to use it up . . . but not in my vehicle!" He spun around and came face to face with Andi. His eyes widened and his cheeks burned. He stammered, "Oh, hello."

"Wally." She smiled at him. "Please say hello to Jennifer for me. And, please, let her know that I'd be glad to help again if the Library Board needs anything."

"Sure. Of course." The older man pushed past her and out the door. Andi stared after him, missing her old life for just a moment. Until she remembered that not a single member of the Library Board she'd served on for two years had even bothered to send her so much as a sympathy card since Chad's death.

Unfazed by Wally, Marge looked up from her crossword puzzle as Andi set her ice cold Coke on the counter. Even after six years, she looked at Andi with suspicion. "That all?"

Andi nodded as she pulled two bills from her purse.

Marge kept her head lowered and peered at Andi over her glasses. "That new Jeep o' yours sucks gas, I betcha."

Andi glanced outside and grinned. "It does, but it's a lot of fun."

"Chrysler is darned proud of them Jeeps. Where'd ya get the money for it?"

Lots of locals were blunt, but this old gal took the cake. She said what everyone else thought but wouldn't voice. Andi said, "My husband died."

Marge's left eye twitched, but she didn't glance away. "Sorry deal, that." She slid the change across the counter, then flicked her eyes back down to her crossword puzzle.

"Mind if I leave it here for a bit? I'm riding somewhere with a friend."

The stout woman behind the counter grunted and nodded. The driveway alarm sounded with a ding and Marge looked past Andi. "Cheap transplant. Foreigners like him come in here and think they own the place, too cheap to pay full price. Know darned good and well he makes more money than us."

Andi shook her head at the older woman's gall, then turned to see Paul as he wheeled into the lot in his yellow Wrangler. She pocketed her change and pushed through the glass door. He had on a t-shirt and a faded denim jacket, and his light brown hair poked out from beneath his Red Sox ball cap. His tan gave him a healthy, natural look, and he swung out of the Jeep with the easy manner of a man comfortable in his own skin.

He greeted her with a light hug and gave her a peck on the cheek, as if they met like that every day. His hand reached for hers with ease and he turned to lead her towards the stack of old lobster traps heaped against the side of an rickety shed where chipmunks scurried about.

“Got to stop and see these little guys before we take off.” His infective enthusiasm charmed her, and the warmth of his hand enveloping hers was soothing and comfortable. “I feed them every time I stop in here. Check this little fella out.”

He squatted down and pointed at a tiny chipmunk, chubby and bright-eyed, his little tail flipping up and down. He sat at the very edge of the pile, torn between curiosity and fear. Andi’d never seen a baby chipmunk before, and thought he was about the cutest thing she’d ever seen.

Paul reached in his pocket and pulled out some sunflower seeds, then opened her hand and poured some seeds in. He squatted and whispered, "Hold your hand out and keep still."

She knelt and extended her hand, not daring to even breathe. The little creature crept forward, his nose twitching. Finally, his tiny little feet tickled her fingers as he grabbed a seed, then retreated to the safety of a trap. She giggled and Paul smacked her lightly on the arm. "See there! He trusts you."

She flinched at the sudden touch and her laughter died as memories of Chad flitted through her mind, but he didn’t seem to notice. His eyes were glued to the baby chipmunk perched just out of reach. He gushed, “Awesome, huh?”

“Yes – awesome!” She laughed, determined to push thoughts of Chad away. Just then, Burt Davis charged out the back door of the auto shop and scared the little chipmunk away.

The old mechanic glared at them as he jerked open the door of the old shed, sending little chipmunks scurrying for cover. Andi stared at the jumble of boxes and cartons stacked haphazardly in the building, amazed that nothing fell on Burt's head as he scrounged through the mess.

Paul pushed to his feet, grabbed her hand and led her towards his Jeep. "We can take mine this time, and we'll take yours next time. Deal?" He opened the half door for her.

"Deal." She decided to just go with it. The sun shone brightly, the crisp salty air reminded her of how lucky she was to live on the ocean, and the gorgeous guy paying attention to her made her feel young again. But was she being unfaithful to Chad? She shivered involuntarily.

He slid into the driver's seat and looked at her. He asked, "You cold? There're jackets in the back seat if you need one."

"No, I'm fine. Just had a chill."

He reached into the back seat, leaning towards her. His chest brushed her arm. She stiffened at the casual touch and swallowed hard.

He sat back in his seat and handed her a pink ball cap. "Here, you might want to wear this. With the top off, it gets pretty windy."

She accepted the cap and settled it on her head. The new pixie cut would be perfect for Jeeping.

Bonus.

The rest of the day passed like a dream. She couldn't have asked for a more perfect outing. They chatted as they drove north on Paradise Hill Road. Tall cedars stretched up on both sides of them. He wheeled into the concrete lot and parked far away from the visitors center.

He pulled a small cooler and a blanket from the back of the Jeep. She took the throw and folded it over one arm. He grabbed her free hand and led her to the start of the carriage trail. The flat, easy trail led them to picturesque Witch Hole Pond in minutes. Several bicycles passed them, and they met a handful of other hikers.

He stepped up onto one of the large flat rocks that lined the trail. "Do you know what we call these?" He held out his hand.

She took his hand and let him pull her up beside him. "No, what?"

"Rockefeller's Teeth." He hopped off and pulled her towards him, away from the trail. He led her along a barely noticeable path until they reached an outcropping of rock smoothed by centuries of harsh Maine winds.

The blue sky opened above them as the trees thinned a bit. A beaver splashed into Witch Hole Pond, then swam away, leaving a V-shaped wake behind him. Andi's mouth gaped open. "This is absolutely enchanting. I've never seen anything like it." Lily pads nearly covered the lake, and two more beavers scurried around their dam on the north side of the pond, oblivious of their audience.

He helped her spread the blanket out and they settled on it. They nibbled on ham and cheese sandwiches and he offered her an orange soda. With a grin, she accepted the aluminum can. "This reminds me of being a kid."

He popped open one for himself. "Does me, too."

He leaned towards her as they talked, interested, and drew her out with questions. She found herself telling him about her childhood, pets, and family. After she tucked her trash in the paper sack Paul had brought along, she stretched her legs out and leaned back. The lichen covered rock was smooth and cool under her touch. She let her head fall backward and watched the wispy clouds drift across the blue sky.

He took a long drink of soda, then asked, "How do you like your job at the welcome center?"

She ran her tongue over her teeth before answering. "I like it. I knew there were a lot of tourists in the summer, but never realized just how many until I started working there."

He gazed out at the blue-green water stretching to the south. "We need to do a better job of catering to the upper class tourists. More money there."

She thought about the harried families who stopped in at the center. "I don't see many upper class tourists."

"There used to be lots of them. You know, the Harbor Fest was a great start, with the addition of fine art."

Her heart swelled under his praise. Chad had never thought her capable of anything, never noticed all that she did. The wind picked up and ruffled her short hair. It still felt new.

"I'd love to see Buccaneer Bay do something more high class, like lunch on the lawn at Jordan Pond. I'll take you there sometime." Paul squinted as he studied her. “So, what do you really want to do?”

She blinked and cocked her head to one side. “What do you mean?”

“Surely you want to do something else – I mean, usually the job at the welcome center is filled by retired folks who just need a time filler."

She stiffened, “I know it’s nothing big, but it pays the bills.”

He reached over and patted her thigh. “No, don’t take that the wrong way. I’m not putting you down. See, I'm an executive with the Chamber of Commerce and want to make sure we're not wasting talent."

She laughed it off, but her skin tingled where he had touched her. Maybe he could help her get a better job. With bills stacking up, a raise would sure help.

Paul studied her for a moment and seemed to recognize the change in her. He dropped the subject and launched into a story about a local businessman. "At one of my first big events, we hosted a reception for a businessman visiting from the Middle East. I sent an email to everyone who was invited with a list of etiquette tips, but one pillar of our community - I won't say who - didn't read the email. When I introduced him to the visiting dignitary, he extended his left hand."

Andi's eyebrows arched, "And that's bad?"

Paul leaned towards her and confided, "In their culture, the left hand is reserved for, well, hygiene."

Her eyes widened when she put two and two together, "Oh, no! How offended was the man from the Middle East?"

"Very. He refused to shake hands and turned his back on the American."

"Ouch." Andi cringed and shook her head. It was good to hear about someone else's screw ups for a change. A shadow passed over them and she looked up at the dark clouds rolling in over the lake. "Maybe we should pack up and get those pictures taken."

He followed her gaze and nodded. They worked together to clean up then walked down the carriage path to the Jeep. She held the passenger seat up for him so he could put the cooler back in the Jeep. His arm brushed against her breast, and she felt a tingle all the way to her toes. She slid into the seat and he leaned close, his ice blue eyes intense as the Maine sky on a summer day, and she felt sure he could see all the hopes and fears and secrets hidden deep within her own. His lips brushed her lightly and her heart raced. She pressed her hand against his chest, and his heart pounded just as hard as hers.

He pulled back and smiled and, just like that, she fell for him.

And hated herself for doing so.

Fact was, she didn't want to be alone. Even being married to someone like Chad was preferable to being alone. But think how good it could be with someone like Paul, a polite man who knew how to treat a woman.

They walked around and took quite a few pictures. The two worked well together. She pointed out things that appealed to her as an outsider, and he found creative ways to change the perspective. By the time they were finished, they were both satisfied with the results.

As they drove south towards Buccaneer Bay, the trees closed in around them, sometimes nearly blotting out the sky completely. As they neared town, she glanced over at him and said, "What about your wife?"

His head swung towards her. "I'm sorry?"

Her fingertips brushed her lips as she thought of the kiss. "You told me you and your wife are separating."

His chest rose and fell with a heavy sigh. "We are."

"Have you moved out? Or are you still living together?" There was a tan line on his left ring finger. Why hadn't she noticed that sooner?

"We're still living together, for the sake of convenience, but the marriage is over." He tapped his fingers on the steering wheel. “And what’s your story? Ever been married?”

“Yes.” After a pause, she added, “I was. For six years.”

"Was?" He glanced at her, then returned his focus to the road. "When was the divorce final?"

Wind tugged at her hat. She pulled it down tight. "He died."

Traffic ahead of them slowed, so he tapped the brakes and looked at her, eyes wide. "I'm so sorry. How long ago?"

She chewed her bottom lip. "Not long."

"How did it . . .?" His voice trailed off. The warm smile faded.

"Accident."

"I'm sorry," he said again, then he recovered and accelerated as the traffic in front of them began to move. Suddenly, he snapped his fingers. "Wait! Andi Adams – I knew I recognized your name! Your husband was Dr. Adams - he was that dentist that fell onto the rocks, up by the Clifftop – oh, man, how horrible. I'm so, so sorry."

"It's okay." She shrugged and swallowed the lump in her throat.

He reached over and squeezed her hand. Goosebumps pebbled her skin, and she shivered. A day did not go by that she didn't remember that night. The sound of his screams haunted her.

They didn't speak again until they reached Caddy's Quick Shop. She slid out of the Jeep, and he did, too. Sort of. He stood, one leg on the ground, the other inside, half-sitting on the driver's seat.

"Listen. I don't want to push you. I didn't realize." His voice trailed off. He shrugged and one corner of his mouth twitched upward, "But I like you a lot, and I'd like to see you again."

She nodded and smiled. His smile spread across his face and her knees felt like spaghetti. She liked the fact that his front teeth were slightly crooked. It gave him character. "I'd like that, too."

"I'll call you, then."

"I'd like that." Maybe she needed to invest in a thesaurus. She hopped into her Jeep and drove away, glancing at the rearview mirror at his reflection until the road curved around and she couldn't see him anymore.

19

Andi spoke to Dana on the phone several times after the trip to Witch Hole Pond, but hadn't confided in her yet about her day with Paul, whom she had also spoken to on the phone several times. Her heart felt like a balloon, pulling her up, lifting her mood. Just the thought of Paul made her smile.

She met Dana at the Black Sails Diner for lunch that next week, and the secret of her budding romance (dare she think of it like that?) had her ready to burst, so after Maggie set their salads down, Andi said, "Remember me telling you that Paul and I were going to Witch Hole Pond last weekend?"

Dana paused, fork in midair, dressing dripping from the lettuce. Her eyes pinned Andi's. "Just the two of you?"

"It's not what you think. It was for work," Andi insisted. "And he and his wife are getting a divorce."

"Work. Right." Dana stuck her fork in her mouth and chewed slowly, then, "Getting. Not gotten."

Andi plunged forward, "I'm not looking for a relationship. Besides, it's flattering to have someone pay attention to me."

Dana nodded. "I know. And I know things weren't as perfect as they seemed between you and Chad."

Andi's body tensed as the unwanted memories returned, wondered how much her friend noticed over the years. Did she notice the bruises? Did she wonder why Andi wore sunglasses so often? Did her friend believe she was that clumsy? Did she know how it felt to cower in the corner while a man out of his mind with rage ranted and raved because the soup cans weren't alphabetized?

Andi closed her eyes and shivered, then pushed the memories away. She met Dana's gaze and said, "I know what you're thinking. That Chad hasn't been gone long. But here's the thing. I've waited for so long to be happy, I don't want to waste time."

Concern softened Dana's features. "I just don't want you to get hurt."

"Believe me, I don't want that either." *In more ways than one*, Andi thought. How could she explain that she wanted to put Chad firmly in her past? That she wanted to pretend the marriage never happened?

Dana's eyes focused in on a point behind her friend, and Andi turned to follow her gaze. Paul and a beautiful raven-haired woman walked in the door, and waited to be seated. His hand spread across the small of her back, and her head tilted intimately towards him. She brushed her hair back with her left hand, and a huge diamond glittered under the diner's lights.

Her wedding ring.

His wife.

Andi turned slowly back to Dana, and smiled, trying to hide her pain behind a façade that she hoped wouldn't crack. At least not until she was alone.

"See. Not even bothered." She stabbed a slice of hard-boiled egg with her fork. "Now, tell me about what's going on with your life. You told me you and Derek are seeing a lot of each other lately."

"Yes, I think he might be *the one.*" Dana paused and tilted her head, her emerald eyes narrowed. "You sure you're okay with listening to this?"

"Absolutely. Fill me in." Andi imagined Paul's face on the other half of the hard-boiled egg and stabbed it. She refused to even glance in his direction, and focused on her friend for the remainder of the meal, though she only heard a few words here and there.

A couple of days later, she curled up on the sofa with a bowl of Rocky Road ice cream smothered with chocolate syrup. With Chad gone, she could enjoy it guilt free. After a long day at the tourism center, with a group of elderly couples on a bus trip wanting to know every detail of every attraction in the area, she relaxed into the cushions. She closed her eyes and rolled the creamy sweetness in her mouth, savoring it. The doorbell rang and her eyes sprang open.

She peered through the peephole and saw a middle-aged man wearing a polo shirt. She'd seen him around town, but didn't know him. She opened the door and said, "Can I help you?"

He grinned. "I hope so! My wife has wanted to live in this neighborhood for ages and I just noticed the for sale sign."

She shook her head, but he forged ahead. "I realize it's rude for me to just stop in without calling first, but can you tell me how many bedrooms there are?"

Her heart sank. Even if she turned him away, he'd just call the agent. There was no escaping the fact that her house was for sale. "Three bedrooms, two full baths."

He leaned out and looked to the side. "Looks like there's a basement. Is it finished?"

She sighed. "Not completely. My husband used it as a workshop."

The man rubbed his beefy hands together. "A man cave."

She shrank with every word he uttered. "I'm sorry, but this isn't a good time. Perhaps you should call the agent and make an appointment."

"Of course," His large head bobbed. "I didn't mean to impose."

She shut the door before he stepped off the porch. The house might be for sale, but that didn't mean she had to offer tours for drop-ins. The sofa was calling her name, so she settled in to watch TV. She tucked her feet under her and snuggled into the corner, just as the opening scene started. The phone rang and she debated on letting the machine pick it up, then shrugged and picked up the handset from the end table.

"Hello?"

"Hey, there."

Her heart chilled at the sound of his voice, just like the icy coldness of the bowl cupped in her left hand. Retorts raced through her brain, but none of them traveled along the right pathways to her mouth.

"Hey, there, yourself." *Brilliant.*

His voice was low, seductive. "Sounds like it's going to be a beautiful weekend. Want to go for a boat ride, take some photos of the lighthouse? We can take my boat out."

"Don't you have plans with your wife?" For a moment, she wondered if she'd really said it out loud.

"She and I don't do anything togeth-"

She cut him off, "Really? You don't eat lunch together?"

His breath caught. Her thumb hovered over the red end button, but she couldn't bring herself to push it. Weakness made her angry, and she wasn't sure who was weaker – her, for allowing herself to fall for a married man, or him, a lying asshole who cheated on his wife.

The low seductive quality in his voice disappeared, replaced by a clipped tone reminiscent of her cousin's from Boston. "Yes, we did have lunch together. I just can't – I haven't-"

"What?" Her temper flared. She'd been ready to forgive him for anything, ready to give her heart to him. She broke in, unable and unwilling to hide her irritation. "You don't have the guts to tell her it's over?"

He continued, his voice barely more than a whisper. "It's complicated, and I, well, I think I'm falling for you."

She bit her lip and closed her eyes, wanting him to need her so badly, and hating herself for that. Since Chad died . . . hell, since long before Chad died . . . she had been so lonely. And here was a wonderful man, good-looking, funny . . . would it be so bad to see what happened? To be a friend to him? To be more?

"Are you still there?" he asked.

"Yes." Her blood pounded in her ears.

"Look, I hate doing this over the phone, where I can't see your face. Can I come over?"

"I don't know. Probably not a good idea." She sat the bowl of ice cream on the coffee table and hugged her knees to her chest.

"Just to talk. Promise. Nothing more. Just for a little while?" He was pleading. He needed her. It felt so good to be needed.

She gave in, but promised herself she wouldn't change anything, wouldn't do anything, and sure as hell wasn't going to primp for him. She punched the end button and laid the phone on the arm of the couch, then took a big bite of rapidly softening ice cream. The creamy coldness soothed her hurt feelings.

20

Within fifteen minutes, her doorbell rang. Though her muscles tensed with the urge to run to the door, she took her time washing and drying her hands after she rinsed her ice cream bowl, then pumped a little dab of lotion into the palm of her hand and massaged it in as she forced herself to walk to the front door.

He stood on the front porch, like a lost puppy dog with droopy eyes and down turned lips. He held up a grocery bag. "I come bearing ice cream."

"I just had some." She pushed the door open and motioned him in.

"Mind if I stick it in the freezer?"

She led him to the bright, cheery kitchen, then opened the freezer door of her stainless steel refrigerator. He stuck the carton in and volunteered, "Nothing comforts like ice cream, right?"

Without a word, she led the way to the family room. He followed, silent. She gestured to the couch, and then settled into her favorite overstuffed chair. He was nervous, and she did not intend to make it easy for him.

The inane chatter from the television filled the room. His eyes darted around, taking inventory of their surroundings. Finally, he made eye contact and the sadness in their blue depths touched her.

The tales of his wife reminded Andi of her own frustrations with Chad. Verbal abuse, how she used sex as a control, how she handled their financial affairs. One story sounded painfully familiar. Her sympathies were with him as he related the story.

"For instance," he began, "We went to the big charity dinner in the spring, you know the big whing-ding out at Wild Flower Stables? She's on the Board of Directors for the Denim & Diamonds Dinner, so we went. It's a western event, so I wore my cowboy boots and Stetson hat. Well, she didn't tell me until we got there that it was a catered dinner, coat and tie. She laughed at me the whole evening, called me Tex. She flirted with all the men. I caught her chatting with our neighbor, Patrick Evans."

That last bit struck a nerve. "There's nothing wrong with your wife talking to another man."

He shook his head and said, "No. No, that's not what I mean. She leaned in towards him, gave him a great view of her cleavage. When I stepped up to join them, she rolled her eyes and patted me on the arm like I was some doddering old fool that didn't know what was going on. She told Patrick I'm fifteen years older than her, and can't keep up with her. Then she laughed and said, 'I'm referring to tennis, of course.' It hurt, and she didn't care. She never cares."

Andi's eyes narrowed. “So why are you still with her?”

He leaned forward, his elbows on his knees. “It’s complicated. A long story, you know?”

She settled back in her chair. “I’ve got time.”

He cupped his hand to the back of his neck and rubbed, “I know money isn’t everything, but I’ve fought hard for us to get to the point where I can take time off, enjoy myself. She would fight me tooth and nail, and make my life a living hell if I asked for a divorce.”

Thoughts of her own marriage bubbled up, those times she'd wondered if divorce was an option. It felt unrealistic in her situation. Chad kept her on a short leash, and he controlled everything from the household budget to the groceries in the cabinets. Even paying for an attorney would be difficult. Paul didn't have that problem, though. She asked, “Do you really think it’d be that bad?”

"Yes." He nodded slowly, then lifted his eyes to meet hers. “She’s a mean, vindictive person.”

She couldn’t imagine any man not standing up to his wife. Couldn’t imagine those roles being reversed. It made no sense. She scoffed, “Oh, come on, she can’t be that bad. You file for divorce, and let the attorneys work it out.”

"She'd ruin me," he snorted. “She had a salesman at a Best Buy in Portland fired when he sold her a modem that didn’t work. She flat out installed it wrong – her mistake, not his - but she insisted that he gave her bad advice and caused her computer to crash. She called a sorority sister of hers at the corporate office and had him fired. Not his fault. And he lost his job.”

She nodded her understanding. So, they had bad marriages in common. It made her think twice about why she didn’t file for divorce. Though her marriage was horrible, divorce wasn't an option. Her parents raised her to believe that marriage is "'til death do you part." Was that reason enough to stay?

She sighed and acknowledged, "She sounds awful. So why not file for divorce?"

"I'd lose everything. My house. My retirement. Plus I'd have to pay alimony." He shifted on the couch so he was facing her. "I don't know how to put into words what I'm feeling, and I know it's wrong. But what it boils down to is that if I stay married to her, I live my life. I picnic at Jordan Pond, I take trips, I do my own thing. We sleep in separate rooms and lead separate lives. I'm not ready to rock the boat yet."

Andi swallowed the lump rising in her throat. She knew exactly what he was talking about. Chad and she had gone through that, too, even down to sleeping in separate rooms for a while. She'd convinced herself life wouldn't be much different, married or not, and it really wasn't – she still did all the cooking, cleaning, shopping. But it was so much easier without him around. And she had to admit, if she was honest with herself, the fact that Chad was dead and not an ex-husband that could – no, *would* – make her life hell, made her life now much easier.

Paul slid off the couch and leaned forward, so he was kneeling, and put his hands on her knees. His piercing blue eyes were beautiful, though sincere and pained. Her own difficulties and struggles reflected in their depths. She could see into his soul at that moment, and knew they were meant to be.

He smiled and fine lines crinkled his tanned face. "I know this is happening quickly, but I think we could turn into something special."

She put her hands on his. God help her, she was falling in love with a married man. What the hell was she doing? Was she so desperate to be loved? She'd been unhappy for so long, wasted so much of her life . . . was it possible to make up for lost time?

"Please be patient with me," he whispered. Even the wrinkles around his eyes and mouth appealed to her. His skin was that of a man who spent his life outdoors, and a tear slid down his cheek, over his tanned skin and along a few light scars on his left cheek. she reached forward and traced the scars with her index finger, and it hit her. Long, manicured nails left those marks.

"You've got to leave her," she whispered, her voice catching in her throat.

"I know." He bent his head forward and rested his forehead on her knee. She stroked his thick, dark hair, and made soothing sounds. After a moment, he looked up at her. "I think I'm falling in love with you."

There was no doubt in her mind that she was falling, too, but she couldn't take her eyes off the gold band encrusted with diamonds on his left ring finger. Then she glanced at the wedding set she still wore on her left ring finger out of nothing but simple habit. She could draw upon her strength to create a fresh start and plan her future. Maybe one day Paul would wear a ring like that for her and she would have a ring that really meant something on her own finger.

But it had to be done right. She sat up straight and lifted her chin.

He whispered, "You know yourself how difficult it is. I suspect you know exactly what I mean."

"You need to go," she said, more abruptly than she intended. "Go back to your wife. And when you are able to leave her, come and find me."

"Tell me, have you gone through Chad's things, or are his things still here?" He kept his hands on her knees and rose so that his face was inches from hers. "It's not easy to get rid of someone who is a part of your life, who has been a part of your life for so long."

Her breath caught at the sudden change of subject. He had her, and he knew it. She shook her head, and he pressed on. "Have you gone through his closet, his drawers? What about his desk? His papers?"

Her eyes filled with tears that threatened to spill over if he said another word, and she whispered, "Not yet."

He stood up and said, "I'll come over and help you. It'll be easier to do if you're not alone. I'll haul the stuff to the Salvation Army for you. Promise me you'll call when you want to get rid of his stuff?"

She nodded, and he smiled, his lips pressed together tightly. He gave a curt nod and said, "Before I go, I need to know how you feel about me."

She cocked her head to one side, "My feelings for you have nothing to do with your marriage. If you want to leave her, leave her. But don't make that decision based on me." The strength she felt surprised her. She straightened her spine and lifted her chin proudly.

He nodded and held out his hand. She took it and he pulled her to her feet. She led him towards the front door. As she put her hand on the doorknob, he grabbed her shoulders, turning her towards him. He kissed her, really kissed her, for the first time. The electricity in that kiss shot through her body, and her toes tingled and her heart skipped a beat. Her body molded to his as his body responded. It only lasted a few seconds, but it felt as if time stood still.

He spoke, his breath warm against her ear, "We can still go exploring, right?"

That throaty voice melted her resolve and, in spite of her conscience screaming no, she nodded.

He jogged down the steps to his Jeep. He got in and started it up, then put it in gear. As he reversed out of the driveway, he turned and raised a hand. She waved back, then shut the door and slipped her wedding ring off. She trudged up the stairs and to her bedroom, rubbing the warm metal between her thumb and finger. She dropped the ring onto the crystal ring holder on the dresser and crawled into the king-sized bed alone.

21

Andi pushed through the front door of the Black Sails Diner and paused for a moment to let her eyes adjust after the harsh glare of the midday sun. She spotted Dana at a table in the back, studying a menu. The tinkle of the brass bell above the door sounded as the door swung closed behind Andi. Dana looked up and waved, a wide grin splitting her face.

"You look like the cat that ate the canary." Before Andi even sat down, she narrowed her eyes and smiled. "What's up?"

The redhead grinned and held out her hand, palm down and wiggled her fingers. There, on her ring finger, was a beautiful round solitaire.

“Oh, my God! He proposed! You’re getting married!” Andi turned to the woman at the next table and thumped her on the arm, “Hey! My best friend just got engaged!”

Several people in the small restaurant smiled and clapped and offered their congratulations. Pink crept up Dana's cheeks and she shushed Andi, while she thanked the well-wishers and ducked her head in embarrassment. Andi sat down across from her and grinned. Jill Price, their waitress, sashayed over and congratulated her, too, before taking their orders.

"You are such a goof!" Dana said, shaking her red locks in mock disgust, but the look on her face belied her thrill at the fuss being made.

"Hey, we gotta make a big deal of this. We've got to go celebrate and," Andi looked around at the cheesy pirate-themed diner filled with tourists, leaned forward and whispered, "*this* is not the place to celebrate. Let's meet after work and go out."

She shook her head and said, "I can't. I'm meeting Derek tonight for dinner. We're going to tell his parents tonight."

Though Andi's feelings of good will toward her friend were genuine, she felt a niggle of fear that her best friend would be caught up in her new life, with no time left for friendships. In spite of her misgivings, she gushed, "Oh, my God. I don't believe this! So, tell me, how'd he do it?"

Dana's grin widened as she related the story, "We'd gone out to dinner at the Clifftop. " A shadow crossed her face and she paused in mid-thought.

Andi made a rolling motion with her hand and smiled. "It's okay. Go ahead."

"It was wonderful, we were both drinking wine and laughing, just a perfect night. After we ate, he suggested we go for a walk. I figured he just wanted to walk before driving because we'd both had a drink with dinner. He started getting all mushy, telling me how much he loved me, and I told him I'd better drive home because I thought he'd had one too many."

Andi laughed – she could picture it, and could just imagine how nervous Derek had been. He was always such a clown, it would have been hard for him to do something so serious. The two of them seemed so in love. Hopefully it would last longer for them than it had for her and Chad.

Dana continued, "He bent down and started messing around with his sock and I tugged on his arm, thinking he was being really weird, but he pulled a little blue velvet box out of his sock and told me I'd make him the happiest man in the world if I'd marry him!"

"Oh, wow. In his sock, huh?" Andi took her friend's hand and examined the sparkling gem. "And I'm guessing you liked the ring so you said yes?"

She laughed. "Of course I said yes! I said yes before he even got the box open. He's finally making an honest woman of me!"

They had been living together for months, largely due to the economics of sharing one household when they were always together anyway, and Dana had confessed during one of her and Andi's Saturday morning coffee dates that she didn't think they'd ever get married. "Have you talked about a date? The location? Colors?"

Dana ducked her head and pretended to examine the menu. "We're not going to do a big church wedding since it's a second marriage for him and I'm older than the traditional bride-"

"Bullshit!" Andi looked up just as Jill arrived with the food and felt her cheeks burn with embarrassment. She lowered her eyes and murmured, "Sorry."

"Shoot!" Jill set their plates down and waved her hand. "Honey, I've heard worse!"

Andi pulled the tomato off her tuna salad and Dana pulled the pickles off her sandwich. They traded. Dana stuck the tomato in her sandwich and went back to wedding talk. “Let’s face it, I am older than the traditional bride, and with Mom and Dad gone, I just don’t want to do the big church wedding, so we’re thinking about going to Atlantic City.”

“Seriously? Like an Elvis wedding or one of those little chapels?”

Dana waved that idea off quickly. “No! Of course not! But remember the wedding pictures I showed you of that attorney that used to work in our office?”

Her portraits were gorgeous, with the waves rolling onto the beach, the wedding party standing in sand, and a boardwalk behind them. Most of all, the pinks and oranges and reds of the sunset made the bride absolutely glow.

Andi shook her head. “That couldn’t have been A.C.”

She grinned. “Sure was. And we can do a package deal, so it won’t be as expensive as a big church wedding, and that way we can put our money towards that farmhouse we’ve been looking at on the cove.”

Memories of Andi's own wedding flashed through her mind. The extravagance of the affair had highlighted the differences between her family and Chad's. Her mother couldn't afford it, but Chad's mother insisted and paid. Of course, that also meant that she planned the event. Maybe Dana had the right idea, keeping it simple. “Wow. You’ve thought this through.”

Dana continued to talk about Atlantic City, and the chapels and hotels, while Andi half-listened. Images of the vaulted ceilings of the cathedral, the sunlight filtering through the stained glass windows, and all Andi's hopes and dreams -- it seemed so perfect at the time. When Chad slipped that gold ring on her finger, she thought it was happily-ever-after come true. And now her finger bore the marks of wearing that ring for the past six years. Even with the ring off, the faint indentation remained as a reminder of her marriage.

Dana's voice broke Andi's reverie. "Hey! You tuned me out!"

The corners of Andi's mouth twitched up. "I'm sorry. Just zoned out for a moment."

"Thinking about Chad?" Dana rested her elbows on the table.

Andi looked down and nodded.

"I thought so." Dana gestured towards her friend's left hand. "I noticed you're not wearing your wedding ring anymore."

Andi rubbed the dented area on her ring finger and shrugged. "It was time to take it off."

Dana brightened and said, "Hey, I've already talked to Kelly Anderson about being my wedding planner. Are you free Friday afternoon to go for an appointment?"

"She owns Blissful Beginnings, right?" Andi took a sip of iced tea.

"Yes, and she's agreed to find me a gorgeous vintage gown."

Andi smiled. "That is so you." She pushed down the worry about money. How could she afford a bridesmaid dress, a gift, all the other stuff that came along with a wedding?

Dana grinned. "I know, right?"

Friday afternoon, the girls met at Blissful Beginnings, located in a quaint little white cottage just west of the harbor. The sisters who owned the business built up quite a reputation for putting together weddings on a budget, featuring "pre-enjoyed" dresses. While Kelly selected dresses that met Dana's style requests, Dana filled Andi in. The meal with Derek's parents went well, and they welcomed her into their family with open arms. They pretty much had already, one of the reasons Andi was so happy for her friend. Since Dana's parents died when she was in her early 20s, she felt like an orphan, but didn't fall into the traditional child orphan category. Holidays were always tough for her, and Andi had been relieved when Derek's parents invited her to join them for Thanksgiving and Christmas.

That had always been a sore spot between Chad and Andi. She invited her best friend to join them for Thanksgiving the previous fall, but he pitched a fit, claiming it interfered with his plans, that he worked hard and deserved some time alone and didn't want to entertain anyone. He forbid Andi to invite her friend to join them, but she'd already done so. He didn't care, and sneered, told her that if she didn't tell her friend not to show up, he'd make sure the rest of the holidays would be miserable. The fact that Derek's parents invited Dana to their holiday get-together saved Andi the embarrassment of having to uninvite her.

"Hey! You're doing it again!"

Andi started. "What?"

"You're zoning out." Dana frowned, concern in her eyes. "You know, if you don't want to be my maid of honor, it's okay. Really. I know this is difficult for you."

Andi glanced at her friend and grinned. "Your maid of honor? Of course, I'd be, well, honored!"

"And you're looking forward to going to A.C. with us?" The excitement in her friend's voice bubbled over.

"It'd be fun. I've always wanted to go. Chad went a couple of times . . ." Her voice trailed off as she remembered the credit card receipts in his dresser. He could afford to go, surely she'd be able to find a way to. She ran a hand through her short hair.

Dana reached out and touched Andi's forearm. "You okay?"

Andi shrugged. "I found receipts in Chad's stuff. He was seeing someone in Atlantic City."

"How can you be sure? I mean, he went to conferences right? So he'd keep receipts for his taxes, right?"

"Receipts for double rooms? For steak dinners at romantic restaurants? I'm not that stupid."

"I'm so sorry, Andi." Dana paused. "But you kind of suspected, didn't you?"

Andi's lips pressed into a thin line and she stared at her friend through narrowed eyes. "Did you know?"

"No." Dana answered quickly, then shrugged and looked away. "Maybe. I mean, I suspected. But didn't know for sure. If I'd ever known for sure, I would've told you. You know that, right?"

Andi nodded. She'd had her doubts, but hadn't had the guts to confront him about it. Couldn't blame Dana. Or herself. Chad was the one who'd cheated.

"So, will this be too tough for you? Going to a wedding so soon, I mean?"

"No," Andi shook her head firmly and met her friend's earnest gaze. "This is for you. Chad is in the past.

Over and done with. I'm moving on with my life, and not looking back."

"Good for you." Dana pulled a binder of invitations off the table and flipped through it. Just then, Kelly and Noelle entered the room, each laden with gorgeous gowns. They made the pair feel like real VIPs. The friends sipped on champagne and nibbled on hors d'oeuvres while Kelly talked to Dana about what she wanted, the feeling she wanted to convey with her event. The consultants treated Dana like royalty, and had her try on several gowns. Dana grinned from ear to ear the whole time, but when Kelly helped her into a flowing ivory gown with a deep v-neck, Dana absolutely glowed. The column of elegantly draped fabric, with incredible crystal detail at the waist and a slight flare at the foot, fit the redhead perfectly, as if it were made just for her. Andi wiped away a tear when her friend turned and the skirt swirled around her. There was no question – that was the dress.

And then it was Andi's turn. She tried on dresses from designers, but she and Dana agreed that the one-shouldered pale pink dress that hit her just above the knee was the best fit. The simple, elegant gown hugged Andi's rounded hips and generous bust as if it were made for her. And to Andi's relief, she could afford it. Thank goodness for vintage!

The two women congratulated themselves on finding their dresses, then Kelly came in with a selection of veils and shoes. Dana tried several veils, but didn't find anything she liked, until Noelle brought in an elegant pearl and crystal headband decorated with a delicate feather flower. They turned their attention to shoes, and took turns trying them on and walking like models, but they opted for white flip flops accented with crystals. Both consultants assured them modern brides often opted for casual footwear, that eliminated the chance for falling down the aisle.

Before they knew it, everything was picked out and the pair finished shopping. It had been such an enjoyable experience, a welcome escape from the everyday stress of life, Andi almost hated for it to end.

The friends toasted their good fortune at finding their dresses while they waited for the dresses to be hung up and accessories bagged. Dana reached for her purse, but Andi stopped her and pulled out her MasterCard. She could pay it off a little at a time.

She handed the credit card to Kelly. "This is on me."

"No," Dana shook her head, and pushed a stray ringlet of red hair behind her ear. "There's no way I can let you do that."

"Yes, you can. I wouldn't have gotten through the last couple of months without you. Your friendship means a lot to me, and this is my wedding gift to you."

Dana smiled and hugged Andi. When they pulled apart, a tear ran down Dana's cheek and Andi's heart swelled.

Kelly appeared in the doorway. She smiled apologetically and handed the card back to Andi in two pieces. Dana gasped. Andi frowned and looked at the woman with rounded eyes, torn between confusion and anger.

Kelly said, "I'm so sorry, Andi, but your card was declined. When I called to check on it, they instructed me to destroy the card, as it's a frozen account and no longer valid."

22

"I don't understand." Andi's jaw dropped. She'd never been so much as late with a payment, and paid on the account every month since Chad's death. Of course, before that the account had been paid in full every month. Now all she could pay was the minimum payment, but still. She paid on time, and the balance was small.

"You're welcome to use our telephone if you would like to call your card issuer," Kelly said, gesturing to the phone on the glass-topped end table next to the sofa.

Dana opened her wallet and interrupted, "Here, just use my card for now and we'll straighten this out later."

Andi blinked and nodded. The woman took the offered card and left to process it. Stunned, Andi flipped the card pieces over and held them together so she could make out the customer service number. She dropped onto the sofa and dialed the number. After navigating the automated maze, she finally reached a live customer service representative and explained the situation.

To Andi's utter horror, the representative explained the account had been frozen. In heavily accented English, he said, "We received the notification from the cardholder's attorney informing us that the cardholder has become deceased."

She swallowed the lump in her throat. "Yes, that is correct. My husband is deceased, but I am his widow."

With a bored voice, the representative explained, "There is nothing further for to do, since the cardholder is deceased. The account is frozen and not to be used."

Finally, after trying in vain to explain, Andi hung up, frustrated and irritated and embarrassed. How could this happen? Every time she started to feel happiness, Chad reached out to hurt her yet again.

Kelly returned and Dana signed the charge slip. Andi hovered in the background as the other two women discussed the arrangements to have the dresses and accessories delivered to Dana's house.

As they walked out of the store, Dana said, "Still okay if we stop by the jewelry store? Maybe it'd be fun for you to have your wedding ring reset?"

Andi glanced back at the store front, still smarting from the embarrassment of having her credit card destroyed. She lifted her chin and patted her purse, where she'd put her wedding ring just that morning. "You read my mind. I'd been considering doing just that."

They drove past the harbor and pulled into Jewels by the Sea, where they started in the bridal section, and Dana tried on several beautiful rings. She kept going back to a thick gold band sprinkled with diamonds. It was unlike anything Andi had ever seen before. The price tag made Andi's eyes pop, but the saleswoman, Josephine, pointed out that a wedding set is something you wear every single day, with every outfit, for life, so it should be something that you really, truly love.

Perhaps that was why Andi had been disappointed when Chad surprised her with her ring. The solitaire was huge and her wedding set wasn't what she would've picked. It looked more like a fancy cocktail ring than a wedding ring. It stuck up too high from her finger and caught on everything. Not practical, not beautiful. Her mother described it as ostentatious.

After Josephine helped Dana, she turned her attention to Andi and asked if there was anything she could show her. Andi explained that she wanted to reset her wedding ring and engagement ring. Given the recent credit card fiasco, she hoped it wouldn't be too expensive.

The woman nodded and said, "Ah, yes, we see a lot of divorced women come in to have their stones reset into right hand rings or pendants, or even earrings."

Andi caught the word divorced, and saw Dana wrinkle her nose. She'd caught it, too. Apparently widows didn't usually have their stones reset. But Andi wasn't an average widow. Her wedding ring didn't hold happy memories. She pulled the box from her purse and flipped it open. The diamonds sparkled under the bright lights of the store displays.

"I was thinking something in a pendant," Andi said, almost as a question.

The saleswoman took the ring out of the box, then produced a jeweler's loupe from her pocket and held it up to her eye. She squinted and said, "Oh, I think we can find something special for you to commemorate your lost love."

The door chime rang. Andi glanced up and felt her heart drop. The raven-haired beauty she'd seen with Paul walked towards her. No, she didn't walk. She floated. Her thin t-shirt and skinny jeans clung to her slender form, long lashes framed dark chocolate eyes, and her flawless complexion completed her perfection. Her straight, black tresses reached nearly to her waist. Her face broke into a wide smile as she approached, and Andi froze.

23

Andi swallowed hard, and wondered what to say to the woman, but she walked right past, never even so much as making eye contact. Her eyes focused at a point at the rear of the store. Andi let her breath out in a rush, and blinked as the woman glided past.

Dana's fingers gripped her arm, squeezing tightly.

"Here we go, ma'am. Perhaps we could do something in platinum?" The saleswoman pulled out a couple of empty settings while Andi watched the images in the mirrored wall.

Andi shook her head, "No, I don't think I can afford platinum. Perhaps something in silver?" She looked over Josephine's shoulder as Paul's wife greeted a lanky, scruffy looking man with wavy blonde hair who looked even younger than she did. She tipped her head up and presented her cheek for him to kiss, then he put his arm around her shoulders in a casual gesture of protectiveness, and they bent to look at watches in the case.

Andi half listened as Josephine chattered on about the various settings that would work with the stones from her ring. She nodded and mmm-hmmmmed, while she continued to watch the mirror with curiosity as Paul's wife – it occurred to Andi that she didn't know his wife's name - selected a matching set of Citizen watches, and paid with a gold credit card. The two of them admired their new purchases as they walked past Dana and Andi and out the door, the chime merrily announcing their exit.

Andi felt frantic with the need to follow them. Maybe this meant Paul was telling the truth about his marriage. She rubbed her temples and said, "Dana, I'm sorry, but I've suddenly got a horrible headache. I'm going to go out and get some fresh air."

Dana looked at her sideways and frowned, but followed Andi out the door. As soon as Andi pushed through the door, she looked to her right and saw the handsome couple strolling away, arm in arm.

"What are you doing?" Dana demanded. She stepped in front of Andi.

Andi pushed past her, shrugged and tracked the couple so she wouldn't lose them in the meandering tourists that filled the sidewalks.

Dana hissed in a loud whisper, "Are you out of your mind? Don't get caught up in this. It's a tangled up mess, and you don't need any part of it."

Dana grabbed Andi by the arm and spun her around. Her green eyes flashed, her cheeks flamed and her lips pressed together in a thin line. "Would you get your head out of your ass, just for a moment? I have put up with your sorrow, your guilt, your whining and going on about messing around with a married man, but I am *not* going to let you ruin my engagement."

"I'm not-" Andi protested.

Dana cut in, "Oh, yes, you are. We came up here to pick out my wedding ring. You drag me out of the jewelry store before I'm ready, and now you want me to tag along with you while you chase after your lover's wife?!"

Andi jerked her arm away, feeling her own cheeks burning. "First of all, he is not my lover, and second of all . . . "

"Second of all, what?" Dana's fists perched on her hips, green eyes flashing.

Suddenly, Andi deflated.

Her best friend was right.

Dana deserved to be the center of attention today. Andi shook her head and sagged. "Damn. I don't know. I'm sorry."

Dana stuffed her hands in her jacket pockets and turned to walk toward the Jeep. Andi followed, feeling like a heel, but couldn't help glancing back down the street one more time. She spotted them a couple blocks down, where they disappeared into another store. There was a sandwich board outside. Whoopie's. Andi quickened her step, and caught up with her best friend just as Dana put her hand on the passenger door handle.

Andi grabbed Dana's arm and said, "I'm sorry. Do you want to go get something to eat, then go back to the jewelry store?"

Dana sighed. "I don't know. I'm sorry, too. I shouldn't have blown up at you like that. It's just that I saw Chad treat you like dirt for so long, and now I can see the same thing happening with Paul, and-"

Andi protested, "Oh, no, Paul treats me great-"

Dana's red curls swung as she shook her head. "No! No, he doesn't. Can't you see that? He's *married.*"

Andi latched onto the only thing she could. "To a woman who's cheating on him." She lifted her chin stubbornly.

"And he's cheating on her. Sounds like an upstanding guy to me. Perfect marriage material." Her best friend's voice dripped with sarcasm.

To Andi's surprise, her temper flared. She took pride in the fact that she and Paul hadn't let it get physical. The muscles in her jaw clenched. "He's not cheating on her. He and I are just friends."

Dana snorted. "You may be just friends now. But he'd sleep with you in a heartbeat if you gave him the signal. And who knows how many other 'friends' he has."

Andi did not like the way the conversation was going, so she tamped down her anger. "We'll have to simply agree to disagree. What are you hungry for?" Seemed like she was always trying to placate those around her, trying to keep them happy, avoid confrontation.

"Fine. Soup and a sandwich, maybe?"

"Want to just walk over to the Harbor and get something from the Crab Shack?" How long had it been since she suggested a restaurant? With Chad, he chose. With Dana, they always ended up at the Black Sails.

Dana hesitated, then said, "Sure."

Things remained tense between the two friends but they relaxed as they ate. After they finished, they returned to the jewelry store. Dana looked at wedding rings for a little bit, and Andi finally settled on a new ring. She chose to have the center stone reset, with the little diamonds channel set on either side, with some added tourmaline. She went with sterling silver, in spite of Josephine's upturned nose. At least it was something she'd wear. And something she could afford. Josephine promised to call when the jeweler finished it. Andi knew she might have to pawn something to pay for this new ring, but it would be worth it to get rid of the wedding ring.

Andi invited Dana back to her house for a drink, but she opted out, saying she was tired and just wanted to go home. When Andi reached her subdivision, she noticed a familiar dark sedan about a half a block behind her. She frowned into the rearview mirror and continued on home. The car followed the whole way, then parked just up the street as she pulled into the driveway. Just when she started to relax, something happened to jerk her back to reality. Fear niggled at her as she glanced over her shoulder at the vehicle rumbling quietly down the street.

As she turned the lock, she noticed a bouquet of bright spring flowers sitting on the corner of her front porch, tucked against the house. She picked the arrangement up and plucked out the card. It read simply, "With love, P."

She inhaled the fresh scent as she slipped her key in the lock, then placed the vase in the center of the hall table, with the card tucked so that it was just peeking out. A smile lit on her face at his thoughtfulness. Chad hadn't ever sent flowers. She peered out the front window. The dark car was gone.

24

The next couple of days dragged along. Out-of-towners kept her busy at the tourism center, but Andi spent every spare moment dreaming of what her life could be like. It felt like a blank canvas. Life with Chad had been dull, boring, black and white. Since his death, her life was colorized. When he was alive, she walked on eggshells around him, and felt like an empty hull. Now, she felt energy coursing through her and could scarcely wait for the adventure that awaited her.

One afternoon after work, she walked through the big empty house and felt it was time for a change. Cutting her hair had been a great first step, and she loved how free she felt with her new pixie cut. She could scarcely wait for Paul to call every day, as she knew he would. This time, she would be ready when he called. He asked every day about going through Chad's things. She would prove she could let go of the past.

Clearing out Chad's closet took priority. She wasn't sure why it took her so long. It wasn't that she was holding on to him – it was more a matter of not wanting to be bothered with it.

She went into the bedroom and flung his closet doors open. She hadn't been in there since the day she selected a suit for him to be buried in. Her thoughts had been foggy then. She'd jumped at every shadow, sure someone out there knew her secret and would come forward. But it had been months. The insurance company still hadn't paid, and the police detective followed her around sometimes, but that had gotten to be nothing more than a nuisance. It felt like time to clean things out and put the past behind her.

She flipped through the clothes hanging on the rod. She tugged the dress shirts off the hangers, then folded and stacked them neatly on the bed. She had just turned back to the closet and the telephone rang.

The male voice on the phone was overly friendly. "Hi, there! May I speak with Mrs. Adams, please?"

"Speaking."

"You may have seen me in the neighborhood. I live across the road and down a few houses, the little white cottage with the green picket fence?"

She frowned, cautious. "Yes?"

"My wife saw the sign in your yard and we wondered if you might be willing to sell without going through the real estate agent? See, we're expecting our first child and are looking for a larger home, but because of the baby coming, money's tight and--"

"I'm sorry," She cut in. "But you'll have to work through the real estate agent."

"But--"

"I'm sorry," She repeated, then clicked the end button as she shook her head. As if it wasn't bad enough having her house sold out from under her . . .

With a sigh, she turned her attention back to Chad's clothes. All were nice, most were name brand and like new. They would make someone very happy. A sad smile crossed her face as she touched his worn brown leather jacket. He had worn it the night he proposed. So soft and supple. She ran her fingers over the smoothness, memories of a happier time flooding back.

He'd surprised her with a weekend trip to Boston over the Christmas holiday, then wined and dined her like she'd never experienced before. They'd only been dating a few months at the time. The romance began when she was waitressing at a barbecue place in Kansas City during college.

She'd been completely shocked when he slid the box across the table to her just before dessert was served. He smiled and asked, "Will you marry me?" in the most everyday voice, as if came natural to him.

Of course, after her wedding, she suspected he simply didn't care all that much. It was his mother's idea after she found out they were sleeping together. He likely found it a convenient way to keep her close and under his thumb. Leaving college after her junior year seemed stupid in hindsight, but at the time, he promised to take care of her and she happily believed him.

She snorted and shook her head. Even the good memories were tainted now. The Salvation Army would be able to make good use of all of Chad's things. Even the leather jacket. She checked the pockets and pulled out a pair of driving gloves, a little pack of tissues and a pale pink linen business card. She turned it over. It was simply a name, Portia, and phone number: 207-631-5555. She didn't recognize the prefix. She shrugged to herself, then stuck the card in her jewelry box.

The name reminded her of one of her favorite movies, A Fish Called Wanda. Portia was the name of the daughter of the barrister played by John Cleese. Silly, the way a mind connects things sometimes.

Quickly, she checked the pockets in all his jackets, and found several useless items, a lot of trash, a few receipts that she sat aside to file, and several wads of cash. When she counted it, it came to over $2,000 in small bills. She wrapped the money in a sock and stuck it in the back of her underwear drawer. With Chad gone, she needed an emergency fund.

The telephone rang as she flipped through the phone book looking for the number to the Salvation Army.

"Hello?"

"I know what really happened," The voice was slow, like a tape dragging. "And that will be our secret if you give me the papers."

"What papers?"

"You know what papers." The speaker clipped off the last word, not pronouncing the "R." Mainers did that all the time, but this accent sounded different.

"Who is this?" She strained her ears to identify the vaguely familiar voice.

"If you don't give them to me, I'm going to tell everyone what you did."

She clicked end and looked around as if someone might be watching, swallowed a lump in her throat, then jumped when the phone rang again.

"Hello?" A tremor sounded in her voice.

"Hey, lover," Paul's gravelly voice greeted her. He waited a beat, then said, "You sound funny. Everything okay?"

"No." A part of her hated herself for wanting him to come over so badly, for needing him. "Someone's been making prank calls, and with me being here all alone, I'm starting to get freaked out about it."

Without hesitation, he volunteered, "Want me to come over?"

She took a deep breath, then said with a waver, "No, I'll be okay. There's just been a couple today-"

"A couple?" He paused, then asked, "Are you sure?"

"It's not a big deal." Her voice broke. She hated being alone almost as much as she hated being scared.

"I'm on my way over."

She sat the phone down and felt a little thrill at his protectiveness. The smile faded when the phone jangled again.

"Hello?"

"I want the papers back that Chad took from me. I'll call back with details of the drop."

"I don't have any papers! I don't know what you're talking about!" Why did this person keep calling? Why wouldn't he believe her?

"Don't hang up on me again." Laughter crackled across the phone line and his voice lowered dangerously. "I'll get them from you . . . over your dead body, if that's the way you want it. You get the papers and I'll call back with instructions."

She clicked the end button and threw the phone across the room, then sank to the floor and hugged herself. Her chest rose and fell as she sucked in deep breaths. She didn't have any papers, didn't know what he was talking about. Even if she gave him all the papers from Chad's desk, what would stop him from going to the police? She'd be exposed. Everyone would think she murdered her husband.

The doorbell chimed, jerking her out of her stupor. She rubbed her eyes, then hurried down the steps to answer the door. She hesitated and looked through the peephole to make sure it was Paul before she let him in. The door creaked as she opened it just a crack. He looked great, as always.

The more she thought about it, the more he reminded her of Pierce Brosnan. Absolutely gorgeous, and those piercing blue eyes melted her very core.

He cocked his head and opened his arms as he stepped towards her and enveloped her in a hug that made her feel safe and secure. She imagined greeting him like that every day when he got home from work, and snuggled in closer. He always smelled so fresh and clean, never artificial. In contrast, Chad smelled like Eternity. She squeezed her eyes shut, and breathed in Paul's scent. She hadn't realized until that moment how deeply she hated being alone.

Something bumped her side and she looked down to see a plastic grocery bag hanging from his wrist. He held it up and grinned. "Ice cream."

Nothing comforted like Rocky Road.

Slowly, he walked her backwards into the foyer, and pulled the door shut behind him. He leaned against the door and flipped the deadbolt, then tilted her chin up with one finger so they were gazing into each other's eyes.

"Now, tell me when this started."

She shrugged and looked away. "A couple of days ago."

His dark eyebrows pushed into a V as he took hold of her hands and pulled her close. "Well, I'm here now so don't worry. What does he want?"

"Nothing." She wanted him to hold her, take care of her, make it all better. She played the damsel in distress, and he served as her knight in shining armor. A part of her hated that, but she quickly suppressed that voice.

"He's got to want something." He traced her jawline with his index finger, then ran it up and around her ear. "Maybe you should give him what he wants and be done with it."

"No, really, I've already turned the phone off. I don't want to deal with it today. I just want to get my mind off of it. And now that you're here," She wanted so badly for him to stay, so she went for the one thing that she could count on to get a man's attention. She slipped her index finger under his belt buckle and tugged. "You can help me get my mind off of it."

He laughed and shook his head, but the laughter didn't touch his piercing blue eyes as he looked over her shoulder. He frowned and said, "Who do you think the caller is?"

She waved the question off. "Oh, probably somebody Chad owed something to. He wants something he says Chad took from him, but I have no idea what he's talking about."

He brushed a stray tendril of dark hair back from her face and said, "Now that I'm here, want me to help you go through your husband's things? We can work on it together. Maybe we'll find whatever that guy is looking for."

She shook her head. “I started packing things up already. Figured it was just something I had to force myself to do.”

He blinked and the lines in his tanned forehead deepened. “I told you I would help you do that.”

She focused on his belt buckle and rubbed her thumb over the smooth metal. “I know, and I appreciate that, but-“

One corner of his mouth twitched up in a half smile. “Did you get much done?”

She shrugged. “Got through most of his clothes.”

He placed his hands on her shoulders, spun her around and began to knead them like a cat. “Did you find anything?”

“You mean besides lint?” She looked back at him and smiled. It felt so good to have someone close. To touch someone. To be touched. Since he hadn't responded to her attempt at seduction, she thought the next best approach was his stomach. "Want some ice cream?"

He grinned, displaying his dimples. "Thought you'd never ask."

She took his hand and guided him towards the kitchen. She dipped two bowls of ice cream and held up the chocolate syrup. He nodded and she swirled the dark liquid over the ice cream. They carried their bowls into the living room. She curled up on the couch and he sat next to her. The ice cream was smooth and creamy, with chunks of gooey goodness that added just the right crunch. They sat facing the big picture window, and looked out at the blue-green harbor stretched below them.

As they ate, he relaxed visibly. She finished hers and sat the empty bowl on the coffee table. He sat his nearly-full bowl next to hers and said, "Okay, enough relaxing.

Let me help you go through Chad's things so you can put that behind you."

"I don't want to even think about him right now. Come on," She leaned towards him. "Distract me."

"I can't stay long." The smile melted from his face. "Besides, the last time I was here, you insisted I leave my wife."

Panic bubbled up. Maybe she pushed him too hard. "You can't blame me for trying."

"Then you were distant with me when we talked on the phone last week. And you didn't want to go with me Saturday." He pulled back and looked away from her.

He sounded quarrelsome and she didn't like that. Desperation pecked at her, persistent and annoying. She didn't want him to leave, didn't want to be alone. She pulled him closer and they sank into the supple leather. She touched the frown lines that creased his forehead, smoothing them with her index finger.

"I wanted to be able to see you on Saturday, but I had plans with Dana." Her voice caught in her throat. "And I'm having a really hard time with the fact that I'm falling for a married man."

He smiled sadly and shrugged. "I can't do anything about that right now. Caren and I have a . . . unique relationship. But I can tell you it makes me very happy to hear that you're falling for me."

Her heart thudded in her chest so loud she was sure he could hear it. She shouldn't have told him that. She caught her lower lip in her teeth. He ran his fingers through her thick hair and tilted his head. "This is such a good look for you. So sexy."

Her heart thumped as he leaned forward and kissed her, his lips barely brushing against hers. Her breath caught in her throat. She hesitated a moment, then responded. His hand roamed up her side, then towards her chest where he cupped her breast gently. Her heart rate quickened at his touch and a soft moan escaped her lips. She began to explore his body as his hand moved under her shirt. Their clothes seemed to fall from their bodies almost of their own accord, and she nuzzled against his neck, letting his dark stubble tickle her nose.

They spent the afternoon exploring each other until the sun dropped so low that the beam from the lighthouse swept across the room every minute or so. To their credit, they stopped short of making love, but they crossed the line acceptable for fidelity in a marriage.

The clock chimed and he glanced at the mantle clock, then swore under his breath. He ran his fingers roughly through his hair and said, “I need to get going.”

“So soon?” She leaned back down to pick up her shirt from the floor where it had fallen. She held it over her chest, suddenly embarrassed at how quickly things got out of hand. She felt 16 again, so anxious to be loved that she’d do anything. As her heart rate slowed, something began to bother her, but she couldn't put her finger on it.

“Yes, I’m afraid so. Caren will be home from visiting her grandfather soon.” He buttoned his shirt.

She followed suit, pulling the shirt over her head without bothering to find her bra, which seemed to have disappeared in the throes of passion. “You never mentioned her name until today. Pretty name.”

“She spells it with a ‘c’, which I always thought was cool,” and he laughed, a harsh, humorless sound. “I guess I’m probably showing my age by saying cool, huh?”

Something nagged at her. Where else had she heard about someone who spelled their name like that? She laughed, but it came out wooden and stiff. "Sounds like you really love her. I was under the impression things weren't so good between the two of you."

He tilted his head and looked at her. Gold sparkled in his eyes like flakes in a clear blue mountain stream. This guy was really getting to her, and she couldn't fight the desperation rising within her. She wanted this to be real, and it couldn't be as long as he was married.

He shrugged, "Like I said, we have a unique marriage. It's not perfect by any stretch, but I can't ask her for a divorce. She'd never go for it. She'd kill me first."

She recalled his wife and her lover arm in arm. Either Paul had no clue or he was in denial. "I just meant, you're here with me. How do you know she's not out with someone?"

He shrugged. "She'd never do anything like that."

Her eyebrows arched at his confidence. "You're sure?"

"Of course." He looked at her and his eyes narrowed.

She took a deep breath and plunged forward. "I saw her with a man today, at Jewels by the Sea."

He shook his head as he slipped his boots on. "I've really got to get going. I'll come by Saturday and help you go through Chad's things. We'll box it all up and get it out of here."

She nodded. He was in denial, and was using her dead husband to distract her. He leaned down and pressed his lips against her forehead.

"Don't do anything more until I'm here to help." He rested his hand on the doorknob and said, "And don't eat all the rest of the ice cream tonight."

She shrugged and leaned towards him. "No promises." Suddenly, without warning, Chad's voice popped into her head, warning her about the calories. Pointing out the weight she'd gained. She pulled away, self-conscious.

His smile evaporated as he cocked his head and stared at her intently. Finally, he gave a little laugh and promised to talk to her soon.

After he left, she ferried their bowls to the kitchen. The garbage disposal churned when she dumped his ice cream down the drain. She shook her head. What a waste.

She filled the remainder of her week with work, trips to the Salvation Army and various other charities, but her time at home was anxious. The telephone didn't ring again until Friday night. She flipped through a guide on Acadia National Park, planning a day trip and the phone rang. She answered.

The first sound she heard was breathing.

"I know what really happened." The naggingly familiar voice again. Something about the way he said "know."

"What do you want?" she demanded.

This time the phone line didn't go dead.

25

She asked the question again, in the firmest, most confident voice she could muster. His breath filled the silence, and faint clicks jittered along the lines stretched between her and the mysterious caller.

"What do you want?" She repeated. She hated the tremor in her voice.

"I want the papers your husband had."

Her eyes widened as she probed. "What papers?"

The disembodied voice hissed through the telephone, "You know exactly what I'm talking about. The find at Big Bear Cove. I know you've got them and I want them before the old man dies."

She hated feeling weak and vulnerable. Chad had done that to her enough to last a lifetime and she was determined not to continue her life that way. Her voice rose. "Who? What old man? What papers?"

"You know what I mean." The caller barked a laugh, sarcastic and biting, then, "Get the stuff together and be ready for instructions."

"I don't have any papers!"

The line went dead. She stared at the buzzing handset. What was she going to do?

She hung up and noticed her hand shaking. Her fist clenched until the knuckles turned white. She hurried from room to room, and checked every window. She yanked the curtains closed and locked all the doors. Once satisfied she'd done all she could do, she dropped into her favorite chair and listened.

Every creak sounded like a footstep, branches scraping the siding of the house sounded like someone trying to raise a window, and the wind became a whisper. Her ears tingled with the strain of listening as she tried to discern real threats from imagined. She pulled a throw around her shoulders to calm her shivers.

Her stomach growled, loud in the quiet of the empty house.

She laughed self-consciously and padded down the hallway to the kitchen. The cheery yellow room chased the imaginary demons from her thoughts. She stood with the refrigerator door open as she debated whether to make something or go out. Though she craved a meal out at a nice restaurant down by the harbor, she couldn't bring herself to leave the house. It was too much of an ordeal. Not only was she afraid to leave – afraid that whoever was calling might be waiting for her – but worse than that, she was afraid to go alone. The thought of sitting at the Black Sails or Whoopie's by herself, surrounded by couples focused on each other, terrified her.

One evening earlier in the week, she'd braved the Black Sails, armed with a paperback book as Dana suggested. It had been horrible. Seemed that everyone who walked through the door looked with her with pity, suspicion or a mixture of both. The book made a flimsy shield, useless at holding the world at arm's length.

She perused the shelves of the refrigerator, peeking over the jug of milk and behind the leftover pizza. She popped the lid open on the cottage cheese and sniffed, then immediately drew back at the sourness of it and tossed it in the trash. A bowl of cereal, eaten over the sink, served as dinner.

She swallowed the last scoop of cereal, then tipped the bowl up and gulped down the cold milk. The empty bowl sounded with a hollow clink when she placed it in the dishwasher, bits of cereal still clinging desperately to the side. Her sweet tooth wasn't satisfied, so she pulled out the ice cream left that Paul brought over and dipped a few scoops into a clean bowl and drizzled chocolate syrup over it. Rocky Road was her favorite. He'd picked well. She moved into the living room and flipped on the news while she ate.

The evening news led with a story about a real estate mogul rushed to the hospital with chest pains. File footage of him with various presidents and senators flashed across the scene, and then the reporter said, "And a source close to the Board had confirmed that the company will be taken public if Mr. Woodson does not survive. He is staunchly opposed to such an offering, but it appears that his health may not allow him to stand in the way much longer."

The screen switched to a man in silhouette who spoke anonymously, "Mr. Woodson does not understand the speed with which companies must move in this day and age to keep up with the competition. There are several undeveloped properties on the outskirts of Acadia National Park that need to be developed as soon as possible in order to compete in the current economy."

So that was August Woodson. Seemed like that name met her at every turn.

She flipped the television off and called her mother, which she hadn't done in weeks. As always, her mom couldn't wait to gossip about kids she'd gone to high school with.

"And you remember Pam, that girl that was a year behind you? She had another baby!"

Though she usually enjoyed hearing about folks back home, this time it made her feel more isolated. She could feel herself shrinking as her mom continued. "And Romy was in charge of the high school madrigal, and Monty and Kim finally got married. Oh! Did I tell you that Sadie earned her black belt?"

After a pregnant pause, she said, "Honey, why don't you come back home?"

Andi mumbled something noncommittal, and her mother continued, "No shame in moving home when you're going through such a difficult time."

Though Andi assured her she'd consider it, she knew she wouldn't. Couldn't. They talked for over an hour, long enough to keep the line tied up so no other calls could get through.

Later that night, she crawled into the big, empty bed. Hours later she woke with a start, and felt restless the rest of the night. The bed felt so big. She stretched to take up as much of it as possible, arms flung wide.

The days ran together now that they were in full vacation season. The job at the tourism center gave her a schedule with longer hours, and she perused the internet learning more about the history of the area and studying gemology. She made photocopies of some Chad's papers and jotted notes in the margins.

The semi-precious gem industry thrived in Maine, and the rock hounds took it very seriously. For many of them, it was more than a casual hobby – it was a second job, and their chance at the gem lottery. Casual rock hounds came in the visitors' center frequently, so her research served a dual purpose – she got better at her job while she pieced together the secret life that Chad had led.

Mildred at the Chamber office encouraged Andi's research, and often emailed Andi links of interest to tourists. Andi straightened the racks of brochures, and rearranged them by geographic area. It wasn't an exciting job, but Andi found it intriguing and not as stressful as many jobs she could've gotten. More than once, she thanked her lucky stars she'd taken this job and not had to work for a private investigator - the only other job she'd found in the want ads that she was even remotely qualified for.

She stared out the window at the harbor, watched the boats drift in and out, the dock workers hefting crates, the tourists sauntering along the waterfront. Watched life pass by as she imagined what it would be like to share her home and life with Paul, waking up together, spending Sundays in bed reading the newspaper and sipping coffee.

If Caren were out of the picture, it would become reality.

Even at home, her thoughts revolved around Paul. She used her days off to scout and research the Island so she'd sound knowledgeable when they spoke. With Paul's help, she cleansed her home of things that reminded her of Chad. Bit by bit, pictures of Paul replaced pictures of Chad. Her new guy was shy about having his picture taken, but one of her favorites was one taken on a trip to Cadillac Mountain. The day began with the sun shining brightly, but as they drove up the rocky trail the fog rolled in, shrouding the evergreens in gray. The cold mist reached them even inside the Jeep. At the top, they got out to admire nature's majesty. Being up there was like being in another world. The large outcropping of rock was smooth and rolling, a perfect perch to see in all directions. Wispy white clouds stretched through the blue sky like bits of cotton candy. There's nothing like sucking cool, crisp air deep into the lungs.

That day, she'd been standing on a bald knob of rock when she snapped the picture. Normally, he would put up a hand or turn away when she had the camera, but that day he was focused on the myriad of rocks strewn around the summit and hadn't even noticed. He squatted down to pick up a rock as he often did while they were up in the interior of the island. In the picture, the rocky path snaked down the mountain behind him towards the blue-green sea. That picture gave her chills. It reminded her of how she felt up there, surrounded by the awesome power of God and nature. Nothing else compared to that, certainly nothing back home in Missouri, and the fact that she and Paul shared that experience meant a lot to her.

The drive home had been tense, though. Just after she'd snapped that photo, Paul glanced at his watch and cursed. "Damn. I didn't realize how late it is. We've got to get going."

As they walked towards the Jeep, Andi asked, "The day's still young. I think I'll start cleaning stuff out today."

Paul's head snapped to his left and he frowned at her. "What stuff?"

"Chad's things. There's no sense in putting it off any longer." Andi stepped up into the Jeep.

"I've got to go to a dinner party with Caren tonight." He turned the key in the ignition and the engine rumbled to life. "I'll see if I can get away tomorrow. I don't want you doing that on your own. Just leave it to me."

"No." She shook her head. "It's not your place. I'll take care of it."

"No!" His knuckles whitened as he gripped the steering wheel. His chest swelled as he sucked in air, then he huffed it out. "I'm sorry. I didn't mean to yell. But, seriously, I don't want you going through anything until I'm right there with you, helping you."

His outburst that day shocked her, but she'd seen much worse from her husband. She decided to ignore his raised voice and focus on the fun she had with him.

Their excursions throughout Mount Desert Island provided great pictures to frame and display. The trips gave her a welcome break from the reality of being a young widow. She even enjoyed the research. It also fit in well with her job with the Chamber of Commerce, so she told herself it was for work and not solely because of Paul.

After spending her day off framing recent snapshots, she crawled in bed feeling satisfied. It had been several days since she'd heard from the mysterious caller. Though she still turned Chad's pillow sideways every night to mimic a body, and ate most meals over the sink, she held out hope that being alone would be temporary. Growing up and getting married and having a family was the proper way of things. Being alone simply was not an option.

The next morning she parked and walked into the tourism center, surprised to find it nearly empty, with the exception of Mildred. The older woman perched on the stool behind the counter like a bird ready to take flight, a deep frown settled into her wrinkled brow. She stood when Andi pushed through the glass door.

Andi greeted her cheerfully, but the other woman's impassive face caught her off guard. Mildred snapped, "I'm sorry to have to be the one to tell you this, Andi, but your services are no longer needed."

Andi stopped dead in her tracks, and blinked. Her jaw dropped and her lips moved, but it took several attempts before intelligible words came forth, "What? I'm being fired?"

Mildred's jaw jutted forward stubbornly and she stared at Andi through narrowed eyes. "Yes, I'm afraid so. I am here to make sure you get your things and turn your key in."

Andi ducked her head, and felt her cheeks burn with embarrassment. This job had become an integral part of her life, part of her schedule, part of what kept things normal. Panic began to rise. She needed this job. Especially with her house for sale, and no credit cards. How would she pay her bills? How could she pay for food? A roof over her head? "What? I don't understand why-"

Mildred looked over her glasses, then leaned forward and whispered, "I was instructed not to go into details, but there was a report that you're skimming money from the map sales."

Andi laughed and looked around. Was it a joke? She'd never heard such an absurd accusation. "Map sales? The maps we sell for seventy-five cents? Someone thinks I am 'skimming money' from those sales?"

The other woman shrugged and finally looked at Andi, her watery blue eyes filled with disappointment. Andi abhorred pity, and refused to be the subject of it. But the poor lady probably *did* pity her, if she thought Andi's desperation had driven her to steal what amounted to loose change.

Andi's world crumbled around her. Her chest hurt and she felt as if she'd been kicked in the gut. She squeezed her eyes shut and took shallow breaths, then pulled her keys from her pocket. Her fingers shook as she struggled to separate the split silver ring, then slipped the worn office key off and tossed it onto the counter.

All her hard work had been for naught. Her first job and she failed. Her temper flared. She'd done nothing wrong. Someone had set her up. But who?

No one at work knew about her and Paul, but she wondered if he knew she'd been fired. She walked the waterfront for a bit, breathing in the salty air and listening to the groan of the piers as boats pulled and tugged on them. She wove through the throngs of tourists, oblivious to them as they jostled her. She could ask Paul, see what he knew, if he knew who had accused her. The sea gulls swooped around her, cawing and squealing. Waves crashed against the rocks.

By the time she returned to her Jeep, she'd decided not to ask him. Though she told herself she didn't want to drag him into her problems, the fact was, she didn't want him to know that she'd lost her job. That she'd been accused of such a horrible, absurd crime. After worrying that she'd be accused of killing her husband, this turn of events seemed like a cruel joke.

She drove home, determined to find another job. Hopefully she wouldn't have to end up waitressing, but if that was all she could find, that's what she'd do. She spent the rest of the morning looking through the newspaper and calling about jobs in the classifieds, with no luck. With her frustration mounting, she turned her attention to the job of cleaning, dusting and vacuuming and scrubbing, determined to reclaim some sense of normalcy. By that point, she should've known normal was impossible. Shortly before noon, her doorbell chimed. She went to the front door, peeked through the peephole, and debated on whether or not to open the door.

Detective Johnson stood on her porch, glaring at her.

26

He rapped his knuckles against the wood, then punched the doorbell again. She sagged against the wall, then straightened her back, squared her shoulders and opened the door.

He didn't bother to smile. "Mrs. Adams, may I come in?"

She stepped back, but made no move to leave the entryway. He pulled his sunglasses off, cocked his head sideways and stared at her. She fought the urge to collapse into a heap of quivering flesh. He shifted his weight and cocked his head the other way. He blinked first, and she raised her eyebrows.

Finally, he said, "I hear you lost your job today."

Her eyes narrowed, then she remembered that Mildred was friends with the Sheriff's secretary, the town gossip. "Guess that means Tess knows."

It was his turn to nod. "That it does. Want to tell me your side of the story?"

She feigned indifference and shrugged. "There is no story. I'm not sure what the real reason is I was let go, but I can tell you I certainly wouldn't risk my only means of income by stealing a few measly cents here and there. So unless you've got proof enough to charge me with something, I need to get back to looking for a job."

"Fair enough." He took a step towards the door, then turned back and said, "There's been a police report filed on the matter and I'll be checking into some things. Don't leave Buccaneer Bay without checking with me first. I may need to ask you a few questions."

She fumed at his insolence as he slipped his mirrored aviators back on and nodded curtly before he stalked out the door. Andi thought of police as the good guys, but this detective gave her the creeps and she second-guessed every interaction with him. Was she being too smart with him? Should she've been nicer?

The telephone jangled and demanded her attention.

"Hello?"

"I know what you did."

Her nerves were already tingling and she shifted from fear to anger. She hissed, "What do you want?"

"I want those documents." He breathed heavily into the phone. "You thought they were worth killing for and I have no problem doing whatever I have to do to get you out of the way."

The phone was heavy as a brick in her hands. "I have no idea what you're talking about."

"The exact location of samples and results of the geological tests. The deed. The stocks. I will have those papers in my hands before August Woodson dies, even if I have to turn you over to the cops to get you out of the way. You are running out of time."

The line went dead, and she was left to wonder who, what . . . it made no sense. The mysterious caller thought she murdered Chad for some documents, but she'd found nothing that would warrant killing someone for. Perhaps he knew about the legal stuff, but that had been taken care of with the attorney. The Will had been filed with the court, and certainly didn't leave her any fortune. Maybe the deed to the property bordering Acadia? But that went into the Trust just like the rest of Chad's assets.

Unless the caller needed Chad's notes about gems . . . the find might be destroyed if Woodson Enterprises proceeded with development.

Or was the development a cover for the gemstones?

She was tempted to stop answering the phone, but couldn't. Paul had an aversion to answering machines and wouldn't leave a message, so she began simply hanging up as soon as she heard the tell-tale breathing. She hoped the blackmailer would tire of getting a dial tone and give up, though she knew that was nothing more than a pipe dream. The phone calls ratcheted up her blood pressure, but she couldn't figure out how to deal with the caller. The fear that he might call the police was paralyzing. For the first time in years, her life was her own, and the thought of losing her newfound freedom terrified her, made her feel desperate.

On Friday, she arranged to meet Paul at the Harbor. She arrived early and decided to peruse Jewels by the Sea, with the goal of finding out more about the rough stones she'd found in the safe deposit box. When she asked Josephine about unpolished gems, the woman nodded enthusiastically. "You should talk to my husband. He's an amateur rock hounder, and frequently sets semi-precious stones that he finds."

She went into the back and within minutes her husband appeared. Andi blinked. "I think we've met."

His eyes widened as recognition dawned. "Yes, at the Clifftop."

A shiver ran down her spine at the memory of that night. "I didn't put it together. That you owned a jewelry store, I mean."

"Josephine and I have run the store for years." His smile faded. "Please accept our condolences on the loss of your husband."

"Thank you." She glanced around, then said, "I was wondering if you can tell me anything about local stones, what is found around here."

He gladly showed her some tourmaline crystals, and told her about two boys who discovered a major source of the crystals near Mount Paris, Maine. The only other people in the store were at the opposite end, engrossed in Pandora charms, so Andi pulled the little cloth sack from her purse and dropped the pink and green crystals onto the glass counter. "Are these worth anything?"

“Wow,” he whispered. “Where’d you get these?” He looked up at her with wide eyes.

She glanced nervously around and shrugged, “I don’t know. My husband had them.”

"That night at the Clifftop, that wasn't the first time we'd met." He hesitated for a moment, then picked up one of the stones and turned it over, examining it carefully. He shifted his weight from foot to foot, then finally said, “He came in here with all kinds of questions about mineral rights and mining. He hinted that he’d found a wicked big producer, but wouldn’t tell me where. Said that it was his ticket to a better life.”

"Do you remember anything else? Anything about where he'd found the stones?"

"No, but he did say that his girlfriend's grandfather-" his eyes flicked up and he said, "Sorry."

"It's okay. The wife's always the last to know." She shrugged and motioned for him to continue.

He glanced at Josephine before he continued, "Anyway, he said his girlfriend's grandfather owned the land, and that he hoped to buy it for a song. That's why he wanted to know about mineral rights."

The door to the store opened, and the wind chimes jangled in the breeze. Paul strolled towards them. "Thought that was your Jeep back there."

She scooped the stones up, stuffed them in the bag and dropped it in her purse. She thanked the man for his help, and turned to Paul.

His smile crinkled his tanned cheeks and his piercing blue eyes sparkled as he caught her in his arms, then gave her a quick peck on the cheek. His lips barely brushed her skin, but it still sent aftershocks all the way to her toes.

He kept one arm possessively around her while they looked at the tourist trinkets in the store. She commented on a simple hematite band displayed next to the cash register, and he slipped it on her right ring finger. Her breath caught in her throat.

"Fits perfect," she breathed.

At that moment, she couldn't have been happier with a diamond from Tiffany's.

He took her hand and ran his thumb over the ring as he pulled a bill from his pocket. He laid it on the counter, never breaking eye contact with her. To Carl Franklin, he said, "Keep the change."

The two held hands and swung them like school kids as they walked out of the store. She had to keep from skipping down the steps as they walked out to the parking lot. Suddenly, she felt optimistic. The stones tucked safely in her purse were worth something. Maybe there were more where those from. Maybe she could sell them to the man at the jewelry store. Paul opened the car door for her and she hopped in his Jeep, feeling lighter than she had in quite some time, equipped with her camera, maps and a sweatshirt. She held out her hand, fingers spread wide, and admired her new ring as they headed south and left Buccaneer Bay behind them to shoot some photos for a new brochure.

Their destination was Otter Point. The weather, beautiful for an late summer day, buoyed her spirits. Though tourist traffic slowed them, it just meant they'd be together longer. The wind ruffled her short hair and she reveled in the feeling of freedom.

He hooked his thumb over his shoulder. "You want to grab me a Pepsi from the cooler? There's an Orange Crush there for you, too."

She grinned as she reached into the back seat and opened his before handing it to him.

"You didn't have to do that." He grinned at her and dimples formed in his cheeks. "But, thanks!"

She beamed. Doing little things like that had become habit during her marriage. Chad trained her to think like a servant and it became second nature, but he never thanked her like Paul did. She wondered if Caren ever did things like that for him. Probably not, gauging from his reaction. She slipped her thumbnail under the tab and popped her own soda open.

The cool sweetness slid over her tongue. "It's been a long time since I've had a soda, much less anything not diet. Much sweeter than I remember." She sat the orange can in the cup holder.

He tapped her can with his finger. "You'd better drink up. It's better when it's ice cold."

With a smile, she grasped the can and guzzled the sugary drink. A droplet of soda slipped down the side and onto her finger. She frowned and held the drink up. "Must be a hole in the can somewhere. It's starting to lose its fizz."

He glanced over at her and frowned. "Do I need to get you another, or can you drink that one quickly?"

She laughed. "It's fine. I'll just drink quick." She tipped the cold can up and took another gulp, then another. When she finished the soda, she tucked the can in the plastic bag they'd brought along for trash, then held her hand in her lap, palm up, to keep from getting the stickiness all over.

He pointed at the glove box. "There's some wet wipes in there."

As she wiped off her hands, she let him guide the conversation, which he turned to her husband before they reached the turnoff from 3 onto Park Loop Road. He drove with his left arm draped casually out the window. He spoke loud to be heard over the rush of wind, "Thought maybe we'd go back to your house when we get back to Buccaneer Bay. We can go through some of Chad's stuff."

"I've been chipping away at it."

"Thought you were going to wait for me." His knuckles whitened on the steering wheel. "Have you gotten through most of it?"

She shrugged. “Some. It’s going to take quite a while, and there’s a lot to go through, so I’m just taking it one step at a time.”

He glanced over at her with those piercing blue eyes and cocked his eyebrow. “Finding anything of interest?”

Thoughts of the Will and the mysterious accounting papers flitted through her mind. “Just a lot of old memories. Even the good memories have lost their sparkle, though, so it feels good to get rid of them.”

“No marriage is perfect. By the way, did you get any more calls from that creep?” He fiddled with the radio.

“A couple. No big deal.” She glanced at him. “I’m a big girl.”

He frowned and adjusted his rear view mirror. “I know. I just don’t like it.”

She felt a little thrill at the show of protectiveness.

He continued, "Why don't you just give him what he wants?"

"I don't know what he wants." She frowned, anxious to turn the attention back to imperfect marriages. Surely, it wouldn’t be long before he grew tired of this sneaking around and left Caren, especially when she was cheating on him. It couldn't be a secret for long in a small town like Buccaneer Bay. “So, how was your week?”

"Same 'ol', same ol'." He downshifted as they neared the next turnoff. “I told you - I'm going to help you go through Chad's things. You don't need to do that by yourself.”

He turned the radio up and they drove in silence the next several miles until they reached the turn for the parking lot at Otter Cliff. He signaled then pointed the Jeep west. The sun warmed their backs, and the forest and rocks rose up around them, gorgeous, majestic in their ruggedness, deep green. They parked and crossed the road, then made their way down the rocky path. About a quarter of the way down, she felt off-balance and stepped wrong. Paul caught her elbow just as she stumbled. She shook her head. "I don't know what's wrong with me today."

He grinned at her. "The height can be disorienting sometimes."

She nodded, then looked out. The blue-green ocean spread out before them, absolutely incredible, and boats floated in the distance.

“Breathtaking, isn't it?” he whispered. There was a strange inflection in his voice that she couldn’t quite figure out.

“Yes. Beautiful.”

“Easy to forget how dangerous they can be, though, right?” He waved towards the waves crashing against the craggy red rocks.

A wave of nausea threatened to end the trip prematurely. She swallowed and shrugged in an effort to be casual. “I guess-“

Paul glanced at her, his face blank. “I’m sorry. I shouldn’t have said that. That's how your husband died, right? Falling onto the rocks from a cliff?”

She gazed to the south. “Yes. He fell over a guardrail.”

His voice was rough like sandpaper, “But it wasn’t an accident, was it?”

27

It took a lot of self-control to keep her eyes focused on the rocks underfoot. She sucked in a deep breath of salt air before answering. "Of course it was an accident."

He dipped his head towards hers. "I mean, it wasn't a wreck – a car accident? Was it?"

Relief swept over her like the frothy waves rolling over the rough rocks below them, "Oh, no, it wasn't a wreck. But it was an accident. Of course, it was a horrible, horrible accident. He just stepped back and went over the guardrail-" She clapped her hand over her mouth, feeling the horror all over again.

"I'm sorry," he said quickly. "I didn't mean to bring up bad memories. Tell me what your brochures and maps say about these cliffs."

The exchange dampened her mood the rest of the day, and she couldn't shake the unease that settled in the pit of her stomach. Something had changed, and she wasn't sure if it was her or him. She'd convinced herself that he was the one, the one she'd live happily ever after with. He filled her dreams, but now she was unsure. She focused on taking pictures during the trip, and kept the discussion on safe topics. Neither of them made any effort to touch the other as they explored the shoreline.

As they walked the concrete path towards Thunder Hole, she glanced down and felt her head spin. Heights usually didn't bother her, but this did. She wrapped her hand around the handrail and held on tight, then asked, "Did you know I was fired this week?" It came out more confrontational than she'd intended.

"What?" He grabbed her arm and turned her towards him, then leaned back against the steel support. "I'm sorry. I didn't know."

She glanced at a couple of tourists that stepped around them. "They accused me of stealing."

He jerked his head back and lowered his eyebrows. "What? That's crazy."

No offer to check into the situation for her. She laughed, sharp and humorless. "I'll be fine. Just have to find a new job." And soon. She either had to buy the house she lived in - an absurd situation - or find another place to live. Laughter bubbled up, unbidden. She clapped her hand over her mouth to stop the giggles.

What was wrong with her?

He slipped his arm around her waist and guided her down the narrow steps. She gripped the handrail with her right hand and took in the awesome sight of Thunder Hole. The roar of the water rolling in and crashing into the narrow cleft in the massive rock did indeed remind her of thunder. Wave after wave rolled in, sending up a spray of salt water each time. The rolling motion made her feel queasy. She blinked and swayed as if she'd been drinking. Her side struck the support and she pressed against it in an effort to stop the steps from pitching from side to side. She looked out to the east and focused on the horizon.

He shouted over the roar, "This is pretty good for summer. It's usually pretty calm!"

She swallowed hard. "It's awesome!" she shouted back.

They were standing just above the end platform when the first stab of pain struck. She straightened, thinking she might've pulled a muscle on the walk. It hit again, this time nearly blinding in its intensity. Paul was a step below her, facing the roiling sea, when she fell to her knees. Waves of nausea passed over her, and she lost her lunch. She spat. He turned to look at her, and she retched again.

It hurt so bad, it didn't even bother her to have him see her like that. The massive boulders tilted around her, and the edges of her vision clouded. The pain doubled her over. Just before she lost consciousness, she saw Paul leaning casually against the guardrail as two people she didn't know hovered over her. Their faces blurred and then everything closed in around her.

Andi woke up in the emergency room, barely covered by a dreadful cotton gown, with a plastic tube snaking from her right arm up to an IV bag. Hospitals have a buzz about them no matter the time of day, but the lights in the cubicle were dimmed. All around her voices competed with the beeping and chiming of machines. A nurse swept the curtain open and strode in, then took Andi's vital signs without so much as an introduction. The woman's heavy gray brows pushed together and she tipped her head back to peer through the bottom half of her glasses at her watch as she pressed her fingers against Andi's wrist.

"Excuse me, but what's wrong with me?" Andi remembered the horrendous pain she'd felt while at Thunder Hole but was blissfully pain free at the moment. She raised her head, but the room tilted dangerously, so she dropped back down.

The nurse tucked a loose strand of gray hair back into her bun and mumbled, "Kidneys."

Andi blinked in surprise. She'd never had any problems with her kidneys before. "Am I going to be okay?" Everything was delightfully foggy.

"Remains to be seen." The older woman wrapped the blood pressure sleeve around Andi's arm and nodded towards the IV bag, "Pumping you full of fluids to try to flush the alcohol out of your system."

The sleeve tightened around her arm until it felt like it would explode. "Wait. What?" She tried to pull her arm away from the pressure, but her muscles didn't respond.

"You were really out of it when the bus brought you in." The nurse tugged the pressure sleeve from Andi's arm and tapped the results into the laptop mounted on the wall. "Looks like you really tied one on."

"I didn't have anything to drink." Andi struggled to keep her eyes open and glanced around the room. "Was anyone--did my--is my -- friend still here?"

"Not that I've seen and I've been on duty since you got here." The nurse shook her head and examined the clear plastic bag hanging on the silver pole at the side of the bed.

The door burst open and a white-coated doctor pushed through. "Calcium oxalate crystals in the urine!"

"Dr. Cavanaugh. I was on duty when you were brought into the ER." The tall doctor strode over to the bed and squinted at Andi. "What did you have to drink earlier today?"

"That's what I been trying to tell her." Andi shook her head when she heard the slur in her words. "Nothing."

The nurse snorted and the doctor frowned at her, then turned his attention back to his patient. "I'm not talking alcohol. I mean anything liquid. What did you drink before you were brought in?"

She laid her head back against the pillow and closed her eyes, "A glass of water first thing in the morning. I had a cup of coffee in the morning." Her eyes popped open. "I had an orange soda."

The doctor said, "Did it taste funny?"

She ran her tongue over her teeth as she recalled the sugary sweetness in her mouth. "It was really sweet."

"When did you drink it?" The young doctor looked up at the clock on the wall.

Andi blinked as she tried to remember. It was after they left Buccaneer Bay, but before they got to Thunder Hole. They'd already turned off of Highway 3. "Late morning, maybe 11 or so."

Dr. Cavanaugh nodded. He and the nurse exchanged a knowing glance, then the nurse shook her head, "You're thinking antifreeze poisoning?"

Andi blinked. The sweet orange soda? "But that's not possible. How could antifreeze have gotten into a can of soda?"

Twin lines formed in the young doctor's forehead. "There haven't been any other cases, but we need to make sure this is an isolated event. Where did you get the drink?"

Andi's arms shook as she tried to push herself up. The nurse gently put her hand on her patient's shoulder. Andi dropped back. "I don't know where he got it."

The doctor asked quickly, "Who?"

An image of Paul and his piercing blue eyes flitted through Andi's mind. "My boyfriend. I don't know where he got it. Maybe Caddy's Quick Shop when he stopped to get gas."

Suddenly her room was abuzz with activity. He picked up his pad and scribbled with the stylus. "I want to push fluids, then start a course of Antizol. 15 mg over the next 30 minutes. I'm going to alert the police."

The nurse sprang into action, immediately checking the IV bag. She darted out the door and returned shortly with a vial and syringe. Andi watched as the woman held up the glass vial, inserted the needle and withdrew the clear fluid. After she cleared the air bubbles, she inserted the syringe into a small tube in the IV. A tiny air bubble formed in the tubing and slowly traveled through the clear plastic, snaking its way towards Andi's hand.

Her head rolled to the side as she wiggled her fingers. "Is that a problem?"

The nurse dropped the used syringe in the bright red sharps container. "What?"

"There's an air bubble in my IV tube."

"It's OK. Not like it is on TV."

Andi giggled nervously, and looked around the room. The blinds were closed and the sliver of window around them was dark. “What time is it now?”

“Almost 7." The nurse pulled the blanket up and tucked Andi in.

She could almost picture it. Paul dropped her off at the emergency room, but made no effort to stick around and make sure she was going to be okay.

The nurse tapped more information into the laptop at the station next to the bed. Andi's side began to ache and the pain wrapped all the way around from the front to the back. She moaned and shifted in the bed. The older woman glanced up, "Feeling pain?"

Andi nodded and bit back a moan.

"I'll get you something for it."

The rest of the night was spent in a dreamless sleep, for which Andi was thankful. The next morning, she picked up the telephone to call Mildred at the Chamber office to let her know she'd need to find someone else to work, but stopped in mid-dial. She didn't have a job anymore. She thought about calling her mother, but didn't want to worry her. She couldn't call Paul because his wife might answer. Finally, she called Dana.

"Oh, my God! Are you okay?"

Andi pressed the button to raise the head of the bed. "I'll be fine. They said it was antifreeze poisoning."

"Antifreeze poisoning? I didn't think that was even a thing anymore. Manufacturers are required to make it taste bitter, because so many pets died."

"I think I remember that." Andi scrunched her face at that horrible thought. Something niggled at her memory, but she couldn't put her finger on it.

"When will they discharge you?"

The doctor hadn't really said anything about her prognosis. "Not sure yet." She glanced at the IV bag. Nearly empty. The nurse had returned several times overnight to inject more antidote to be pumped into her veins.

"I'll come by after work. If they discharge you before that, call me."

At least Andi wouldn't have to take a cab home if they let her go. She had just placed the handset in the cradle when Paul stuck his head in the door. His forehead wrinkled with a frown as his piercing blue eyes swept around the room, then settled on her.

"Hey, there. How're you feeling?"

She lit up at the sight of him, "Better than yesterday."

He stepped in and pushed the door shut behind him. As he dragged the chair closer to her hospital bed, he said, "I was pretty worried about you, but you seemed to be in good hands. I figured it was better just to get out of the way and let the doctors do their thing."

She nodded, and told him about her night. "Hey, where'd you get that soda? They think it was antifreeze poisoning."

"Really?" His dark eyebrows pinched together and his left eye twitched. "What makes them think that?"

An image of Paul leaning against the guardrail floated through her memory. Other faces crowded close to her while they were at Thunder Hole. Other voices asked if she was okay, but he hadn't. Had she been that out of it?

He pulled a plastic bottle of chocolate milk from his pocket opened it, then handed it to her. He shrugged, "Thought a little chocolate might make you feel better."

She took a sip of the sweet liquid and sighed. "Thanks. All they've given me so far is ice chips."

He glanced around the Spartan room. The news was just coming on the television as he reached over and pushed the off button.

"You need rest and quiet, so you can get all better and get out of here." He jumped up and continued, "Let me get you another pillow."

"Really, I'm--"

"Not a problem," he interrupted, as he opened the narrow closet at the foot of the bed.

She heard something metallic jangle, and cocked her head. His back was to her, and he dug around in the closet. "Did you drop something?"

He straightened and glanced over his shoulder at her, then pulled a pillow from the top shelf of the closet. He fluffed it and said, "No. Not-- I just dropped your keys in your purse. I had a friend go out with me to get your Jeep from Jewels by the Sea and take it home."

He held her arm and helped her lean forward as he arranged the pillow behind her. It took her a moment to catch her breath after the exertion. "Oh, well, thanks. You didn't have to do that, but thanks."

"Not a problem." He nodded and smiled, hands stuffed deep in his pockets. "No problem at all. Any idea when you're going to get out of here?"

"Not yet. Haven't seen the doctor today, but I'm sure he'll be in soon."

"Right." He pointed to the closet. "Want me to keep your keys and check your mail or anything?"

She shook her head, "I doubt I'll be here that long. I appreciate the offer, though."

He made a show of looking at his watch, then gave her a peck on the cheek and said, "I've got to get going. I'm late to the office."

There was something off, but she couldn't put her finger on it. His eyes darted around the room, swept the floor. She asked, "Call me later?"

He rocked back on his heels and nodded. "Drink up, now. Milk is good for you."

She held up the chocolate milk in a salute. "Thanks for everything."

He blew her a kiss just before he stepped out of the room, and she took a deep breath. The scent of him still hovered in the room. Fresh, clean. Like a mountain morning. She took another drink of chocolate milk and smiled at his thoughtfulness. He'd acted so oddly though.

Probably nervous that someone would recognize him and tell his wife he'd been to visit her.

Within the hour, Dana arrived and promptly announced that she would stay throughout the day, in spite of Andi's protests. Shortly after she arrived, she said, "This isn't exactly what I had in mind, but I did want to get together and talk about wedding plans. Didn't you get my message yesterday morning?"

Andi pushed herself up in the bed. "No. I went exploring."

"Really? With him?" Dana's lips pressed into a tight line.

Andi's head dropped back into the soft pillow. "Yes. But no judgments, please. I just can't do that right now."

"Fine. No judgments."

The nurse returned with a small glass bottle on a stainless steel tray. She nodded to Andi. "It's time for the next round of Antizol."

Dana moved to Andi's side and squeezed her hand. Together they watched the nurse as she readied the medicine and inserted the needle into the clear IV bag hanging from the metal post above Andi's head. Dana's face paled as she watched the nurse empty the syringe.

Andi asked, "Is that for the poison?"

The nurse nodded as she finished the injection, then she dropped the used syringe in the red sharps container next to the sink. "Someone'll be in shortly to draw blood again. We'll see how your counts are and then the doctor will decide what happens next."

Dana filled the cup on the plastic tray table with water from the pitcher and handed it to Andi, who sipped the cool liquid. Dana walked around the room. She rearranged the pitcher and cup on the tray table, threw away the empty bottle of chocolate milk, then straightened the blanket at the foot of Andi's bed.

Andi raised her eyebrows as she watched her friend. "What's on your mind?"

Dana shook her head. "Nothing that can't wait."

"Spill it."

Dana grinned and sat on the edge of the bed. "Anyway, I started to tell you that Derek and I picked up our wedding rings yesterday. So, we decided we don't want to wait. Can you get away next weekend? Assuming the doc says you're okay to go?"

Her friend's enthusiasm was catching. "Next weekend? Did I hear you right?"

Dana beamed. "Yup! Edward has offered to pay for my way and my maid of honor's way. How can you turn that down, my maid of honor?"

Andi laughed weakly as relief flooded through her. She couldn't afford a trip to the mainland, much less a trip to Atlantic City. Edward's generosity overwhelmed her. "Write down the details so I don't forget anything in this drugged haze."

They decided to meet for lunch one day to finalize things, because Dana had about a dozen brochures for weddings at different casinos and couldn't decide which she wanted. As she told about her day with Derek, Andi's mind began to wander to her afternoon with Paul.

And then she wondered why he'd acted so oddly when he'd visited.

What was he doing in the closet?

The doctor came in just then, and Dana cocked an eyebrow. Dr. Cavanaugh's head nearly touched the top of the door and his shoulders were wide like a football player, with dark hair and a dark complexion. He stood inches from the bed, reviewing the medical chart. After a moment, he looked down at her, with dark brown eyes framed by long dark lashes. "I'm concerned with your numbers. Your electrolytes are still low, but it looks like we caught the poisoning in time."

Andi cocked her head to one side. "In time?"

"Before permanent kidney damage." Dr. Cavanaugh examined the monitor beside her bed. "How're you feeling now?"

"Better."

"Good. I'm going to move you to a private room and give you at least one more Antizole treatment by IV, and want to keep flushing the fluids through you." He flipped pages back and forth, and frowned. "Looks like you've had a rough life, Mrs. Adams."

She swallowed hard, and focused on keeping her countenance neutral. "Sorry?"

"Your X-rays. Looks like you've had a couple of fractured ribs, and your arms have had several hairline fractures."

28

Dana sat up straighter, but Andi kept her focus on the handsome doctor and shrugged, "Not that I recall."

He nodded but his eyebrows pushed into a deep V. "Well then, you must be quite accident prone. You'll be moved shortly, and the remaining treatments should go well. It's too soon to say, but it looks like the Antizol is doing the trick."

Andi gulped. "Let's hope it works."

After he left, Dana leaned close and whispered, "He wasn't wearing a wedding band."

Andi noticed, too, but she responded with a shrug. The edges of the room began to soften, thanks to the pain medication. Should she give up on Paul? Would anyone else be interested in her? Handsome, successful Paul. When she closed her eyes, she could imagine them leading the perfect life.

She let herself drift away.

"Andi!"

Andi blinked slowly and tried to focus on her friend's green eyes. "What?"

"You were talking in your sleep, crying almost."

With effort, Andi opened her mouth and licked her lips. Her tongue felt too big, and she felt deliciously relaxed.

"The injuries. Chad did that to you, didn't he?" Dana didn't wait for a reply. She moved next to the bed, her forehead furrowed with concern. "Why didn't you leave him?"

Andi shrugged. "Couldn't. Never would've let me go. If only I'd been a better wife--"

"That's bullshit."

With effort, Andi opened her eyes. "Could've done better. Should've done better."

"You're so much better than that." Dana shook her head. "You don't even see it. You don't need a man."

Andi's head bobbed. "But I do. Happier, more complete." Her tongue filled her mouth, making it difficult to speak.

Dana sighed and turned away. "I've got to get going. I'll check in with you later."

"Don't leave like this." Andi tilted her head and smiled at her friend. "Please."

"Get some rest. I'll talk to you later." Dana opened the door and looked back. "Call if you need anything."

After her friend left, Andi drifted off. Sleep was uninterrupted by dreams and she felt rested when the nurse opened the blinds the next morning. By late morning, she felt better and the handsome doctor ordered another round of blood tests. Shortly after a lunch of hospital Jell-O and a smuggled cheeseburger (thanks to

Dana), he announced that her numbers weren't as good as he'd hoped.

He frowned as he looked at the terminal screen. "This doesn't make sense. Your numbers should be lower than this if we're correct that your exposure was nearly 24 hours ago."

Andi caught her lower lip with her teeth, then ventured, "What does that mean?"

He shook his head and twin furrows appeared in his forehead. "It means that we need to continue the Antizol. I don't want you eating or drinking anything unless you are absolutely sure of the source."

By the next morning, her numbers had improved. To her delight, her doctor ordered the removal of the IV and catheter and released her with strict instructions to drink a lot of water -- and nothing else.

Dana drove her home and worried over Andi like a mother hen. After many assurances that she would be fine, Dana left her alone to rest. The truth of the matter was that Paul hadn't called as he promised, and Andi was afraid of what that might mean. After she engaged the deadbolt, she trudged up the steps, put her hand on the doorknob to her room and froze. Their bedroom door was never shut. The doorknob turned in her hand with a squeak, loud in the empty house. She glanced over her shoulder, and stared into the shadows. After a moment's hesitation, she laughed at herself and pushed the door open. She crawled into bed, alone and exhausted.

As she laid there staring at the ceiling, the reality of her situation began to sink in. She'd been poisoned. How? And she needed a job.

Maybe she could wait to get a job after things were settled with Paul. They'd probably move anyway, to get away from Caren, so there was no sense in looking for a job here.

Earlier that evening, the real estate agent called to say another couple was coming to look at the house. She'd lost her job. She had no credit cards. The detective thought she was a murderer and, more importantly, so did someone else. Just as she was about to give up and take a sleeping pill, the phone rang. She hesitated, but the ringing continued. She couldn't stand to not answer in case it was Paul.

As she feared, she was greeted by the blackmailer's voice. "I know what happened that night. Time is running out. The old man is dying, and I need those documents before he dies . . . and I swear to God, I'll give the police everything they need to put you away for the rest of your life."

A chill ran down her spine. "What documents are you talking about?"

"The deed and the stock certificates."

"What? What deed? What certificates?"

He huffed. "The stock certificates."

"What? I don't know what you're talking about! What stock certificates?"

The line went dead, and she wondered what this man thought she had. All she had in her possession was a bunch of poor photocopies. But how could she convince him of that?

She pushed the blackmailer out of her mind. She'd been unhappy for so long, and the doctor's reference to her old injuries brought all that frustration and fear back to the surface. She'd wasted so much time with Chad. Maybe Dana was right. Maybe she should've left him. But being alone wasn't an option. She couldn't imagine life as a single woman, widow or otherwise.

On a whim, she punched in Paul's phone number, then put her hand over the mouthpiece. The phone rang twice, then a woman answered, her voice melodic and smooth. There was a man in the background, but it wasn't clear enough to be sure if it was Paul or not. The woman said hello again, then hung up.

Andi was so frustrated.

She needed Paul.

Caren didn't.

29

She woke up shortly after four in the morning, unable to sleep. After hours of restlessness tossing and turning, she finally rolled out of bed. She dragged herself to the bedroom and took a long, hot shower. It felt good, with the soothing water rushing over her body. After her shower, she popped another pain pill then went to the bedroom to get dressed and noticed the red message light blinking on the answering machine.

It was that voice again. She listened to the message, and then listened again, to see if she recognized the caller. She didn't, so she listened yet again.

"I know what really happened."

Damn.

She dropped onto the bed. What the hell was she going to do? And why did that voice sound so familiar? Something about the way he said "know," clipped off.

A noise downstairs piqued her attention, so she went to the door to listen. Everything was quiet, but she slipped into her clothes and went downstairs to check things out. A car pulled out of the driveway, tires crunching in the gravel, but was gone by the time she got to the living room window. She ran to the door and opened it, hoping to get a look at the vehicle. Her bare foot landed on a big white envelope that slid on the polished wood floor, and her arms cartwheeled in an awkward attempt to keep her balance. She succeeded, but barely, and glanced around to see if anyone was watching.

Mrs. Harrison stood at the edge of her driveway, a newspaper gripped in one hand. She fluttered her fingers in a wave. Andi waved back, then scooped up the envelope and ducked inside.

The block print on the envelope simply said Mrs. Adams. She slipped her thumb under the flap and opened it. Inside was a glossy 8 x 10, grainy, black and white. It was a rainy night on a dark road. A man and woman stood on the shoulder next to a dark-colored SUV.

The photo fell to the floor, and she was right behind it.

The room spun around her, her breath came in short gasps. The rug had been pulled out from under her. She blinked and swallowed hard, covered in a cold sweat. Goosebumps pebbled her arms and she rubbed them vigorously, trying to warm up and get some sense of reality.

Dear God, someone out there really *did* know what happened.

She wheezed, struggling to suck in air. There wasn't enough oxygen in the room. She squeezed her eyes shut, but the dizziness got worse and images flashed through her mind of that stormy night. The room spun and she fought to maintain control. Her mind raced and she struggled to be rational. It was her only hope if she wanted to survive.

Who would have been out there on a night like that? And even if someone happened to be out there, who would have a camera? Thoughts swirled like a tornado and she forced herself to look at the picture analytically. The photo was black and white, grainy, as if it had been taken from a distance with a telephoto lens. The only light that night had been from the moon.

She picked up the photo and examined it. Neither of the faces were clear by any stretch of the imagination, but the license plate was readable. A road sign in the background was visible, 2 miles to the Clifftop. It wouldn't take a huge leap to figure out who was in that photo. She flipped it over and looked at the back. Kodak paper, but that could be purchased anywhere. The quality of the print was good, but with home printers these days, it could have been printed anywhere.

Sweat beaded on her brow. Her heart thumped so loud against her ribcage, it took a moment for her to realize the telephone was ringing. She stared at the hall table where the telephone sat, then just before the machine picked up, she crawled forward and snatched the handset off the base.

"Hey, girl! You sound out of breath. Did I catch you at a bad time?" Dana's cheerful voice greeted her.

Andi sagged against the wall, "No, no, not at all. I was just coming in from outside and ran for the phone."

"Outside?" She was probably looking at her watch. "You know it's only a little after 8, right?"

Andi laughed, hoping it didn't sound as forced as it felt. "Guess I was feeling productive today. What's up?"

"How are you feeling?"

"Tired, but better." She repeated, "What's up?"

Dana puffed out a breath. "Well, I just wanted to tell you that I've decided where we're staying while we're in Atlantic City. Want to hear now, or want to wait until lunch?"

Andi clutched the photo in her fist. No one could learn about this. The fact that she was all alone in the world hit her like a ton of bricks. Even her best friend couldn't understand the gravity of what she'd done. It had been an accident. At least, that's what she'd told herself. But looking at the images in black and white made her wonder.

Her friend's voice jolted Andi out of her head, "Hey! If you want to wait, it's no biggie!"

Andi shook herself, and squeezed her eyes closed, but the images from that night swam on her eyelids like the projection of a movie, "No, I absolutely want to hear now. What's the plan?"

"We're staying at the Tropicana! Woo-hoo! Doesn't that sound awesome? They've got a bunch of packages, so I want you to help me pick out which wedding we're going to have. Want to meet at the Black Sails at noon?"

Her enthusiasm coaxed a smile from Andi. "See you there."

"See ya!"

Andi hung up and looked down at the photo clutched in her hand. Dana's excitement was contagious. Starting a new chapter in life had that effect on folks. As Andi looked around at the heavy traditional furniture and dark walls that Chad picked out, she thought that perhaps the time had come for her to do the same.

Maybe Paul would want a change of scenery, too, after finding out about Caren. Missouri wouldn't be bad. That would be a change of scenery, that's for sure, and her mother would be thrilled. Before she could think about that step, though, the blackmailer had to be dealt with. She tapped the edge of the photo against her leg and chewed on her lower lip.

The phone rang again and Andi snatched up the receiver, thinking it was Dana calling to tell me another wedding detail. It wasn't.

"My patience is wearing thin."

She was torn between fear and frustration. She demanded angrily, "Who is this?"

This time she got a response. The slow voice said, "Do you like the picture I left for you?"

"Who are you?" Her voice rose with tension.

Silence hummed over the line, so she repeated the question. Still, silence. She heaved a sigh. "What do you want? Tell me what you want, specifically, and I'll get it for you, or leave me the hell alone!"

"Ahhh, now you're getting the picture." Slow laughter followed, which gave her goosebumps. "Chad had the coordinates, an unrecorded deed and stock certificates. I want them. You have no right to them."

No right? Anger flared. "Chad was my husband!"

The voice remained calm, but smug. "So you admit your wrongdoing?"

"I admit nothing. This conversation is over." But she couldn't bring herself to hang up the phone. Her knuckles whitened and her heart raced so fast it hurt.

"It's not over. Not yet. But I'll let you have your fun first. Go to A.C., have a good time. We'll take care of business when you get home." He paused and she heard faint breathing. "You'd just better hope the old man doesn't die before you get back, or the cops'll be waiting for you to land."

Click.

She stared at the phone and shivered as a chill ran up her spine.

30

The rest of the morning passed like molasses. She kept the blinds closed, and turned the ringer off on the phone. When she left the house to go to lunch, she looked around as casually as she could and tried to take note of every vehicle on the street.

Mrs. Harrison hunched over the strip of flowers between their houses. She waved, "Did you hear about Bruce Peabody?"

Andi opened the car door. "No, what about him?"

"Had a heart attack and died in his sleep." Bruce was a lobster fisherman, a fixture on the harbor front. The old lady grinned and turned back to her weeding. "Good way to go!"

Andi shook her head at her neighbor's obsession with death and hopped in the Jeep. She backed out and headed towards town. Her eyes drifted to the rearview mirror, looking for a tail. A blaring horn broke her reverie and saved her from a head on collision at First and Pine. She shook herself and blinked back tears. The blackmailer wouldn't be following her to lunch.

She didn't think so anyway.

Lunch was a casual affair, thankfully. Andi found it difficult to focus, and she caught bits and pieces of conversation. Dana had brochures and talked about the amount of time in the chapel and the slider buffet and the champagne toast and a premium brand open bar and chocolate fondue. Then she mentioned that her fiancé wanted to go with one package, but she wanted the cheaper package. She mentioned a showroom and IMAX and then it was back to the chapels and their creams and greens and wouldn't that be pretty for a wedding.

The only colors Andi could think about were black and white.

The colors of the grainy photograph stuffed between her mattress and box springs at home. The colors prisoners wear who do time for murder.

Finally, thankfully, the minute hand on the clock on the wall inched up until it pointed toward the 12. Dana glanced at her watch and frowned.

"Damn! Lunch hour just isn't enough. And I did not mean to talk the entire time. Look, I didn't eat hardly any of my lunch." Dana glanced at Andi's plate, then at Andi. "And you didn't eat any of your fries. I've never known you to skip fries when Chad wasn't-"

Dana's mouth hung open for a moment as she caught herself. She snapped her mouth shut. Andi smiled sadly and shrugged. Chad's habit of criticizing every bite of food that went in her mouth used to embarrass her. At least that's one thing she didn't have to endure anymore, but he was right. Every bite she put in her mouth went straight to her rounded hips.

Dana leaned forward. "Oh, God, I'm sorry. That just popped out. I'm so sorry."

"Not a problem. Here, it's on me today." Andi tossed a twenty and a five on the table as the two pushed their chairs back. Andi tugged her shirt down over her hips, self conscious of their fullness. Dana walked towards the law office, and Andi headed home, wondering what might be waiting for her. More pictures? Messages on the machine?

The mail had come by the time she arrived home, but it was just the usual – junk mail and bills. Again, she took note of the vehicles around, but didn't see anything out of place. Once inside, she flipped the deadbolt and headed upstairs to the darkened bedroom to check the machine. Light slipped in around the blinds. The red blinking light gave her pause, and she considered pressing delete, but couldn't. She pushed play and sat down on the bed to listen.

A quiet, vaguely strained voice said, "You there? It's me. Thought I might stop by after work and check on you. Call me at the Chamber if you get in before 4."

The sound of Paul's voice surprised her. The computerized voice after his message said he had called at 1:12 pm. She glanced at the clock on her nightstand. She hadn't missed him by much. She played the message again, and again thought he sounded a little off. Maybe he'd found out about Caren's infidelity. The corners of her mouth curled up.

She punched in the Chamber's number and asked to be transferred to Paul Thompson. He answered briskly.

"Hey, lover," she said in her sexiest voice.

"Hey, yourself. Been out today?"

"Just got back."

"Really? Why?"

She blinked, taken aback at his tone. She fought her first instinct to apologize for going out, and instead straightened and said, "My best friend Dana and I were talking wedding plans."

"Oh, right. You're going to be her maid of honor."

Was the fact that she was involved in a wedding bothering him? Jealous? Nervous? "Yup. That's me. You want to stop by after you get done there?"

"Sure. It'll be a little after 4."

"Great. See you then."

After she hung up, she went through the house room by room, checking the windows to make sure they were locked. Being alone freaked her out. She wasn't good on her own. She kept going over the conversation. His voice sounded a little stiff, and there was that comment 'been out today?' She shrugged it off, then reminded herself not to read too much into it. Between the years of Chad's constant monitoring of her whereabouts and the surprise delivery of the photograph, she was on edge. It would be good to spend a little time relaxing with Paul, and it would give her a chance to make sure he knew how good life could be with her.

With that in mind, she went to the closet and picked out fresh clothes. She pulled on black jeans, to make her butt look smaller, and a pale pink blouse so she could leave an extra button undone. With a dab of product rubbed between her palms, she ran her fingers through her short hair and tousled it. The fresh look made her look younger, spunkier. With a smile, she admired her look, glad she'd taken the plunge and cut her long locks. It might be a cliché, but she felt like a new woman.

And it was time for a new start.

She skipped down the stairs and lit a couple of candles, then chose a bottle of wine to chill. After she selected a couple of goblets from the wine cart and set them out so they would be ready, she flipped through CDs to look for something to set the mood until the doorbell rang. The clock on the mantle said 3:30, and Paul had said after 4. Instantly, her breath quickened and her stomach clenched. She padded as softly as she could to the front door and looked through the peephole. Paul stood there, shoulders hunched up as if trying to stay warm.

Or hidden.

She opened the door and stepped back. He came in, pushed the door shut behind him and kissed her. It was a deep kiss, his lips taking hers - so unlike his usual greeting. It took her breath away. Her eyes opened wide, and she felt her body respond before she even realized what was happening. She melted against him, until he pulled away abruptly, grabbed her hand and led her to the family room.

"We need to talk," he said as he pulled her down beside him on the sofa. He sat leaning forward, elbows on his knees, face in his hands.

"What's wrong?" She kept her face a blank slate, impassive. But would she appear uninterested? Her eyebrows pushed together in a frown.

He let his hands drop and looked at her. "I think Caren is having an affair."

She patted his thigh and said gently, "Well, sweetheart, is that such a bad thing? I mean, you are, too."

His forehead wrinkled as his eyebrows shot up. "That's different."

Typical man. Of course he thought it was different. "Is it?"

He blinked twice, rapidly. "Yes."

His ego was bruised. She probed gently, "How?"

"It just is."

She felt like she'd been punched in the stomach. This wasn't the reaction she hoped for. Then again, what man could ever conceive that his wife would cheat on him? She scooted closer and draped her arm over his shoulders.

She lowered her head and asked, "What makes you think she's screwing around on you?"

His piercing blue eyes flashed as he said, "I think she's taking trips with this guy."

"How do you know?" She held her breath, wondering how much he would share with her.

He shrugged her arm off his shoulders and stood. She hesitated a moment, then pushed to her feet. His back was to her. His broad shoulders rose and fell, and she yearned to touch him but was afraid to. If he rejected her, she would die.

He whispered, "Did you ever cheat on Chad?"

She gasped. "No! Absolutely not!"

"I never meant for this to happen. I never meant to fall for you."

Perhaps a nudge could swing the balance her way. "I never meant to fall for you, either."

He turned to look at her, and she gazed into his eyes. Those eyes were like pools of deep water, and she wanted to drown in them. She stepped forward and put her arms around his neck. He didn't pull back. She tipped her head back and stretched up to kiss him. He responded, then stiffened.

And not in a good way.

His voice thickened. “What are you doing?”

“Your wife is cheating on you. So why not?” She let her hand trail down his arm, then took him by the hand and led him to the stairs. He stopped with one foot on the bottom step.

“I can’t do this. I am a married man. It’s different for you. Your husband is dead.” He motioned to the wedding photo still displayed on the console table. “You can’t even get rid of all of his stuff. Won’t let me help you do it. I have a wife at home waiting for me, and right now I need to be with her.”

He pulled away, then walked out the front door.

Andi stood at the bottom of the stairs, deflated. With Chad dead, she was free to get on with life. She'd wasted so much time with Chad, and felt as if time was ticking away far too quickly. Paul would be a dream come true, and he was slipping away. All she had to do was get rid of Caren.

And stay out of jail.

31

She stayed up until nearly one in the morning, worrying. Someone out there knew – or thought they knew - the truth about that accident. She'd been so caught up in life - worrying about money, her home being sold, having no credit cards, losing her job, worrying about Paul's marriage, she'd nearly forgotten about it until the pictures and phone calls.

She went to bed but laid awake until nearly dawn, thinking about ways to track the blackmailer down. Most blackmailers were looking for payment. This one wanted something she didn't have. She needed to figure out who he was and find something on him. Everyone has a skeleton in their closet.

The next morning, she got up, showered and dressed quickly. With a mental list in mind, she was ready to get to work. She sipped on cup of strong coffee while she made a list of stops to make.

Her first stop was Chad's office. Jennie had done a good job of cleaning the place up before she dropped the key off with Andi, but the realtor hadn't found anyone who wanted to buy it yet. Chad's office contents had been boxed up and stored in the building. She intended to sell the contents to a new dentist. Jennie had told her Chad's personal effects and papers were packed in bankers boxes stored under his desk. Andi pulled the first box out and sat down on the floor to look through it.

Part of her suspected the photographer was a private eye that Chad hired to follow her. She couldn't imagine anyone could just happen to be out on a stormy night with equipment like that. Surely he would've noted that in his papers somewhere.

Most of what she found was mundane. There wasn't even any personal correspondence or notes. Had Jennie culled out what she didn't want Andi to see? She put everything back in the first box and shoved it under the desk. She went through the second box and found more of the same, mostly handbooks and newsletters and journals relating to the field of dentistry. About halfway through the stack, she found Chad's leather bound agenda.

She leaned back against the wall and flipped through the gold-edged pages. Most were notations about patients, with a few social engagements and business meetings sprinkled throughout. One entry in late March caught her eye. It simply said "P - 2 pm Tiny's Pub." She dog-eared the page. For most of the other entries, she recognized either the names of his colleagues or friends or the locations, but she'd never known Chad to go to Tiny's. She flipped forward to the first weekend in April.

That weekend, he had been in Atlantic City, but told her he went to a conference in Boston. Her blood boiled at the memory of spending her birthday alone. She hadn't even called anyone, because she didn't want Dana or her mother to know she was by herself.

She shook her head as if that could make the memories go away. The notation on that Friday at 5 said simply "AC conf w/ P." There was a smiley face jotted next to the entry.

P, again. He had told her he didn't know anyone going to the conference. Obviously he hadn't gone to a dental conference in Boston. He'd gone to Atlantic City. And apparently the friend wasn't just a one night stand he found there. It was a planned getaway.

She dog-eared that page, too, but wasn't sure what she could possibly do with just an initial. At least some bar, she could go talk to somebody. But his fling just had one initial. She frowned and went back to the agenda. All that was left were the last few entries before the night he died.

Only two days before he died, he wrote himself a reminder, "P's b-day."

She hadn't gotten flowers, a gift or even a card for her birthday. She snapped the agenda closed and tossed it back in the box. As she pushed herself to her feet, her cell phone rang. She pulled it from her purse and answered. It was Dana. "Hey, girl! Just wanted to remind you, I'll be by to pick you up at 9 tomorrow morning."

It took a moment for Andi to remember that she was going to Atlantic City with Dana. While they discussed last minute preparations, she returned everything to the boxes. She paused, opened the second box and pulled out Chad's agenda.

By the time she left the dental office, the sun was touching Cadillac Mountain to the west. With a heavy heart, she decided to call it a day and head home. She checked the mail before going in, and noticed a brown envelope, about 6 x 8 or so. No return address, but her name and address were printed in neat block letters with a Sharpie. Her breath caught and she looked around. Mrs. Harrison's curtain fluttered in her living room window.

Andi hurried inside and locked the door, then went into the kitchen and pulled a Sam Adams from the 'fridge before perching on a bar stool. The envelope sat on the counter in front of her. Her eyes never left it, but she popped off the cap and took three good gulps of beer before she opened it.

32

As she feared, the envelope contained another grainy black and white picture. This one showed her face. This time she held the heavy flashlight like a baseball bat. Chad's profile showed his head back and his mouth open in that horrible mocking laugh that she still heard in her nightmares. Goosebumps pebbled her arms and she shivered uncontrollably. Bile rose in her throat and she ran for the trashcan. She barely got the lid up before she threw up.

Her legs shook so badly, she couldn't stand up. It felt as if she were melting, as the numbness moved up her body inch by inch and she sank bit by bit to the floor. She had blocked out so much of that night, tried to forget, but the pictures brought back images that flashed through her mind like a slideshow. The memory of his scream echoed in her head and her stomach churned harder. She pushed the lid off the trashcan and threw up until there was nothing left, and her sides heaved to no avail.

After she lost the beer and everything else she'd eaten that day, she cleaned up. A long, hot shower was in order. As she let the water wash over her, her thoughts turned to Chad and Paul and Caren. Her life was spiraling out of control, but she felt as if she were floating above, watching things happen. She had to take control, or she wouldn't survive.

If Caren was out of the way, she was sure Paul would be with her. He'd as much as said so earlier. Then she and Paul could disappear. They could move someplace where nobody knew them, and where the blackmailer couldn't find her. She'd never be alone again.

After she dried off, she snatched Chad's agenda from the bar and took it into the den. Her leg struck the desk drawer when she sat down. It was opened slightly, so she pushed it closed, then rubbed her bruised knee absently. The blotter sat slightly askew so, out of habit, she straightened it.

As she tapped the paper against the desk, she considered what to do first. She jumped up and headed to the bedroom. She flipped open her jewelry box and dumped the contents, digging through them until she found the pink business card. Portia.

She grabbed the handset from the nightstand and punched in the number on the card. The phone rang twice, then a man with an British accent answered. He spoke too quickly, so she asked him to repeat it.

"You've reached the Woodson residence, ma'am," he answered patiently.

"Oh, I'm sorry, I have the wrong number."

She ran back downstairs and pulled out the photocopies she'd found in the desk. She ran her index finger down the paper until she reached Portia Woodson's name. A stack of newspapers sat in the rack to the right of the desk. Though she'd passed over them earlier, thinking them unimportant, her eyes settled on the article on the front page of the Sentinel. August Woodson, the real estate entrepreneur who owned three exclusive ski resorts in Maine, recently purchased a piece of land bordering Acadia National Park on Mount Desert Island. Near Black Bear Cove.

A light bulb went on. The vague entries in his agenda. P.

Portia Woodson had gone with him to Atlantic City.

Huh. Interesting. But did it matter? She didn't know. Possibly. A woman like that could certainly have funded him with the money to hire a private investigator. Maybe *she* had been the one to hire the private investigator to follow *him*. That seemed more likely actually, because someone like that would've checked Chad out thoroughly. So, that gave Andi some idea of who her blackmailer was – either Portia Woodson herself, or the PI she hired.

Andi closed her eyes and pressed her fingers against them. Too much to think about, too many details clogging things up. Thousands of voices screamed in her brain, their voices echoing. Her head hurt. All the Portia Woodson element added was the need to get out of town. The heiress wouldn't be after money – she had plenty of money already. All she wanted was revenge.

Andi needed to be able to protect herself in case the blackmailer came back.

She jogged down to the basement. The wooden gun cabinet she'd gotten Chad for their first Christmas together stood against the far wall. She ran her fingers along the top of the case and felt the cold metal of the key. She unlocked the bottom drawer and opened it. Two handguns shone dully in the dim light from the bare bulb that hung from a beam.

Her mother gave her the Walther P22 when she moved down east to be with Chad, and Chad bought himself the Ruger 9 mm so they could go to the range together for target practice. Andi grew up with guns, since her daddy was a hunter, but Chad didn't have much experience and only went to the shooting range with her once. Though he wouldn't admit it, she was a better shot than he and that stung his ego. Dana was a shooter, too, and she was the one who usually went with Andi. Actually, that's how Dana and her fiancé met, at the gun club.

She touched the smooth, cold steel of the Walther, then ran her fingers over the molded grip. She grabbed the gun, then pulled a box of ammo out of the bottom drawer.

33

Something white caught her eye at the top step. She leaned down, picked it up and turned it over. It was a torn napkin, with seven numbers scrawled across it, 2175560 but the number didn't mean anything to her. Maybe a phone number or an account number? She tucked it in her pocket so she could check into it later.

She laid the gun on her nightstand, then went through the house and checked all the doors and windows to make sure they were locked. When she went into the den and flipped the light on, she stopped cold. A brown envelope sat in the center of the desktop, with familiar block print in marker shouting her name. A chill ran up her spine. The blackmailer had been *inside* her house. And might still be.

Why hadn't she kept the gun with her?

She crept upstairs to retrieve the handgun, then thumbed several bullets in the magazine. Just as she shoved the mag into the gun, a muffled crash sounded downstairs.

She hurried to the bedroom door then slipped down the steps. Blood pounded in her ears. Every nerve in her body was on alert. Something creaked, and it sounded like it came from the front part of the house. With her thumb she flipped the safety off and continued down, staying close to the wall. The front door creaked open and she dashed down the last few steps. The door clicked shut just as she reached the foyer. She slipped on the wooden floor, quickly regained her balance and ran for the door. She flung it open and stepped out onto the cold concrete. No sign of anyone. She looked in every direction, listened for some indication of which way the intruder went.

The neighborhood was quiet, nothing out of place, not a soul in sight.

Her chest heaved with the effort expended and her hand found the doorknob. She backed in and shut the door, then flipped the deadbolt. It was time to have all the locks changed. Maybe time for a security system. The .22 was a welcome weight in her hands.

It took a good five minutes for her heart rate to return to normal and for the adrenaline to subside. The envelope would have to wait.

A quick pass through the house revealed no other signs of the intruder. In his rush to leave, the intruder knocked the basket of keys and change off the hall table, but nothing else was missing or out of place. Though she'd already checked the doors and windows before she heard the intruder, she went room by room and checked again. All closed. All locked. All blinds drawn. It made no sense. How did he get in?

After flicking the safety on, she laid the loaded gun on her nightstand so it would be there when she went to bed and returned to the den. She tore the envelope open. It was the picture she'd been dreading. The same black and white, grainy picture, but this time Chad rocked slightly back on his feet as the flashlight connected with his chest. The rain plastered her long dark hair to her head and back. Chad's face turned slightly away from the camera and stared at the black and white Andi in disbelief.

She closed her eyes and felt the cold rain on her face. She heard thunder roll. She heard the muffled thud of the flashlight as it hit his body. She felt the impact jar her arms.

Her eyes popped open with a start.

Oh, dear God, what had she done?

She took a deep breath and shuddered. She'd killed her husband. Goose bumps pimpled her skin as the reality of that night sank in. The photo caught on its way back into the envelope and wouldn't slide in. She blew into the envelope to open it wider, and saw a piece of paper inside. She pulled it out. The same neat block print as found on the envelope slanted across a piece of ordinary copy paper.

"Bring the deed, the coordinates and the stock certificates. Be at the cemetery at 11 tonight."

It felt like her chest was collapsing in on itself. She glanced at her watch. Four hours to go. Great. She reread the note. Her stomach rumbled and she realized that she hadn't eaten anything since she'd lost her breakfast. She slipped the photo and note back into the envelope and dropped them on the desk. There was nothing to do right now. Besides, she'd handle things better on a full stomach. Or at least one not rumbling in protest.

She went to the kitchen, dumped some cereal in a bowl and splashed milk over it. Not exactly meat and potatoes, but faster than nuking a meal. She smiled as she put the milk back in the 'fridge. It had been so nice of Paul to bring her over milk, eggs and bread earlier in the week. He was so much more thoughtful than Chad.

She took her bowl into the family room, curled up at one end of the sofa and flipped on the television. She spent the next two hours watching the minute hand creep forward on the mantle clock. The ten o'clock news had the only item of interest. Woodson Enterprises reported spectacular gains so far for the year. Hundreds of employees received bonuses, and there was talk of expanding the ski resort at Sugar Mountain.

A man shown in silhouette with an altered voice said the company would go public, but a clip of August Woodson showed a frail looking old man who declared no such thing would happen as long as he was alive. The reporter noted rumors of August Woodson's failing health seemed to be confirmed by the rapid weight loss the man had experienced.

Time was running out. She had to find out who was behind the photos before the old man died.

When the clock chimed once to mark the bottom of the hour, she hurried upstairs to change into head to toe black, then tucked her dark hair into a ball cap. She couldn't wait any longer. It was time to meet the mysterious photographer and find out what the hell was going on.

34

One of the life tips Andi's grandma taught her was that information was power. Though she'd been talking about the need for higher education, it applied to life, too. Andi needed power. She suspected her dead husband's lover was on her trail, and was very wealthy, and therefore, very powerful. Portia had to have been the one that hired someone to follow him, so it stood to reason that she had the photos and she knew that Andi killed her husband. Either she chose to blackmail Andi to get back what she gave Chad or the PI she hired took advantage of the situation in an attempt to improve his own financial standing.

The documents in Chad's desk were the blackmailer's target, but turning those documents over didn't guarantee an end to the harassment. Whoever held those photos could make her life miserable, or worse, send her to prison for killing the man who made her life a living hell.

Andi decided not to turn anything over yet, but intended to find out who she was up against. She drove into town where she parked on the street. After looking around to make sure no one was around, she got out, tugged a dark sweatshirt over her head, and walked around the building to the cemetery.

The cool breeze ruffled her short hair. Several decent sized trees provided cover, and clouds rolled past the half moon. The clock in the Jeep had said 10:46, so she had a few minutes before the arranged meeting time. Whoever wanted to meet her probably had the same idea. She veered left, aiming for the southeast corner of the cemetery. A clump of trees on a slight rise looked like the perfect spot to sit and watch.

A shiver ran up her spine, as much from fear as the chill in the air. It smelled like rain, and she glanced at the black velvet sky. Not a star in sight. Tombstones poked up here and there like crooked teeth, some taller than others. She leaned against the rough bark of an oak tree and waited, listening and watching. Though she knew the chances of spotting anyone in the darkness were slim, she hoped to at least get a look at the vehicle.

Boy, if the ladies from the Friends of the Library could see her now . . . she'd come a long way from being Chad's meek wife, afraid to speak her mind, blending into the background.

The clouds shifted slightly, and a sliver of moonlight peeked through. She scanned constantly from right to left and left to right, her eyes playing tricks on her as shadows moved and shifted in the pale light. Chad's tombstone of polished white marble stood out in stark contrast to the older stones. That would be where the blackmailer would be waiting.

A twig snapped to her left, and she froze, moving only her eyes. An orange glow bobbed between the monuments, glowing brightly, then softening and occasionally disappearing. Her eyes ached with the strain, but the clouds parted a bit more and she spotted a black figure moving towards her. She swallowed hard, shivering. She clenched her teeth together to keep them from chattering. The shadow turned slightly, the orange glow making the figure easy to track in the darkness. Once the figure reached Chad's stone, the glow burned brightly for a moment, then dropped to the ground and disappeared. Andi stared, afraid to blink. If he would only light another cigarette, she might be able to get a look at his face.

Finally, a match flared up, revealing a dark moustache. He took a deep drag before shaking the match out. She waited and watched long enough for him to smoke the entire cigarette, but stood rooted in place. The desire to talk to him tugged at her, yet she couldn't overcome the paralyzing fear. Being the wife of a dentist, working with charity groups, planning luncheons - hadn't prepared her for this. What if he shot her? The cold seeped into her bones, the stiffness crept up her legs.

She waffled. Confront him? Hide? If she confronted him, what would she say? Should she have brought something with her to show good faith?

She stuffed her hands in her pockets and crouched, careful not to move her feet. The wind picked up, and an owl hooted in the distance. Belatedly, she realized the orange glow was gone.

She'd waited too long.

She squinted and scanned the cemetery until she spotted a shadow darker than the night moving away from her and to the left. She'd waited too long! As she pushed quickly to her feet, her legs screamed with the sudden movement. She bit her lip and fought the urge to cry out as the blood rushed back into them, sending pins and needles shooting into her muscles. The black shadow slipped between St. Joseph's church and the parsonage. She crept forward, careful to stay behind the tombstones. The wind whispered through the trees, and branches clacked together. It gave her enough cover to allow her to move forward quickly. The shadow never slowed. He reached the street and turned to his right. She peeked around the corner of the parsonage and watched.

Moments later, an engine turned over and purred to life. Tires crunched in gravel and she stepped out to get a better look. The dark shadow of the car drew closer, and she ducked back when the headlights came on. She waited until the car was even with her before daring to sneak another peek. A dark car, a late model sedan, with a dent in the front driver's door cruised past. It looked a lot like her mother's car, an Accord. Nondescript. Something that would blend in. A private investigator would drive a car like that.

She waited until the car cleared the cemetery, then jogged across the street. She reached her Jeep and let it idle for a moment before she put it in gear. Thoughts tumbled through her mind like pebbles in a swift mountain stream.

Portia was behind everything. Andi felt sure of that, but had no proof. With no plan, she had no idea where to start and no one to turn to. She turned ideas over in her head, but didn't like any of them. The Jeep cruised through the darkened town. At that late hour, the Bay was like a ghost town with empty streets and no movement. The chances of spotting the car were slim, but she couldn't go home without trying. Like most small coastal towns, the old houses had been turned into shops with apartments on the second floor, so cars dotted the streets.

As she drove past Caddy's Quick Shop, she remembered the Seaside B&B and turned. She coasted past the mansions and pulled to a stop in front of the Seaside. A black Mercedes with a plate that said WDSN 3 sat in the front circle drive. That had to belong to one of the Woodsons. Portia, perhaps? She pulled into the graveled lot at Jolly Jack's and killed her lights, then cracked her window. A door slammed and she glanced back at the front of the B & B and saw a woman swing her long legs out of the sedan. She grabbed a Burberry plaid duffel bag from the trunk and went inside. Moments later, a maroon Honda Civic pulled up and parked behind the Mercedes. A man dressed in dark clothes and wearing a ball cap got out and went inside. A red Mustang convertible wheeled into the drive and parked by the front door. The white roof buzzed up slowly and the young couple got out, laughing. They walked arm in arm, then he backed her against the white column and kissed her. He raised her arms above her head and she raised one leg and wrapped it around his. His hand disappeared under her shirt, exposing a triangle of tan midriff. They put on quite a show before they finally pushed through the front door and disappeared.

Belatedly, Andi realized the maroon Civic was gone. She left the Jeep in the parking lot, then hurried across the street and up the drive. After a moment's hesitation, she pushed through the front door. The young woman at the desk spoke with a French accent, and was friendly and helpful in spite of the late hour.

Andi smiled and stepped forward. "I'm sorry to bother you, but I'm meeting a friend in Buccaneer Bay, but think we must've gotten our wires crossed. I wondered if maybe she checked in here instead of the B&B I thought we were going to?"

"I'm sorry, but we can't give out information about our guests." She tilted her head and raised her thinly drawn eyebrows. "Have you tried calling her?"

Andi tried to look as earnest as possible. "Yes, but her phone's going directly to voice mail, so I think her battery must be dead." Andi pointed to the door. "It's getting late and I'm getting worried. I'm certain that's her sister's car out there, so she must be here."

The dark haired girl shook her head and spread her hands, palm up, "I wish I could help."

"She would've just arrived." Andi swallowed hard. "Ms. Woodson?"

The girl looked at the iPad on her desk and tapped her fingers for a moment. "Portia?"

Bingo! "Yes! Can you direct me to her room?"

Her smile faded as she shook her head, then her dark eyes brightened as she pointed to the sitting room. "She said she would come down for a glass of wine after she settled in. You're welcome to wait for her."

Andi smiled and thanked the desk clerk, then walked into the beautifully decorated parlor. The roaring fireplace felt good after the chill she'd gotten in the cemetery. This might be just the advantage she needed. Portia would be caught off guard, relaxed and alone. Alone in the room, Andi sank into an elegant wing chair facing the fireplace.

A well worn Lea Waite paperback sat on the table, so she picked it up and pretended to read. Perhaps Portia wouldn't give a second glance to a fellow guest with her head in a book.

The door creaked and Andi glanced over the top of the book. Portia Woodson walked in. She was tall, maybe 5'9 or 5'10, and slender as a reed. Her dark brown hair pooled around her shoulders, contrasting sharply with her silver pashmina.

She glided past Andi without so much as a glance and looked out the big bay window at the darkness of the ocean. Andi shook her head, hating the heiress for every perfect movement. Chad slept with this woman, planned a new life with her, with no thought whatsoever to his wife of six years. She peered over the paperback as she considered her words, now that her husband's lover was so close.

The tall woman seemed oblivious to Andi's presence. After taking a deep breath and gathering her courage, Andi sat the book down and strode across the room. Fists clenched at her side, she stood less than a yard from the other woman.

35

Portia turned, and her features sharpened as confusion morphed into recognition. Her eyes widened and she spat, "What are you doing here?"

All the fear, frustration and anger of the past couple of months coiled up in her belly and gave her strength. Andi hissed, "I'm here to tell you to back off."

"Excuse me?"

Her heart thumped in her chest. Boy, the gals from book club would be so surprised if they could see her now. "You heard me. Whatever your beef is with me, it ends now."

Their heiress laughed, and her sapphire blue eyes narrowed, "Why should it?"

"Just tell me what you want and let's get it over with."

"I want you to pay for what you did." The other woman lifted her chin.

Andi held her back ramrod straight. "I didn't *do* anything. Besides, you have no idea what he was like. What my life with him was like."

"I have a pretty good idea."

"No," Andi shook her head, disgusted with the other woman's naiveté, "You don't. Tell me, how'd you meet him?"

The brunette's eyes lit up, and she said wistfully, "My brother-in-law introduced us. They've been friends since college. The four of us had so much fun together . . . "

Her voice trailed off, and Andi let that last word hang in the air for a moment, then said, "So, you had fun with a married man. Great way to build trust. Now it's time for both of us to get on with our lives. What's it going to take to get you to leave me alone?"

"It's not about money. I have plenty of that." She turned and faced Andi, toe to toe. "You took him away from me. He was leaving you for me. And you couldn't stand to lose him."

Blood rushed in Andi's ears as she glared up at the heiress. "You're full of shit."

The woman brushed by Andi and waved a hand in a dismissive gesture, but Andi grabbed her arm and spun her around. "I'm telling you, it stops now. Get on with your life and leave me the hell alone."

Andi dropped the woman's arm like a hot poker and stalked out of the B&B, letting the door slam behind her. At least she said her piece. Her blood ran cold and her heart thumped like mad. She couldn't believe she'd actually had the nerve to confront Portia.

The door slammed again and Andi turned to see the brunette stomping towards her. “You have some gall, following me--”

Andi cut her off, “What?! *You* are the one following *me*.”

The woman sputtered, “I’m on vacation.”

“Why Buccaneer Bay?”

The young woman's chest heaved, and Andi wasn’t sure if it was from the exertion or worry. She hadn’t noticed that inside, but she'd been focused on the woman's face. It made Andi feel good to know she could make Portia a little nervous. A smile tugged at the corners of her mouth. The heiress probably thought she looked quite mad, like a killer. Andi tilted her head and repeated the question.

The other woman settled her hands on her hips and glared. “You know damn good and well why I’m here.”

“You want the stock certificate stuff and the deed, but I don't have them.”

"Wait! What?" Portia stopped, jerked her head back and blinked. “I’m here because of Chad. I know what you did to him. You killed him!”

Andi shook her head. “It was an accident. A horrible, terrible accident.” A shiver ran up her spine at the memory.

The brunette's eyes narrowed. “I’ve seen the pictures.”

Andi jumped on the girl's words, determined to get to the bottom of things. “What pictures?”

“The pictures of you and him that night. The night you killed him,” Her sapphire eyes flashed with anger. “You know exactly what pictures I’m talking about.”

Andi crossed her arms. “How’d you find out about the pictures?”

The young woman glared, but Andi held her gaze. Finally, the other woman sighed. "I'm the reason those pictures were taken. Daddy hired a private investigator to find out . . ."

Andi blinked in surprise, then cut in and demanded, "To find out what?"

Portia looked like a poised adult, but sounded like little more than a child. Her chin jutted forward defiantly, "To find out what was going on with Chad. Daddy knew something was- I don't know - off."

Andi pressed on, "What's your connection with Chad?"

"He was my boyfriend."

She laughed, "Your boyfriend? Are you kidding me? How old are you?"

The brunette tilted her chin up, "I'll be twenty-three next week."

"And it didn't bother you that he was married?"

Portia squeezed her eyes closed and a single tear slipped down her perfect cheek. "I didn't know he was married. At least not when we started seeing each other."

Andi shrugged, suddenly deflated. It didn't really matter anymore. All that mattered was that a horrible man was dead, and she was finally free of him. But now she wanted to be free of this spoiled little rich girl.

She walked down the drive, then stopped and looked over her shoulder at the other woman. "Look, I'm sorry you got caught up with him, but trust me, he is not worth what you're putting yourself through, or what you're putting me through."

The girl bit her lip and frowned, "Someday the authorities are going to figure out what you did."

"I didn't do anything. It was an accident. Please, just let it go and get on with your life." Andi smiled sadly, opened the car door and turned the key in the ignition. The brunette stopped at the end of the drive. As Andi pulled out of the lot, she glanced in the rearview mirror and saw the girl still standing there, alone.

36

As soon as Andi pulled in the garage, she went in and checked the machine. She had two messages, one from Paul and one from Dana, but didn't return either. It was too late to call Dana, and she couldn't call Paul, regardless of the time. She went downstairs to the basement to put the gun back in the gun cabinet. She felt guilty for even carrying it. If push came to shove, she wasn't sure she could pull the trigger, especially now that she knew Portia was just a kid. There had been enough pain without inflicting more.

She opened the lower drawer and laid the gun inside. When she closed the drawer, the gun caught. She tugged the drawer open and moved the pistol forward a little.

Something was off. The front of the drawer was deeper than the back.

She pulled the drawer out. It was heavy and she sat it on the floor to take a closer look at it. She removed both guns and set them on the floor, then ran her fingers over the soft green felt covering the bottom of the drawer. The fabric wrinkled where it met the back of the drawer, and pulled away from the wood.

Andi ran upstairs and rummaged through the junk drawer in the kitchen for a nail file, then hurried back downstairs. She worked the file along the back edge of the drawer. The thin wood popped up with little effort. The false bottom popped out to reveal a thick white envelope.

She removed the papers from the envelope and spread them out on the floor. It was like getting a glimpse of a man she didn't know. The man she lived with for years, the man she slept with every night. How had he managed this? The thickest document was something called an Operating Agreement for Flatlander Holdings, and there were certificates of membership in the company. There were also stock certificates for Woodson Enterprises dated just a few days before the accident. Her eyebrows arched.

So these were the certificates the blackmailer wanted.

She flipped the membership certificates over. Chad had signed a transfer on death clause, dated a few days before the accident, stating that on his death his membership interest would be transferred to his trust. The typing was slightly blurry. She ran her index finger over the print and felt the uneven texture of white out. She held it up to the light and saw the faint outline of other printing. He'd changed the TOD clause to his trust, but she couldn't make out what it replaced.

She picked up the Operating Agreement and skimmed it. The Agreement named Chad as the sole member and manager.

Naturally.

There were also maps of the area, with a few pencil marks, most near Black Bear Cove. Notations filled the margins of the map, about pegmatite, elbaite, terminated crystals, and numbers that looked like GPS coordinates.

The last thing in the envelope was a smaller brown envelope containing a checkbook with several bank statements folded up and stuck in the cover. She flipped open the register. The first entry was a deposit dated January 4, in the amount of an even $9,000. He'd made other smaller deposits, and a few checks were written out to what looked like building contractors and suppliers.

She examined the bank statements, starting with the January statement and ending with the April statement, which would have been the last one before Chad's death. She'd never seen so many zeroes. Most entries were deposits, all below $9,000, except for one which was a deposit in mid-April for nearly $1.5 million. The notation said simply "sale of condo," which struck her as rather odd since they didn't own a condo. At least not that she knew of, she reminded herself wryly.

Two checks written in January and one in February caught her eye. All three were made out to Woodson Enterprises, and said "Purchase of Condo." The checks were $25,000 each. She didn't claim to have any special knowledge of real estate, but that was a steal. The ending balance on the last bank statement was well over a million dollars.

She turned the checkbook over and shook it. A debit card dropped out. After a moment's hesitation, she stuck the debit card in her back pocket, and returned everything else to the envelope, then put it all back exactly as she'd found it. With a turn of the key, she locked the drawer and stood on her tiptoes to put the key back on top of the gun cabinet.

At least now she knew what the intruder was looking for, what the blackmailer was after. How much did Detective Johnson knew. Did he think she was involved?

The phone jangled above her, so she jogged up the steps and snatched the receiver up on the third ring, just before the machine picked up.

It was Dr. McKenzie, from the hospital. "Mrs. Adams, I'm sorry to be bothering you so late, but I have some disturbing news for you that can't wait."

She chewed her lower lip. "Really? What?"

"We got back the complete blood test results from when you were in the hospital, and the results concern me."

She slid onto a bar stool, worried at the tone of his voice. "What?"

"Your test indicates a steady dosing of high levels of ethylene glycol. This wasn't an accidental, one-off ingestion. Someone is poisoning you."

"Wait. What?" That thought simply didn't process. "Poison?"

"Yes. We've got to figure out where you're getting the substance. Have you eaten anything unusual lately?"

She gripped the phone tighter. "No, nothing I can think of. Where would it come from?"

"Ethylene glycol is usually from antifreeze, but it has a bitter taste added to it now. The police will be contacting you - I've alerted them, and I know they'll want to talk to you. In the meantime, don't eat or drink anything you don't absolutely trust. And if you notice anything with a bitter taste, don't drink it."

"Doctor," Her mind spun, wondering how she could've been exposed. "How bad is this glycol stuff? What's it do?"

"It makes you seem drunk, and," he hesitated. "It can cause death."

She gulped. "I see."

That night she laid awake for hours worrying, turning over what she knew, what she didn't, and realized that the latter was a much bigger bunch of stuff. She felt as if she were putting together a jigsaw puzzle, missing a corner piece.

The next morning, Andi called Dana as soon as she got out of the shower. She looked at the clock – only an hour and half to get ready! Dana's excitement about the trip to Atlantic City was contagious. Andi had gotten so caught up in her own problems, she'd nearly forgotten all about her best friend's impending nuptials. Dana's enthusiasm was catching, and by the time Andi hung up the phone, she was looking forward to the trip, too. A change of scenery might be exactly what she needed - and might get her away from whoever wanted to do her harm, whether that be Portia or the investigator. She grabbed the small suitcase from the top of the closet and tossed it on the bed. A flash of white caught her eye.

Inside was a brochure from the Chapel of the Stars, and a note scribbled in Chad's distinctive neat writing that said "$55 – no blood test – 3-day needed."

The room tilted dangerously, and she felt as though the floor had dropped out from under her.

Her husband had been planning a wedding.

She took a deep breath. Even though her feelings about Atlantic City were tainted now, she decided it would be good to go. She had to, for Dana's sake. She would check out this Chapel and do a little digging while there. Maybe she could find something out, though she had no idea what.

She left the brochure and note in the suitcase, and covered them with her things. Her favorite clothes went in. She intended to look good while there. Just as she flipped her bag closed and latched it, the phone rang. She picked it up and answered.

A gravelly voice greeted her. "Hey, lover."

She couldn't help but smile. "Hey, yourself."

"What are you doing?"

"Packing."

"Packing? For what?"

"I'm going to Atlantic City with Dana. Remember? She's getting married this weekend."

"Oh. Well," He paused a beat, then murmured seductively, "Don't do anything I wouldn't do."

"I think I'm safe in saying I can do that." She squeezed her eyes closed and reminded herself that he was married.

"When will you be back?"

She felt a little thrill at his question, and immediately hated herself for it. "Just a couple of days. We're coming back Tuesday." Dana getting married reminded Andi of how much she missed being a couple.

"I'll miss you."

She couldn't keep the jealous bite out of her voice, "No, you won't. Just snuggle up with your wife."

"Hey," he said, sounding genuinely hurt. "That's not fair."

"Who said life is fair?" She hated the bitterness in her voice. All she wanted was for Caren to disappear so that Paul would be free. After meeting Portia face to face, Andi felt like one big raw nerve.

"She won't be home anyway. I'll be here all by myself, thinking about you."

"You poor thing. Where will she be?" She fought the urge to add, with her lover?

"She's visiting family in Massachusetts."

"And not taking her loving husband?" *Meow.* What was wrong with her? She wasn't usually this catty.

"I've got other obligations. And this way she can go shopping in New York City with her friends one day. That's not my thing."

"I see. Don't suppose you'd want to take advantage of your time as a bachelor and join me in A.C.?" She chewed her lower lip, immediately sorry she'd asked. Desperation wasn't sexy.

He hesitated. "You know I can't do that. Besides, you and Dana need the time together."

She sat on the edge of the bed and examined her neglected fingernails, "She'll be busy with her husband. I'll be free to paint the town red. And since this is my first trip as a single woman, I intend to do just that."

He sighed. "Just be careful. Please."

"Call me Tuesday night?" As soon as the words were out of her mouth, she regretted them. She didn't want to seem needy. She hated that about herself.

After a beat, he said, "Talk to you soon."

Then there was silence.

She stared at the phone for a moment, aching with the desire to be needed and loved. It had been so long since anyone had said they loved her. Chad never said it unless they were within earshot of someone he wanted to impress. And Paul was such a nice guy, and handsome to boot. Being with him was exciting and fresh, yet as comfortable as her favorite pair of faded jeans. She could picture them walking together hand in hand through life, them against the world.

She felt restless and anxious to get going on this trip, to get out of town, but most of all, to get out of the house that constantly reminded her of her dead husband. She ran to the post office to get stamps, then stopped at the grocery store to pick up some chocolate syrup for the ice cream Paul had dropped off, and decided it wouldn't hurt to drive by his house.

It was silly and childish, she knew, but she felt drawn to him. She slowed when she got close, squinting against the glare of the sun on the car parked in his driveway. The glare lessened as she pulled even with their house, and she nearly drove off the road. Sunlight glinted off the back of a black Mercedes sedan, just like the one Portia drove. A horn beeped impatiently, and she glanced in her rearview mirror. A little white sports car hovered right on her bumper. She slowed and eased right to let the coupe pass her.

Surely there has to be more than one black Mercedes sedan in Buccaneer Bay, although she couldn't think of one to save her soul.

There was no traffic coming so she spun the steering wheel to the left and did a U-turn. She made it back to the city limits in record time and didn't slow down until she reached the Seaside B&B. She hit the brakes and pulled up to the gate. Not a Mercedes in sight.

37

Perhaps Portia decided to leave town on the same day that someone with a similar car visited Paul and Caren. She could ask Paul, but didn't want to admit that she'd driven past his house. That seemed a little too desperate and needy, and she didn't want him to think of her that way. She had enough real problems to worry about without creating more.

A horn beeped outside. She pulled the curtain back and looked down to see Dana's Impala in the driveway. Andi grabbed the suitcase and bounced down the stairs, anxious to get this trip started. Between the photos and someone poisoning her, she couldn't wait to get out of Buccaneer Bay. She pulled the door shut behind her, then used her key to lock the deadbolt. By the time she reached the car, Dana had popped the trunk open. Andi dropped her suitcase in next to Dana's, slammed the trunk closed and slipped into the passenger seat.

Dana pointed to the cup holder. "Got you a French vanilla cappuccino."

Andi grinned at her friend, and felt the tension begin to melt away. "Thanks! Are you ready for this?"

She giggled as she backed the car out of the driveway, and said, "Absolutely. I've known Derek was 'the one' from the very beginning."

The hot liquid burned Andi's throat as she swallowed, "Good. And you don't think you'll regret not getting married in a church?" She glanced at the cup in her hands, then at her friend. Dana, she trusted. But who else could she trust?

Dana's long red locks swung as shook her head, "Not a bit. Honestly, it's just a ceremony. Why go through all the stress and expense of a big fancy wedding? Besides, this is Derek's second wedding."

Andi remembered how she'd let Chad dictate their wedding. "But it's your first."

Dana shrugged and waved her hand dismissively. "That's OK. Whatever he wants is fine." She pulled out of Buccaneer Bay, heading north. Oh! Derek isn't going to get there until tomorrow, so you and I will have today and tonight to ourselves. Thought we could hit the spa and salon, get manis and pedis."

Andi smiled and thought about all the preparations for her own wedding, "Sure, that'll be fun!"

"What was your wedding like?" Dana glanced at Andi, "If you don't mind talking about it."

"I don't mind," Andi said, and leaned her head back against the headrest, exhaustion taking its toll. "It was a big wedding, lots of family and friends. It was nice, but felt like such a production."

"And your dress? Your mom took you shopping for your dress?"

"Yeah. We spent a day in Kansas City, and went to the JC Penney's outlet store. I found a dress that I really liked, and it was less than a hundred bucks, so Mama bought it for me."

Dana whistled. "Wow, that's a bargain!"

Andi laughed, "Mama didn't have much money. After Daddy died, she struggled just to keep her head above water, but she insisted on buying my dress."

"That's sweet."

They continued on to the airport, chatting more about wedding memories and what Dana wanted her wedding to be like. Andi's mind wandered and she thought about the credit card receipts from that casino dated in April, the note she'd found, the wedding chapel brochure, and the new Will. What would've happened if Chad hadn't met an untimely end? She had the uncomfortable feeling that she'd barely missed being left behind like so much discarded trash.

Suddenly, she remembered the things she'd found in the gun cabinet. Perhaps Dana would be able to explain it. Andi quickly told her friend about Chad's hidden stash. Dana listened without comment, until Andi got to the part about the stock certificates.

Dana put a hand on Andi's arm and said, "Wait a minute, Woodson Enterprises stock certificates?"

Andi nodded. "Is that important?"

Her friend snorted, "Well, yeah. Don't you ever listen to the news?"

Andi shrugged.

"You've heard that August Woodson is on death's door?"

Andi thought of the deadline the blackmailer had given her, and wondered how long she had. "Yeah, but what's so important about his death?"

"Woodson Enterprises is huge, and the Chairman of the Board of Directors wants to take the company public. If they do that – it's called an Initial Public Offering or IPO – anyone who owns stock initially will be rich." Dana looked at her friend and punctuated her words with raised eyebrows. "I mean filthy rich."

That reminded Andi of the photocopies she'd found in Chad's desk. One of those papers had the words Public Offering circled on it. "So are these stock certificates worth a lot of money?"

"They will be when the company goes public. And the way they are now, if you were dishonest, you could make them TOD to you. They'd be worth millions."

Andi considered that, then her thoughts turned to the blackmailer, the stock certificates, the poisoning. Obviously, *someone* wanted her out of the way so they could cash in on the Woodson fortune.

But that wasn't going to happen. The meek, submissive person who had been married to Chad was gone. She needed to be tough, and figure out how to survive.

As they crossed over to the mainland. Andi pointed, "There's our turn."

Dana signaled and turned into the airport. They skirted around the airport, then found a parking spot. The two women got out and stretched a moment before getting their bags out of the trunk. They headed for their terminal and moved fairly quickly through the line to check their bags. Andi found herself caught up in Dana's excitement. She and Derek had been a perfect couple from day one, and Andi was sincerely happy for her. She told everyone in line that she was on her way to get married, and introduced Andi as her maid of honor, which resulted in congratulations all around. The line moved along quickly, and they were soon waiting at their gate, one of the advantages of a small airport.

"Oh, I almost forgot!" Dana reached into her purse and pulled out a little pink gift bag. "This is for you!"

Andi pulled out the tissue paper and found a little velvet covered box. She looked at her friend with raised eyebrows. Dana laughed and urged Andi to open it. To Andi's surprise, it was the ring that she'd had made from her wedding set that day they were shopping. The day she'd spotted Caren and her lover. With all the drama of the hospital visit and losing her job – not to mention Paul and Caren – she'd nearly forgotten about the ring.

"Thank you!" Andi leaned over and hugged her best friend. "You are so sweet!"

Dana shrugged, "You've had a lot on your mind lately, so I had Derek pick it up for you when he went to get mine."

She slipped the ring on her right middle finger and admired it. Such a thoughtful gift. Soon, their flight was called to board and they made their way to the attendant checking tickets. They walked across the hot tarmac and up the steps to the plane. Dana had never flown before, so Andi let her have the window seat. She remembered all too well how excited she'd been to fly the first time, and how badly she'd wanted the window seat. But Chad preferred the window seat, so she sat on the aisle. A sigh escaped at the memory. She let her head fall back and closed her eyes, thankful that part of her life was over.

It was a short flight, but sodas and peanuts were served. Andi stretched up to see out the window. Dana hadn't said two words since the plane rose into the air, intent on the view. A layover in Philadelphia, and they were on their way to A.C. Dana watched the landscape below, and pointed out casino resorts rising from the edge of the Atlantic. Even in the daylight, it was impressive. Dana grinned from ear to ear, but Andi felt hollow. Did Chad fly in by himself, or did he have his lover in the seat beside him?

They landed and collected their luggage from the baggage carousel. Dana's head swiveled and she said, "There's probably a kiosk around so we can call for a shuttle from our hotel."

Andi put her hand on her friend's arm and pointed to a tall man dressed in black holding a sign that said "Dana, Bride-to-Be."

Dana looked at Andi, green eyes wide, and exclaimed, "No way!"

Andi grinned, glad she'd taken the time to make the call before her friend arrived that morning. It had taken nearly everything in her meager bank account, but the look on Dana's face was worth it. "Yup. Happy wedding weekend!"

They followed the driver out to a black Hummer waiting at the curb. Dana's eyes bulged and she kept murmuring, "Oh, my gosh - I don't believe this."

Andi smiled, thrilled at her friend's reaction. The driver loaded their bags into the back and then held the back door open for them. Andi hopped in and scooted across, and Dana followed. Neither of them had ever been to Atlantic City before, so Andi asked the driver to take them for a tour of the city before taking them to the Tropicana.

The city seemed to stretch out along the beach. They passed so many high rises, monstrosities that reached towards the sky, as well as the Absecon Lighthouse and the Trump Taj Mahal, where Andi knew Dana and Derek had reservations at Il Mulino New York after their wedding ceremony. It seemed surreal, the buildings rising up out of the sand. Kind of a shame, really.

The driver gave the women a list of recommended things to see, and promised that he'd be back the following day to take Dana and Derek to dinner at the Taj Mahal after they were married. Andi tipped and thanked him, and Dana squeezed her arm on the way into the hotel, thanking Andi over and over for arranging the limo service.

"I never expected that!" A bellhop appeared to take their bags and Dana whispered, "I feel like a queen!"

"You are queen for the weekend, and my job as maid of honor is to make it as special as possible for you."

They checked in and went up to the room. It was absolutely sumptuous, decorated in blue and white. Derek was due to arrive the following day, and the two lovebirds had reserved a Premium Suite in the South Tower for their wedding night. Andi'd have the room to herself the remainder of the trip, and she could hardly wait to crawl between the sheets and sleep with no fear of being interrupted by a ringing phone.

They each claimed a bed, and Andi flopped down among a pile of pillows while Dana took a shower to freshen up after their long day of travel. She was nervous. She'd gone through the cash from the attorney in Bangor too quickly, and felt the strain of being unemployed. The handful of bills in her purse would have to last the weekend, and she'd have to eat macaroni for the rest of the month.

The limo was an extravagance she shouldn't have indulged in, but seeing Dana's expression of pure joy made it worth every penny. As soon as she got back to Buccaneer Bay, she needed to make finding a job a priority. She quashed her worries when her friend came out, determined to enjoy the weekend.

38

Dana tried to talk Andi into going to the casino and gambling after they hit the salon, but Andi wasn't in the mood. Andi finally convinced her friend to go by herself, then got on the elevator. As she watched the numbers tick higher, she sank lower. Chad made her life miserable, and now he was doing it from beyond the grave. The elevator door slid open two floors below hers and when a middle aged couple got on, she got off. She waited until the door slid shut, then pushed the down button and got on the next elevator.

She walked through the lavish lobby, and caught a bellboy. "Is the Sapphire Star within walking distance?"

He glanced at her strappy sandals. "Yeah, if you don't mind your feet hurting a bit. Just down the Boardwalk, about a ten minute walk."

He pointed her in the right direction and she stepped out into the late summer heat. She thought about the destroyed credit card and the small stash of cash in her purse, and was glad no cab was needed. It felt like a dream, with all the lights and sounds and people swirling around her as she walked along the Boardwalk. She bumped into several people as she hurried past them, but stopped apologizing after the first few steps. No one else apologized, either. She wanted to see where Chad had been, but had no idea what to do when she got there. Her heart literally hurt with the knowledge of his betrayal.

She reached her destination and looked up at the garish glass and steel monstrosity, taking in the sights and sounds. It didn't look like the kind of place Chad would have chosen. He worried about appearances and that sort of thing. It was difficult to imagine him in Atlantic City at all, much less in a place like this. Music thumped from the open doors, neon signs lit the sidewalk like mid-day, and kids ran every which direction. It seemed to be more of a family destination than the sophisticated casinos. The Taj Mahal or one of the other nicer hotels would have been more his style.

A doorman watched her for a moment, then stepped forward and asked, "Can I help you, miss?"

She started to shake her head, then changed her mind and stepped towards him so she wouldn't have to shout to be heard over the din. She pulled her wallet from her purse and produced one of Chad's business cards with his picture on it. She showed it to the young man and asked, "Do you recognize this man?"

He nodded and said, "Why, of course, that's Dr. Adams!"

She blinked in surprise. "May I ask how you know Dr. Adams?"

He tilted his head and frowned. "Well, he's Miss Woodson's friend." His eyes narrowed as he examined her.

She nearly dropped her teeth then and there. "So he and Miss Woodson visit here often?"

The young man hesitated, then tapped his finger on his chin as he considered his answer. Finally, he nodded. "Every now and then, though I haven't seen him in months. They used to come when Miss Woodson's father was in town. He is a part-owner of the property, you know."

"Oh, right," Andi nodded in an attempt to hide her surprise. Her husband really *had* been leading a life separate from their simple life on Mount Desert Island. She thought back to all the conferences he had attended, all the ball games he had gone to with his buddies from dental school during the last year, all the visits to his parents' home in California. Were they all lies? How could she have been so stupid, so gullible?

The doorman's eyebrows crept up his forehead. "Are you a friend of Dr. Adams?"

She laughed, a humorless bark. "You could say that."

"I'm sorry I can't help you – I haven't seen him in some time. Perhaps he's staying at a different property now."

She nodded and thanked him for his assistance. Just as she started to walk off, he called after her, "But Miss Woodson is here this weekend. You can probably find her in the spa if she isn't in her usual suite."

She smiled and thanked him again, then entered the hotel. She walked numbly through the casino, past the row of dinging, clanging one-armed bandits and between the tables. Lights flashed and shimmered as the machines clamored for attention all around her. She considered trying to find the spa in the chaotic maze, but decided instead to head back to the Tropicana. This was a waste of time. What would it accomplish, seeing Portia again?

Obviously, Chad tired of his boring life with his boring wife and was looking forward to his jet-set life with a young, beautiful heiress. Andi couldn't have competed with that. No way. He would have left her behind in a heartbeat, and it certainly looked like he planned to do just that. A sign for the chapel caught her eye, and she took a second look. The Chapel of the Stars. She'd seen that name on the slip of paper in the suitcase, and curiosity took over.

She approached the chapel area and found a nice older woman at the reception desk who seemed willing to answer a few questions. Andi showed the silver-haired woman Chad's business card and her face registered recognition. She lowered her chin and examined Andi over the top of her wire-rimmed glasses.

Andi widened her eyes and smiled in an attempt to look as innocent as possible, "I'm a friend of his and he told me about the wedding chapel at the Sapphire Star."

The older woman nodded, "Yes, he and Miss Woodson looked at the chapel. Had it reserved and everything, but Miss Woodson called, oh, I don't know, a couple months ago, to cancel it."

Andi smiled in what she hoped was a blissful way. "I imagine they had a beautiful ceremony planned."

"Oh, yes. If I remember correctly, they were going with the Touch of Class package." She smiled, crinkling the delicate skin around her eyes, and continued, "Of course, Miss Woodson's father would have given her the moon, but she and Dr. Adams just wanted a simple ceremony with family and a few friends. Less publicity that way, you know."

Andi felt as though her face would crack with the effort of smiling, "Do you recall what their wedding date was?"

The receptionist flipped the leather bound calendar back a couple of months and ran her index finger through dates, then tapped the book, "Ah, yes, they wanted a spring wedding. It was to be the last weekend in May."

Andi's knees went weak, and a chill ran down her spine. He died little more than a month before he and his mistress were to be married. When was he going to break the news to his wife? Was he even going to file for a divorce first? She thanked the kind woman for her time and hurried through the hotel. It felt as if her heart would burst and she couldn't catch her breath.

When she reached the front, she pushed through the doors before the doorman could open them. Once outside, she sucked in deep breaths of fresh air and waited for her heartbeat to slow. She made her way back to the Boardwalk and began walking towards the Tropicana in a daze.

Her life had been a lie. Her marriage had been a lie. And she had tortured herself for months, feeling bad about what had happened to Chad. For what she had done to Chad. At least his pain had been short-lived. What he planned to do to her would have destroyed her, slowly and painfully, piece by piece.

Who was she kidding? He was still destroying her.

By the time she reached the hotel, her legs felt like spaghetti and her feet ached. She stepped into the elevator with several other people, then leaned against the cool metal wall and closed her eyes. She counted clicks and opened her eyes each time the door opened. Finally, the elevator opened on her floor. She stepped out and fumbled for her key card. The door opened before she could insert the card and Dana stood there, eyes wide with concern.

She demanded, “Where on earth have you been? I was getting worried about you!”

Andi brushed past her and dropped onto the bed.

"I know you're feeling pinched right now." Dana's voice softened, “Lots of people can't afford to gamble. These things happen. It’s nothing to be ashamed of.”

Andi hung her head and let the tears flow. Her friend dropped down next to her and put her arm around Andi's shoulders. Dana waited until Andi's sobs dissolved into hiccups. "What's going on? What's really wrong?"

Andi took a deep, quivery breath, then said, “I guess I’d better start at the beginning, but please don’t judge me until you hear the whole story. Promise me you won’t judge me. And you can’t tell anyone what I’m about to tell you.”

Dana ducked her head to catch Andi's gaze. “Okay.”

“Not just okay.” Andi lifted her head and looked her friend in the eye. “I’m serious. You have to promise me.”

Dana blinked in surprise. “I promise. What is it?”

Andi took a deep breath and told her about that stormy night at the top of the cliff. This time, she didn't sugar coat anything. Dana gasped when Andi told her how it felt when the flashlight connected with Chad's body, but didn't interrupt. Andi told her friend about the Will she'd found, the pictures that had been delivered, the intruder, the late night trip to the cemetery, the confrontation with Portia Woodson, the mysterious package hidden in the gun cabinet, and the Atlantic City wedding that her dear departed husband had planned with his mistress.

When she finally finished, she felt completely wrung out. Her friend held her, and patted her on the back, making comforting noises. Andi was scared to death that Dana would pull away and hate her, and she'd lose the best friend she ever had, but Dana never made a move or said a word throughout the confession and subsequent story.

Andi shrugged her shoulders and deflated. "And that's it. Now I'm scared to death that someone is going to go the police with those pictures and I'll end up in jail. And I probably deserve it."

"No, you don't," Dana said firmly.

39

Dana nodded her head and declared, “Chad was a lying, cheating bastard and what you did to him was too good for him."

Andi's mouth dropped open. “So, you’re not going to turn me in?”

“Of course not! And I’m going to call Edward in the morning and see if he can help us out with that whole Will situation. Working for a lawyer comes in handy sometimes. He’ll know what to do. Don’t you worry about a thing.”

Andi leaned her head against her friend's shoulder and sighed, “Thank you. Thank you for understanding, and not hating me.”

“I could never hate you. And that’s enough depressing talk for tonight. I got us a bottle of wine and you and I are going to have our own little bachelorette party tonight. Forget your worries and help me celebrate!”

Andi felt as if a huge weight had been lifted from her shoulders, if only for a night. Sharing the burden helped. The friends spent the rest of the evening drinking, laughing and talking. Dana did a wonderful job of making Andi forget her problems.

The phone jangled jarringly in the quiet of morning. It was their wake up call, and they were both still fully dressed in their clothes from the night before. Two empty bottles of wine stood watch on the nightstand between the beds and Andi's last glass of wine had tipped over in the bed beside her, leaving a small red stain on the white sheets. Dana saw Andi dab at the stain and shrugged, then pointed at a much larger stain on her own bed, also next to an overturned wine glass. The two grinned at each other and shrugged.

Dana took her shower first, and Andi straightened up the room a bit. She worried about what she was going to do when she got back to reality. The blackmailer wanted those certificates, but she suspected they were leverage and hesitated to let go of them. But the reality was, if she didn't give the certificates to Portia, the woman could go to the cops with the photos. On the other hand, it wasn't like the heiress needed the money, so Andi was afraid she'd turn the photos over anyway.

And since Andi'd lost her job, she had to start looking for something as soon as she got back to Buccaneer Bay. The credit card situation would have to be dealt with, too. She sighed. The weight on her shoulders had returned and was just as heavy as ever.

Maybe it was time to give up and move back home to Missouri. In spite of Dana's confidence in her boss's abilities, Andi worried that this might be beyond his realm of experience.

The phone rang, interrupting her thoughts. It was Derek. "Hey, Andi! Is Dana around?"

The shower shut off, so Andi hollered at Dana to let her know her fiancé was on the phone. While she waited for Dana to come out, she chatted with Derek. "Did you make it in?"

"Yup. Just did. You and Dana stay out of trouble last night?"

"Of course. You ready for your big day?"

"I've been ready since I met her." He sounded just as excited as her best friend was, and Andi was happy for them, yet jealous at the same time. Dana popped out of the bathroom with a white fluffy towel wrapped around her. She took the phone and flopped down on the bed.

Andi slipped into the shower, determined to put her own problems behind her until her best friend was married off.

The pair ordered room service for breakfast. Neither was very hungry, and certainly couldn't stomach eggs, so opted for toast and coffee. As soon as they were finished, it was off to the spa for massages and then to the salon for hair and makeup. By the time they made it to the bridal preparation room, Andi felt like as much a queen as the bride herself.

The gorgeous vintage white dress from Blissful Beginnings hung on a hook, and it made Andi's heart ache, as she wondered if she'd ever wear a dress like that again. She helped Dana into the dress, then got dressed herself. Before she knew it, they were headed for the chapel. Derek, his best friend, James, and Andi stood at the front, waiting for the bride to walk down the aisle to the prerecorded music. She appeared in the archway and everyone oohed and aahed.

Andi imagined what it would be like when she walked down the aisle to meet Paul, and thought that a destination wedding might be just the thing for them, too.

She half listened as the two recited their vows. Hopefully things would turn out better for Dana than they had for her. After they said their I do's, the group gathered for pictures, and then headed to the patio for the reception, where they cut the cake and the best man toasted them, with the sparkling blue ocean as the backdrop. Derek's parents were there, as were Dana's aunt and uncle from Iowa, the closest family she had, and everyone seemed to get along well. Dana and Derek had eyes only for each other.

Andi slipped away as soon as she could, and went back to the room. She pulled on her flannel pajamas, flipped on the television and called room service. Within fifteen minutes, she was in bed eating the biggest hot fudge sundae she'd ever seen, watching a James Bond marathon.

The next morning, though Andi hesitated at calling so early, she gave in and called Dana's room to wish her well and tell her good-bye. Her friend sounded groggy with sleep, but her voice still carried the excitement from their wedding day. Everything was already 'we,' and she promised to spill all the details when they got home. As a wedding gift from Derek's parents, they were going to spend a week in Kennebunkport for their honeymoon. Just before she disconnected, Dana said, "I haven't forgotten about your problems."

Andi shook her head, sorry that she had burdened her friend with such news right before her wedding.

Dana continued, "I'll call Edward today and get his opinion. He'll know what to do. Want me to have him call you directly, or do you want me to stay on top of it?"

"I don't want to bother you on your honeymoon. It can wait until you get back."

"Nonsense," Dana said, giggling. Derek's voice was in the background. "I'm taking my laptop. I'll have him send the results to me, and I'll keep in touch by email. Tell me again – what was the name of that lawyer in Bangor? I'll see if Edward knows him or anything about him."

Andi gave her friend the attorney's name and wished her the best, safe travels, and all that, and they hung up. She checked out of her room and took the shuttle to the airport. Traveling alone made her uncomfortable. People tend to target you and think you're lonely and glad to talk to them, when in truth, you couldn't care less about their trip to see Uncle Harry and Aunt Sylvia. Andi picked up a Paul Doiron paperback at one of the airport shops, stuck her nose in it and waited impatiently for the flight to board. At least the early flights were mainly business travelers, so she didn't have many families to deal with. They boarded and she started reading before they took off.

She'd just finished her little bag of peanuts when a ding sounded and the fasten seatbelts sign came on. The captain announced over the loudspeaker that they were beginning their final descent. She looked down and saw several planes parked on the tarmac. It looked like a traffic jam, which never happened at this little airport. The flight attendant's face pinched as she announced that a plane in Philadelphia had crashed. She warned that the cascade effect was causing significant delays in air traffic.

Andi's heart dropped and goosebumps rose on her arms. Philadelphia. She took a deep shaky breath. That's where Dana and Derek were flying out of. What time was their flight? She couldn't remember. Was the crashed plane flying to Philadelphia, or from?

Andi watched the young woman as she walked to the front of the plane, where she and another flight attendant leaned close and talked. They both dabbed at their eyes, and their makeup stood out in stark contrast to their pale faces. Andi raised her hand to press the call button, but stopped when the captain's voice came over the loudspeaker, and announced that the plane would be landing soon.

She let her hand drop and stared out the window, feeling completely useless. As the plane taxied to a stop, she fished her cell phone out of her purse and gripped it tightly. As soon as they were cleared to make calls, she'd call Dana.

She caught the flight attendant's eye and waved. The woman walked towards her, her features tight and thin eyebrows raised. As soon as she reached Andi's row, Andi leaned towards her and asked, "Was the plane going to Philadelphia? Or leaving?" She crossed her fingers as she spoke.

"I don't know," The blonde shrugged her shoulders and blinked back tears, "All I know is that it was a Destination Airways flight."

A shiver ran up Andi's spine. That's the airline Dana was going to fly. Just then, the captain announced that they could use their cell phones, but disembarking would be delayed while the tarmac was cleared. The flight attendant smiled an apology and turned away. Andi tried to call her friend, but got a fast beeping instead of a completed call. The guy next to her held up his cell phone and shrugged. Only a handful of people seemed able to get through. The cell phone systems were probably overloaded.

They waited on the tarmac for what seemed like an inordinately long period of time before the plane taxied to the gate, though her watch said it was only twenty minutes. Finally, they disembarked.

Andi stopped in front of a television with a group of travelers and watched the images on the screen, the smoke, the fire, the horror. The graphic on the screen indicated that a Destination Airways plane traveling from Philadelphia to Orlando had crashed just minutes after takeoff.

Andi closed her eyes and fought back the tears. They were flying to L.A., via Atlanta. Thank God it wasn't their flight.

A thick woman with a shock of gray hair blew her nose, then glanced over at Andi and apologized.

"Quite all right," Andi murmured as she turned her attention back to the screen.

"All those people," the woman mumbled as she blew her nose again. "They didn't have a chance."

"Do they know what happened?" The images on the screen brought back so many memories of panic, terror. That fear was reflected in the faces of those around her as they watched anxiously.

The older woman shrugged, "I heard them say the flight was delayed due to mechanical problems. The pilot had time to radio for help and turn the plane around, but that was about it. Sounds like it dropped from the sky like a rock."

Andi's phone vibrated in her hand. Dana's voice crackled through the static. “Oh, God! Are you okay? Please tell me you're okay!”

"Yes!" Andi spun away from the clump of people and held her finger in her other ear so she could hear better, "And you? You okay?"

"Yes. Where are you?"

She pressed the phone tighter to her ear, "Just got into Hancock County. Where are you?"

"Still in Philadelphia. Our flight was grounded before we even boarded."

Dana told her they'd been watching MSNBC at the airport. Since it was a Destinations Airway flight, that whole terminal was a madhouse in Philadelphia. Andi thought about her luggage, then felt in her purse for Dana's keys. She'd planned to take Dana's car home for her. She was glad she didn't have to get on another airplane now - or wait for a delayed flight.

Andi said, "Go back to the hotel and wait until it's safe to fly. Maybe you can get on another airline."

Dana laughed, but it sounded forced. "You're reading my mind."

The two promised to touch base later and Andi stuck her phone back in her purse, as she hurried to her friend's car.

Andi just wanted to get home. Suddenly, having to deal with a cancelled credit card didn't seem like the end of the world.

She listened to the radio on her drive home. Every channel carried the same thing, news of the crash. The stories coming in were horrendous. No survivors had been found, and the authorities didn't sound hopeful. She glanced up at the sky. Not a single jet trail crossed the clear blue sky. She couldn't remember the last time she'd noticed that.

The next morning she flipped on Good Morning, America, where the crash was the leading story. She had a hard time watching the screen, listening to the reporters, and reading the scroll across the bottom, given how close this had hit. If Dana had been on that plane . . . Suddenly, she blinked and moved closer to the screen as she waited for the scroll to repeat.

When it finally did, she clapped her hand over her mouth as she read. A spokesman for Woodson Enterprises confirmed that August Woodson's eldest granddaughter, Caren Woodson Thompson, was on Destination Airlines Flight 121.

She watched until it ran again, and made sure she was reading it correctly, then rocked back on her heels.

Another piece of the puzzle fell into place.

40

Andi snatched up the phone and dialed Paul's number. She got his machine, and left a brief message that she'd just heard the news, and told him to call if he needed anything. She didn't leave her name, and didn't expect a return call, but at least he'd know she was thinking about him.

How was it possible that she could be so connected to the Woodson family without even knowing it? Was it a coincidence that she was falling for the man married to the sister of the woman her dead husband had been sleeping with? Things like that didn't happen in real life.

During the next few days, she watched the news trying to catch clips about Caren Woodson Thompson. She thought about calling Paul again, but couldn't bring herself to do it. She wasn't sure how he fit into all this. She was torn. Part of her was angry, because he surely knew about her husband's affair with his sister-in-law, but another part of her was relieved he was free of his wife. She would never, ever, have wished the woman dead, but she was relieved, just the same. After he grieved, they could date properly. They would come out of this just fine, and no one would ever know that they'd had an affair.

Later that morning, a couple stopped by to look at the house. They walked through, commenting about tiny cracks in the walls, small rooms and the lack of an open floor plan. Andi escorted them out and watched through the window as they huddled together on the front walk. The man turned around and rang the doorbell.

When she opened the door, he grinned. "My wife and I agree - this is exactly what we're looking for. We'll give you your asking price!"

Her heart dropped and she swallowed hard. "You'll have to contact Gabby Martin, the agent." She pointed to the real estate sign, then shut the door on the happy couple.

She couldn't put off getting a place of her own any longer. She got in the Jeep and drove around, looking for For Sale signs. On a whim, she stopped at Bunch o' Blooms and ordered a small plant and picked out a sympathy card. She signed it "thinking of you – Andi," and made arrangements to have it delivered to Paul's home. Her next stop was Martin Real Estate. The woman had been polite about bringing customers by to view the house and, after all, the situation wasn't her fault.

Gabby drove Andi around in her white Cadillac to show her several nice houses around town, most little salt block houses. The prices shocked Andi. Until the insurance money came through, she couldn't hope to own anything in Buccaneer Bay proper. None of the houses really did anything for her, either. Gabby showed her quaint houses, which Andi suspected was because she was a single woman. The agent likely assumed a widow wouldn’t need much space, but Andi couldn't fathom a future of living alone.

After the sixth house, the agent sighed and said, “I just can’t think of anything else in town that might work.”

“Okay,” Andi countered, “How about outside of town?”

The woman nodded and thought for a moment, “You know, there is a very nice little cottage just outside of town.”

“North or South?”

“South.”

After a moment’s hesitation, Andi nodded, “Let’s go.”

She couldn’t help but look as they passed Paul’s house. His Jeep sat in the driveway, next to a silver Lexus and a dark green Lincoln Navigator. Gabby kept going for a couple of miles, then turned right onto a narrow blacktop road. They rounded a curve and topped a rise and Andi's eyes widened when she spotted a cute little cottage. The white one story with sea foam green shutters had an unattached two-car garage to the rear of the house. A covered porch ran the length of the house, and flower beds filled with a rainbow of plants made it look homey. Andi knew this was her new home before she even looked inside.

As soon as Gabby dropped Andi off at her Jeep, Andi ran calculations in her head and headed for Harbor Regional Bank.

The loan officer who helped her with the Grand Cherokee loan asked her to fill out a loan application before he took her back to his office. She waited nervously while he reviewed the application, and entered numbers into his computer. He tapped his pencil against the desk and mumbled under his breath. He stared at the screen, then at the application. Butterflies fluttered in her stomach.

Finally, he looked up from his screen. "How much do you plan to put down on this house?"

Her stomach lurched. "I don't have anything to put down."

"Are you waiting for your current house to sell? Because if you are--"

She shook her head. "I'm not. My husband had the house in a trust, and I'm not . . . " Her voice trailed off when she recognized the pity in his gaze.

He shook his head and stroked his moustache. "And you do not have a job at this time?"

She swallowed the lump forming in her throat. "No, sir."

His eyebrows rose and he asked, "Do you have any leads on jobs?"

"No." She shrugged, "But I've been busy and haven't really looked yet."

He blinked several times, then barked out a laugh. "And how exactly do you intend to make a mortgage payment with no job?" He clamped his mouth closed and nodded, tilted his head back as he frowned at the screen again and clicked his mouse. "I can take this to our loan committee, but I'm not making any promises. You should hear from me next week if your loan is accepted."

She hated feeling powerless. "What would improve the chances of acceptance?"

His eyebrows crept up his forehead and he leaned forward. "Get a job."

She left the bank and drove around town, thinking. She needed a real job, not a part time gig like the Chamber of Commerce, but she had no experience and no college degree. What if she didn't get the loan? She didn't have enough to buy the place outright. Her mother didn't have enough money to loan, and neither did Dana. Perhaps Paul? Given his family connections, he had access to a lot of money, but she hadn't spoken to him since she'd gotten back from Atlantic City, and didn't know if he would loan her anything anyway.

And then she remembered the documents in the gun cabinet.

Could they be turned into cash?

41

She returned home, and felt her stomach drop when she saw the bright red sold banner atop the For Sale sign in the yard. How long would she have before she was out on the street? Andi put her key in the lock and the door swung open. Shards of the glass vase sparkled on the foyer floor like glitter and flowers were scattered across the tile. She stepped inside carefully, straining to hear anything out of the ordinary. The grandfather clock ticked softly, but she didn't hear anything else. She picked up the phone in the kitchen and dialed 9-1-1.

The operator immediately instructed Andi to get out of the house. She hurried outside, taking the phone with her. Mrs. Harrison pretended to water her flowers, until

Andi waved and hollered across, "Mind if I wait with you? Someone broke into my house!"

Mrs. Harrison's hand fluttered at her chest. "Oh, dear! You know, Mike Fielding's house was broken into and he had a heart attack."

Andi kept watch on her house as she walked across the lawn. "Oh, no! I'm so sorry, I hadn't heard! Is he going to be OK?"

"Nope." Mrs. Harrison's head swiveled back and forth. "Died instantly. Lucky duck."

Andi nodded as she considered that. Was the burglar still in her house? What was he after? A robbery in broad daylight was awfully brazen. She changed the subject. "Did you notice anything out of the ordinary today?"

The older woman said, "I saw a car earlier in the day that I didn't recognize. A dark red Toyota."

Andi thought about the dark sedan she'd seen pull away from the cemetery. It could have been dark red. "Was it a Corolla, by chance?"

"You know, it could have been. It was a Honda or Toyota. You know, one of those foreign jobs that all look the same."

Sirens interrupted their talk. A patrol car pulled up and Andi walked out to meet the two officers with Mrs. Harrison at her heels. The first officer, a thin man who looked barely old enough to be out of high school, directed them to wait by the patrol car while they checked the house.

Andi waited anxiously, and tuned her neighbor out as the older woman continued to make idle conversation. When the officers approached, Andi excused herself. The first officer took Andi aside, and the second, a thick man that reminded her of a bulldog, took Mrs. Harrison aside.

The officer asked Andi several questions about where she'd been, how long she'd been gone, how she'd discovered the break-in, if she'd had other problems, that sort of thing.

After he flipped is notebook closed, he said, "I want you to take inventory and make note of anything that's missing, and you'll want to notify your insurance company of the loss."

He held out his hand, indicating that she should walk with him towards the front of the patrol car, where Mrs. Harrison and the other officer were standing.

The thick officer turned to them and consulted his notes. "Ms. Adams, your neighbor here saw a dark haired man, average build, go up your driveway earlier this afternoon. Said he was driving a dark red sedan, possibly a Honda or Toyota, with a dent in the rear on the driver's side. Any idea who that might have been?"

Andi shook her head, but felt apprehension rising in her. The private investigator.

The police left, and she had a sinking feeling that would be the extent of the investigation. Mrs. Harrison invited Andi over for dinner, but she declined. She hurried home to see if anything was missing. She checked the gun cabinet in the basement first. It hadn't been touched. She breathed a sigh of relief and went through the rest of the house, room by room. She straightened a few things, but left much of it a shambles. Perhaps the new buyers would renege when they learned that it had just been burglarized.

The last room she checked was the den. A single piece of paper with typewritten words laid on the desk.

> *"Caren's death was hard on the old man. Put the stock certificates in a plain brown envelope in your mailbox before midnight, or you're dead."*

Frustration ate at her. Had the blackmailer poisoned her? What did he hope to gain by killing her? Unfettered access to her home?

Just as she crawled into bed, her phone rang. Paul's gravelly voice greeted her. "Hey, lover."

She curled her feet under her and settled back against the pillows, relieved to finally be talking to him, "Hey, yourself. How're you holding up?"

"Okay. I got your plant. Thanks."

The mere act of talking to him made her toes tingle. "Just wanted to let you know I was thinking of you."

His voice was taut with tension, "Are you busy?"

She practically purred, "No. Just getting ready for bed."

"Can I join you?"

She pictured his mischievous grin and missed him so much it ached. "Come on over." She'd never been good alone. Heck, she'd never *been* alone. She could almost hear Dana chastising her for moving too quickly, but she squelched that voice.

She slipped out of her cotton nightshirt and pulled on her silk robe, then freshened her makeup and brushed her hair, bent over and tousled it. She waited downstairs, and opened the door before he had a chance to ring the bell. She stared into those piercing blue eyes and felt her heart skip a beat. He stepped inside and she pushed the door shut behind him. He spun around and caught her against the door, then kissed her. A real kiss, with heat and emotion. She melted in his arms, and without another word, he led her upstairs.

That was the first and only time they had sex, and it was incredible. Slow, gentle, perfect. His hands ran over her body as if memorizing every line and curve. No direction was needed – he knew exactly what to do to take her to the heights of ecstasy. They connected on the deepest level, and she was sure it was because he was finally free.

The next morning she snuggled up next to him, breathing in his scent. Shame niggled at her, but she told herself his wife was gone. Her conscience wouldn't let it go that easily, though. She pulled away and sat up, tugging the sheet around her to cover her nakedness.

"What's wrong?" he mumbled, reaching out for her.

"I feel bad. Your wife just died." She turned to look at him over her shoulder.

He stared at her with bright, clear eyes, but wrinkles lined his face, making him look older. "I know. This is quick."

"I really am sorry that she died." Her voice cracked with emotion.

He sat up and kissed her bare shoulder, "I am, too, but it makes things much simpler. This way, I don't have to deal with an ugly divorce."

She blurted, "Why didn't you tell me your wife was one of the Woodson heiresses?"

He shrugged, "I never wanted to make a big deal out of it."

"Did you know that her sister was having an affair with my husband?"

He kneaded her shoulders, but didn't answer. She asked again, more firmly, "Did you know?"

He leaned close and gathered her in his arms. "Yes, I knew."

She swallowed the lump in her throat. "Why didn't you tell me?"

He shrugged, “What purpose would it have served? I didn’t meet you until after your husband was killed, so why dredge up bad feelings?”

She turned to look him in the eye, “Is she a nice person? Portia, I mean.”

“Yes. She’s kind, intelligent. Very attractive.”

Andi felt as if she'd been punched in the gut. “That is one piece of information I did *not* need to know.”

“Sorry.” He looked around the room until his eyes settled on Chad’s dresser. Two of the drawers hung half-open, with clothes spilling out of them, “Did you have a little temper tantrum in here?”

She shook her head and told him about the break in, the jimmied door, and Mrs. Harrison’s description of the vehicle and intruder. Almost as an afterthought, she told him about the house being sold.

After she finished her story, she shrugged. “I didn’t feel like picking everything up just so it would look good for somebody to come and buy it out from under me.”

“I saw the sold banner on the for sale sign in the front yard. Guess it won't be long and you'll have to pack everything up and empty this house. Bet you find things you didn't even know you had.” He kissed her forehead and said, "Why don't you go hop in the shower? I'll whip up breakfast."

When Andi stepped out of the shower, the rich smell of coffee drifted through the steamy air. A mug sat next to the sink. After she brushed her hair and dressed, she examined herself in the mirror. She'd used a lighter touch with her makeup. More respectable and mature. She took a sip of coffee, which had just the perfect amount of creamer and sugar.

She felt adored. He knew how to spoil her. Chad never brought her coffee in the bathroom. She sat the drink down and noticed a chalky substance on the edge of the mug. She needed to check the dishwasher and the water softener to see if they were working right.

After she finished the coffee, she practically bounced down the stairs and found the kitchen a mess. She shrugged. She didn't cook much anyway, so she'd figured why clean it up. A morning news show played in the family room. Paul sat on the couch, leaned forward with his elbows on his knees. His own steaming mug of coffee sat beside him on the end table.

He jumped up and flipped off the television when she entered the room. "You look great." He took two quick steps towards her and enveloped her in a hug.

Her cheeks warmed as the flush crept up her face, "Thanks."

"Why don't we go over to my place and I'll fix breakfast for you there?"

She laughed, "I take it you saw the mess in the kitchen."

"Yup. Did he take anything of value?" he asked as he took her hand and led her towards the front door.

"Not that I could find." She started to grab her purse but he gave her a tug.

"Come on, love, you don't need that. I'll take care of you today. You deserve it."

She laughed and gave in. It had been so long since anyone had taken care of her, she was perfectly willing to let him do just that. She grabbed the keys out of her purse and left it sitting on the hall table. As she pulled the door shut behind them, the telephone rang. He gave her another tug.

"Come on, I'm hungry," he urged. "Whoever it is will leave a message."

Before he turned into his drive, she asked him to keep going.

"Why?"

"There's a house up here I want to show you. I'm thinking about buying it."

"Really?" He glanced over at her and asked, "Not to be rude, but do you have enough money to buy a house?"

"No, not yet. But I'm going to get a job and make it happen."

He frowned, "But what about insurance, or the trust?"

She shrugged, "I'm not the beneficiary of the trust."

His knuckles whitened as he gripped the steering wheel. "Who is?"

"I'm not sure."

He reached over and squeezed her hand. "I see. Are you absolutely sure that Chad transferred all of his assets to his trust? Stocks, that sort of thing?"

"That's the way it appears." She thought about the stocks and membership certificates hidden in the gun cabinet. She'd given that a lot of thought, but hadn't quite decided the best way to handle them. But she wasn't ready to share that information with Paul yet.

"And you've searched your house thoroughly to make sure he didn't hide any cash or important papers?" He lifted her hand to his lips and kissed the back of it.

There was something so comforting about him holding her hand. "Yes. And what I didn't search, I'm sure my intruders have. Here's our turn – take a right here."

He turned his Jeep into the long driveway and followed it until the cottage came into view. She couldn't help but smile. She'd fallen in love with the place and knew that she'd find a way to make it hers. Something about it made her feel warm and safe and comfortable. Since the place was empty, they got out and walked around to peek in the windows. The back deck had a great view of the island. She took his hand and led him up the steps to look in the sliding glass doors.

She pointed to the other side of the deck. "And that's where I'm going to put my hot tub, if I can come up with the money."

"I have a hot tub on my deck."

"I know." As soon as the words were out of her mouth, she felt her gut twist.

He looked at her oddly, but let the comment pass. "You'll really enjoy it. I can give you the name of the place where we got ours."

Her smile faded at his casual use of 'we' and 'ours.' She used to be a 'we,' and she so badly wanted to be again. He continued on, not seeming to notice that she had dropped his hand and leaned against the railing. After a moment, she started down the steps and he followed.

"Is something wrong?" he asked.

"No," she answered, trying desperately to squash the hurt feeling centered in her chest. "I'm just getting hungry."

They went to his house and he gave her the grand tour. She felt odd, almost as if his wife's spirit was there listening. Watching. The house was nicely decorated, country French, and Andi could see Caren's touch everywhere. She perched on a bar stool at the island and watched while he gathered up the makings for breakfast.

The buttery yellow kitchen with whitewashed cabinets gave off a cheery ambiance. The blue countertops didn't have so much as a chip or a scratch. A cluster of canisters stood beside the glass top stove like tin soldiers, and a marble mortar and pestle were displayed next to a gourmet spice rack. "You haven't lived here long, have you?"

"No. Just moved here in the late spring. May, I think it was. Caren was quite excited that I was offered this job."

After Chad's death. Seemed like she thought of everything in terms of before or after that fateful night. She asked, "What made you decide to move to Buccaneer Bay?"

"We liked the small town atmosphere, and Caren loves the coast. Being on an island seemed like the perfect solution. "

"I see," Andi stood up. The woman had just died. Andi should be feeling more charitable towards her. "That coffee went right through me."

"You remember where the bathroom is?"

"I can find it." Andi headed down the hallway and found the guest bathroom. After she took care of business she washed her hands and dropped the towel. She bent to pick it up and noticed a crumpled piece of crisp white paper. She picked it up and smoothed it open. It was on a notepad monogrammed with a "W," and said "Jimmy Webster called –207-631-32" and the last two numbers were smudged. The note was signed with a "C" and curlicues accented the slanted writing. Andi sighed. If she and Paul were going to be together, Caren's ghost would be present for some time.

That name, Jimmy Webster, tugged at her memory – he sounded like a two bit gangster. And she was fairly certain the exchange was the same as the numbers she'd found in some of Chad's things.

Bangor.

Again.

42

Paul called out, "Breakfast is ready!"

"Coming!" With an uneasy feeling, she tossed the note in the trash and strolled down the hallway. She glanced into their study, which reminded her a lot of Chad's den. A framed picture on the wall caught her eye and stopped her short. She recognized the group of guys dressed in ski suits, with a roaring fire in the background. The large slanted writing at the top said "Winter Break 1998."

The same photograph that Chad had framed in his dental office. She gulped and a chill ran down her spine. He'd known Chad.

"Did you hear me?" Paul called from the kitchen.

Her heart rate quickened and thoughts jockeyed for position in her mind. She took a deep breath and gathered herself. What did this mean? She hurried down the hallway, and found Paul pouring orange juice into glasses. The smell of omelettes, with diced ham and cheese, just the way she liked them, wafted through the air.

Her thoughts kept turning to that photo, so she asked in the most casual voice she could manage, "Where did you go to college?"

He paused and looked at her, mouth open, fork poised. "The University of Colorado."

She picked up the salt shaker. "I only went a couple of years, to Mizzou. Wanted to be a teacher."

"Ah, the Tigers." He stuck the bite in his mouth and chewed slowly before speaking again. "I started out as a biology major, but ended up switching to business."

"That's funny. Chad was a biology major there, too."

He took a sip of orange juice and nodded. The clock on the wall ticked softly.

A chill traveled down her spine. "What year did you graduate?"

"2002."

"Really? Chad graduated in 2001. Did you two know each other?"

He shook his head, "The University is huge. I may have run into him at some point. How is your omelet?"

She let the subject drop, but turned facts over in her mind and examined them. He was lying to her, but why? What was his motivation?

After they finished breakfast, Paul started the dishwasher. He turned towards her and leaned back against the counter, wiping his hands on a towel.

He was right. It was a big school. Maybe she was reading too much into things. She relaxed and smiled, loving how domestic and comfortable he looked. That was what she wanted, what she needed -- someone to take care of her. Without a man, she felt lost, exposed.

His piercing blue eyes crinkled when he smiled and she knew she had fallen for this guy hard. She wasn't sure it really mattered whether he had known Chad or not.

"What?" he asked as he reached out for her.

She shook her head and went to him, feeling silly. "Nothing."

He pulled her close and nuzzled against her thick hair. "Let's go back to your place. I'll help you clean things up."

She murmured, "You don't have to do that." This wasn't right. Every nerve tingled with danger, but she couldn't let him know she suspected him of anything.

"I know, but you shouldn't have to do it all yourself. And the sooner you clean it up, the sooner it closes. And the sooner it closes, the sooner you can move into your cute little cottage just a stone's throw from me."

She forced a laugh and agreed. "First, I have to get a job."

"Maybe I can help with that. I'll make some calls."

"Oh, could you? I didn't want to ask." Then she remembered the note she'd seen in the bathroom and said, "Did you live in Bangor before you moved here?"

"No. We lived down by Kennebunkport. Why do you ask?"

"No reason," she shrugged, unable to shake the quiver in her gut. That name, Jimmy Webster, still sounded vaguely familiar, and she hated that she couldn't place it. He offered again to help, and she finally relented, unable to come up with a good reason to say no.

Once they arrived back at her house, he wasted no time taking charge. He suggested she start on the second floor while he started on the main floor. She grabbed a couple of trash bags from under the kitchen sink, then jogged up the steps and decided it would be best to start in the bedroom. Pots and pans clanked downstairs, and she was thankful Paul offered to tackle the chaos in the kitchen.

Clothes hung out of every drawer of Chad's dresser, so she started there. As she pulled his clothes out by the handful and stuck them in the trash bags to drop by Goodwill later, she thought about what she'd learned about Paul. Had he known Chad?

She glanced at the doorway. Her nerves tingled with danger, but she brushed the feeling aside and turned to the task at hand. There was no reason to keep any of her husband's things. Other people in the world could use them. She sank into the mindless task, and her thoughts turned to other things. Something about that slip of paper in Paul's bathroom nagged at her, but she couldn't quite put her finger on it. For some reason, she thought maybe she'd come across that name while looking for a job.

She closed the last drawer, then stood and turned to tackle her dresser, and noticed the red message light blinking on the answering machine. Four new messages. She hadn't gotten four new messages in a day since right after Chad's death when people called to express their condolences. She punched the button and listened.

"Andi, it's me. Call me on my cell." It was Dana. Apparently they hadn't made it home yet. The machine announced the date and time – it must have been her calling right as she and Paul had left. Andi was sorry she'd missed her friend.

"Andi, it's me again. Call me as soon as you get this." Dana's voice was tense.

"Andi, where are you? I left a message on your cell phone, too, so ignore this if we've already talked."

In the last message, Dana's voice rose higher. "Andi, it's urgent that I talk to you. It's about Paul."

Andi snatched up the handset and punched in Dana's cell. Her friend answered on the first ring.

Dana was breathless, "Oh, thank God. Are you all right?"

"Of course I'm all right. What's going on?"

"It's Paul, Andi. He's bad news. Remember Amanda Dobbins, the paralegal for the attorney that drew up Chad's paperwork?"

Andi blinked, wondering what the paralegal had to do with anything. "Vaguely."

"She and I went to elementary school together. Used to be good friends. Hadn't talked to her in years, but she recognized my name when Edward called her boss and told him to ask for me."

Andi was confused. Dana meeting up with an old friend wasn't urgent news. "What's the problem? What's wrong?"

"Chad wasn't their main client. They just did the work for him at the request of a client who has them on retainer."

Andi sat on the bed. "I know. It was Portia Woodson."

"No-"

"Or Woodson Enterprises. Whatever. Same-"

Dana cut in. "No, Andi, it was Paul."

Andi froze and looked at the door. No pots and pans clanged downstairs. Goosebumps pimpled her skin. She whispered, "What are you saying?"

"I'm saying Paul and Chad were in it together. Amanda says Paul is a really scary guy. He's the sole beneficiary of Chad's trust."

"What?" Suddenly, it clicked. Jimmy Webster was the PI in Bangor that had the ad in the paper for an assistant. Caren had taken a message for Paul. He was the one who hired the PI, not Portia.

"There's more. Amanda said Paul asked her for a recommendation for a private investigator. She gave him the name of some guy named Jimmy Webster. It's Paul, Andi. Paul is the one who's blackmailing you."

Her heart pounded in her chest as she stared at the open door. She swallowed. "I've got to go."

"Andi-"

She cupped her hand around the mouthpiece and whispered into the phone. "He's here. In my house. I've got to go."

"I'm calling the police."

"Ask for Detective Johnson."

"Don't let him know you suspect anything, Andi."

Andi gently sat the phone back in its cradle and crept down the stairs, listening for anything that would indicate where he was. Her heart pounded wildly against her ribcage. She peeked around the corner. Pots and pans littered the empty kitchen. She eased down the hall to the den. The bottom file cabinet drawer was ajar, and Andi knew she'd closed it after checking for missing items after the break in. Something metal clanged in the basement. She walked to the top of the stairs, and heard something scrape along the concrete floor.

She took a deep breath, tried to clear any strain from her face and walked down the steps. Paul rummaged through Chad's work cabinets against the wall. The third step creaked and Paul looked up, his face flushed and blue eyes wide.

He motioned towards the worktop, “I thought I’d clean up down here before starting on the kitchen. Some of these wood working tools were laying around.”

She nodded and glanced at the wooden gun cabinet. The pistol drawer was ajar. She continued down the steps and walked casually past Paul. “Cleaning upstairs went pretty quick. I went ahead and bagged Chad's things up to be donated. So, I thought I’d come down and help you. I’ll start on this side.”

“Did you come across anything unusual?” he asked as he rubbed the back of his neck.

“No, just clothes. Lots and lots of clothes. How about you?”

“No, nothing but wrenches and screwdrivers.”

He turned his back to her and went back to the tool cabinet. He made a show of putting things back, but she noticed he looked in the cabinets at the same time. She went to the gun cabinet and opened the pistol drawer. The Ruger was in the front and the Walther was in the back, opposite of how she'd left them, and the felt was ripped. She glanced over her shoulder and spotted the big white envelope on the work counter, peeking from underneath some tool manuals. Paul’s back was still to her. She quietly pulled the semi-automatic Ruger from the drawer and checked it. Still loaded. Safety on.

She took a deep breath, turned around and brought the gun up. It was deadly steady.

He faced her, leaned back against the counter, hands up. He smiled that crooked smile and his eyebrows arched up in surprise. “What are you doing?”

She concentrated on breathing and kept the bead on his chest. For the first time in ages, she felt confident and sure. "Getting my property back. Toss that envelope over here."

"What are you talking about?" He pushed away from the bench, spread his hands, palms up.

"The envelope you took out of the pistol drawer. It's just a couple of inches from your right hand. Toss it over here."

His smile widened as his fingers groped across the work bench and closed over the flap of the envelope. He tossed it on the floor so that it slid across the slick concrete towards her. In the split second that she glanced down, he took a step towards her. She flipped the safety off with her thumb and he froze, still smiling.

The envelope was at her feet, but she made no move to reach for it.

Her voice echoed in the cavernous basement. "Move away from the counter. Up the stairs. Now."

He sneered at her, "You won't get away with this. You don't even know what you've got there."

"I may not, but I bet August Woodson does."

"You bitch!" His face transformed into a twisted mask of hate. "You have screwed up everything. I tried to act sweet, to help you clean things out, but you wouldn't let me. I poisoned you with old antifreeze I got from Caddy's, but you didn't get as sick as you were supposed to. Maybe it was too old--"

A crash upstairs interrupted him and booted feet charged down the steps.

"Freeze!"

Paul grabbed a long screwdriver from the workbench and lunged towards her. She squeezed the trigger just as another gun exploded in a bang. Paul's eyes widened and his mouth worked, but no sound came out. He stumbled towards her, and fell, his fingers inches from the blood spattered envelope at her feet.

43

Detective Johnson rushed to Paul's still body and knelt beside him. Andi stood staring, shaking, unbelieving as the Detective put his fingers to Paul's neck, then spoke into his radio, and ordered an ambulance. He turned to her and she handed him her weapon without taking her eyes off of the body at her feet. A uniformed cop stayed with Paul.

The detective scooped up the large envelope still laying at her feet, guided her around Paul's inert body, and took her upstairs.

There had been enough death already. She was glad she and Detective Johnson hadn't killed Paul. Her shot went left, she was certain. She always pulled to the left when she shot. The detective had hit him in the right shoulder. The house flooded with police and investigators and photographers. Johnson took her into the kitchen and fixed her a cup of tea. She shivered as she turned over the events of the past several months, and tried to put the puzzle together. The paramedics had just left with Paul when Dana pushed her way into the room.

Andi rose and reached out as her best friend rushed towards her. The friends hugged, and Andi clung to her as if she were drowning. In a way, she was. And her best friend was there to save her. Detective Johnson pulled a chair out for Dana and sat down with them.

He started simply, "Why don't you tell me what happened?"

There was so much to tell, Andi didn't know where to start. He knew her husband had died, of course, and he wasn't surprised she'd found evidence Chad had an affair with Portia Woodson.

"Then I found several things here in the house that I didn't understand." She pointed to the blood stained envelope sitting in front of him. "It's all in there. Most of it anyway. Stock certificates for Woodson Enterprises. In Chad's den, you'll find a valuation of Woodson Enterprises prepared by an accountant, and some sort of report. You already know that Chad was in over his head with gambling debt."

Dana broke in, "And that's where Paul Varney comes into the picture. He was married to Caren Woodson, Portia's sister."

Andi added, "And Paul and Chad used to be fraternity brothers at the University of Colorado. Chad must have confided in Paul about his money problems, and asked for help. I think that's when Paul came up with the idea to introduce Chad to his sister-in-law."

Dana said, "That's right. A friend of mine is the paralegal that works for the firm that represents the Woodsons. She got to be friendly with the two granddaughters when she handled the probate of their parents' estates. She told me that Portia idolized Caren, and desperately wanted to settle down and have the family life that Caren did. But she had a party-girl image, and didn't want to get serious with any of that crowd. She was afraid they were all gold-diggers. So she asked her brother-in-law to hook her up with a friend of his."

Andi's eyes widened, "And my husband – his old fraternity brother - was the first person he thought of?"

Dana nodded, "He took Chad to see the Woodsons' attorney and arranged to have divorce papers drawn up, a new holding company set up, and got a new Will prepared that left Andi out in the cold, but left everything to his trust, which Paul would control if anything should ever happen to him."

"Chad planned to get a divorce, and get remarried almost immediately," Andi said, then told him about finding the notes about the wedding chapel in Atlantic City, and her conversation with the woman there.

The detective digested all the details, and tapped his pen against his notebook, "If I recall the news reports correctly, those two girls are the sole heirs of the Woodson fortune. August Woodson has spoiled them rotten, and probably gives them anything they want."

Dana continued, "And Portia talked her grandfather into giving Chad a sweet deal on a condo so that he could make some fast money and pay off his gambling debts. He got in good with the old man, and started visiting some of the development sites on the old man's behalf. It was on one those trips that he discovered several tourmaline crystals that had been dug up by a trencher. Paul knew about Chad's find, and offered to put him in touch with people who could put together a mining operation. Woodson Enterprises bought that land along with the mineral rights, but the Board intended to go public with the company as soon as the old man died."

Detective Johnson nodded. "And if August Woodson died and the company went public, particularly given the big tourmaline find, anyone who owned stock in Woodson Enterprises would make a killing." One corner of his mouth twitched up, then he added, "So to speak."

His pen scratched furiously in his notebook. He paused to read back over his notes, then said, "So Paul knew about the tourmaline?"

Dana nodded, "But didn't know where the stones were or the exact location where Chad had found them. He hired a private investigator by the name of Jimmy Webster to follow Chad and find out anything he could about the stones, but the investigator had no leads about the potential mining location."

Andi glanced at her friend as she remembered the pictures Webster had taken in the course of his investigation. "And when the private investigator didn't come through with any useful information, Paul cultivated a relationship with me so he could find out if I had found anything here, and so he could search the house himself."

Detective Johnson interrupted, "We believe he was the one who broke into your house. Your neighbor just identified him today out of a photographic line up."

She remembered how sick she'd gotten. "He borrowed my keys while I was in the hospital. He could have made a key then."

"So he ransacked your house."

"And he was here helping me clean up that mess." Andi couldn't believe it. She thought she'd finally found her happy ending. "Dana called to warn me today, but he was here with me when she told me. He was downstairs, and he did find what he was looking for – part of it, at least – and that's when you showed up."

"We've been putting together a case on him for months. Now we've got enough evidence to put him away for a good long time."

Andi swallowed hard, and kept her eyes down. "And you aren't going to arrest me for Chad's death?" A chill ran down her spine while the grandfather clocked ticked loudly in the hallway. She glanced up at the cop.

One corner of the man's mouth twitched up. "I think you've suffered enough."

Dana reached across the table and patted Andi's hand, "It's over, Andi."

EPILOGUE

Andi never returned to that house. After staying at Dana's for a short time, she moved into her little cottage just outside of Buccaneer Bay, and had been there for about a week when she heard tires crunching gravel in the driveway. She stepped out onto the front porch just as Portia Woodson got out of her black Mercedes.

The young woman shaded her eyes from the sun, "Can I come up?"

Andi hesitated a moment, then said, "Sure."

They sat in white Adirondack chairs, facing the ocean. Andi waited while the heiress chattered on about the view, the salt air, the weather. Finally, she fell quiet.

Andi cut to the chase. "What are you doing here?"

Portia pulled an envelope from her purse and laid it on the table. "I came to apologize. I should have quit seeing Chad as soon as I found out he was married. You probably hate me, and I deserve it."

Andi shook her head. "I don't hate you. My marriage was never a good one."

"Still, I wanted to come and apologize personally."

Her ivory linen sundress showed off her perfect tan, and perfect body. Her dark hair was pulled back in a severe bun, without so much as a hair out of place. But a closer look revealed dark bags under her eyes, and her manicured nails looked as though the tips had been chewed. She lost her parents, her sister and her fiancé, her brother-in-law was sitting in jail, and her grandfather's illness forced her to take a more active role in the family business. It showed.

Andi smiled at her. "Apology accepted."

"Thank you," the girl murmured.

Without another word, she stood and gracefully descended the stairs. She started her car, turned it around and gave a quick wave before she disappeared from sight.

Andi picked the envelope up and slid her thumb under the flap. She ripped it open and pulled out a thick blue-backed paper. She read it carefully, then threw her head back and laughed.

It was the deed to a tourmaline mine.

DEAR READER:

I hope you enjoyed this novel, the first in the Widow's Web series. Read on for a sneak peek at the second book.

Stop by my website and sign up for my newsletter. I won't ever sell your name and I won't bombard you with info - I send out updates a few times a year.

lorilrobinett.com

I'm happy to connect with you on Facebook, Goodreads and Twitter, too.

And if you are so inclined, I would be thrilled if you would pop over to Amazon, Barnes and Noble, or Goodreads (or all 3!) and leave a review. That makes me jump with joy. ☺

The Danger Within:

A Widow's Web Novel

1

Marcus froze in mid-cut, the serrated steak knife still in the meat as blood-red juices pooled on the plate. His eyes focused over his wife's left shoulder and narrowed slightly. Before Sophie could turn to look, she felt the man's presence just behind her.

"Marcus, what a surprise to see you here," the man said. His calm demeanor was belied by his voice, which held an undercurrent of anger.

The metallic clink of the knife striking the edge of the plate sounded loud in the quiet of the dark restaurant. "And why is it a surprise that I take my wife out to enjoy a steak dinner?"

The man stepped forward, inches from Sophie. She could smell the musky scent of his cologne, with a hint of leather. She kept her eyes downcast and noticed the expensive shoes he wore. Loafers, with little tassels on them. He turned towards Sophie and she looked up at him. His blue eyes were clear as a mountain stream, and the streaks of silver at his temples gave him a distinguished air. He smiled at her and took her hand, "If I had a woman as beautiful as this one, I'd take her out, too."

She held her breath as he kissed the back of her hand. The corners of her mouth twitched up in surprise, then she glanced at her husband. The muscles in his jaw worked as he motioned towards the man with his fork, "This is Blake Chaney. He's the executive director of the Foundation."

She looked up at the man and pulled her hand from his grasp. So this was the mysterious philanthropist. She murmured, "Nice to meet you, Dr. Chaney."

Marcus said, "It's Mr. Chaney."

Mr. Chaney smiled at her, a charming smile that exposed a perfect row of white teeth. "He's right. I'm not a doctor. Not a scientist. I supply the money and oversee the facility to make sure everything stays on track."

Marcus looked around the intimate steak house. "Is your wife with you tonight?"

"No, she had other plans tonight." He put his hands on the table and leaned towards Marcus, and lowered his voice, "I'm concerned about the pig that was lost today."

Sophie frowned and watched her husband. His eyes closed for a moment. She knew that look. He was angry and trying to control it. When his eyes opened, his face was relaxed but his green eyes glittered with frustration. "It was a genetic mutation, out of my control. A fluke. "

The man laid his hand on Marcus's shoulder. "I'm afraid this won't sit well with the Institutional Review Board."

Marcus's knuckles were white where he gripped his fork tightly, the only outward indication of his anger. "You are the executive director and sit on the Board. If you endorse human testing, the IRB'll go along with it."

Sophie's eyes widened at the mention of human testing. Although she knew of her husband's research, he rarely shared details. The squat gray building where he worked was intimidating enough without knowing what went on behind those walls.

"I'm so sorry, Marcus, but you know I can't do that in good conscience." His smile widened as he turned towards her. "Your husband is a brilliant researcher. Wouldn't surprise me at all if he won the Nobel prize someday."

He strode away, his leather shoes nearly silent on the polished hardwood floor.

She turned her attention back to her husband and tried to calm his ruffled nerves. "He obviously thinks a great deal of you. I didn't know your research was so far along."

He stabbed a piece of meat with his fork and jabbed it at her. "He has no idea how brilliant I am. He doesn't know how close I am to curing the scourge of humankind. Losing that engineered pig today--"

She reached across and took his hand. It shook in hers, then he squeezed her fingers so tight her knuckles ground together painfully. He whispered urgently, "I have found the cure for cancer. You will see."

The waiter arrived to refill their glasses, giving her the opportunity to pull her hand away. She took a sip of water then remembered, "Oh! I forgot to ask – were you able to get the new insurance card from Jennie?"

He nodded, still frowning, "Yes, yes, she ordered a duplicate for me. It's in my desk drawer. I had other things on my mind today."

"I know. I hate to bug you. I just need to make sure I have that card before I go see the OB again."

He glared across the table at her, "I will get it to you, just quit bothering me about it."

They finished the meal in silence, he lost in his thoughts and her nursing her sore hand as she contemplated her brilliant husband's change in mood.

Less than twenty minutes later, Sophie hugged herself to calm the shivers. The wipers slapped furiously at the rain. Finally, he broke the silence. "You didn't seem to mind when Blake kissed your hand tonight."

Lightning danced across the sky and she jumped when thunder boomed almost immediately. She turned towards him and spoke softly, her voice barely audible over the raindrops pelting the roof of the SUV, "It just caught me by surprise."

"Don't let that act fool you. He's a cad." He grabbed her forearm and squeezed, "You and he aren't seeing each other, are you?"

"Of course not! I'm in love with you. I'm having your baby." She pulled her arm from his grip. The night had been so nice. Marcus had taken her out for a romantic dinner to celebrate her first trimester. He'd opened the car door for her, pulled her chair out for her, ordered for her. And then she'd smiled at his boss. And that was all it took to flip Marcus's switch. He truly was a brilliant man, but his mood swings scared her.

She kept her head down, but glanced sideways at her husband. The muscles in his jaw worked furiously and his lips pressed tightly together. She cleared her throat and said, "Dinner was nice tonight."

He snorted and strangled the steering wheel with his grip. A shiver ran down her spine as the Denali sped down the mountain road, leaving Widow's Pass behind them.

She tried to turn his focus to the one thing he truly cared about. "Blake mentioned human trials. Your research must be going really well if you are thinking about human trials."

"More ready than you can ever imagine. And I'm not waiting around for the IRB. They move at a glacial pace, and the world cannot wait for them to grind along--" A loud rumble of thunder drowned out his words. A sharp bang punctuated the night. The SUV swerved to the left and threw Sophie into the door. The seat belt held her in place, but her head snapped to the right and hit the glass.

Made in the USA
Las Vegas, NV
11 March 2022

45466439R00198